The E[barcode obscured]

Floyd Simeon Root

To Suzanne
Great at what
you do.

Floyd Root

This story is a work of fiction and the names of its characters are the author's creation. Any resemblance to real people are unintentional and purely coincidental.

DEDICATION

Lynne Foster Fife

Lynne was a beautiful person and a brilliant artist. She was able to combine her extraordinary talent with accomplished technical skills and mystical insight. She loved to paint Native Americans and their natural world and understood their spiritual inspiration. But, even more important than her artistry, was her beautiful personality. I can think of no person who truly loved people around her as did Lynne. It was my privilege to work on some projects together, her art and my writings.

It was with great sorrow I learned she had a medical condition which proved to be fatal. She retained her ebullience to the end. I never heard her complain in spite of her suffering. Lynne focused on inspiring and cheering others. She was a meteorite that flashed across the sky and disappeared all too soon. Lynne died in 2007 at the age of sixty two, youthful and angelic. Her body was donated to Indiana University School of Medicine in the hope of helping others. That was so like her.

Her husband Tom, also a beautiful person, wanted her celebration of life to focus on the beauty and love that was uniquely hers, and to be as cheerful and inspirational as was Lynne. Her many friends who came were also beautiful people. They shared the sentiment that she made them each feel special, that when she was talking to them they were the most important person in the world to her at that time. She has been a great inspiration to my writings. I have been blessed to call Lynne and Tom friends.

CONTENTS

ACKNOWLEDGMENTS

There are many who have been helpful in bringing my book to fruition. They are listed in chronological order as they made their contributions. I owe much to each and every one as they helped make this book possible.

My mother, Sylva Dennis Root, who read to me as a child, the Lafayette Word Smiths, Lynne Foster Fife, Rebecca Mullen, The Vincennes Guild, Martha Jane Schoeff, Molly Daniels, Precious Rhea, Alena Rhea, Kay Briskey, William Henry Root, Candice Denning, Langdon Root, Ryndee Root, and Lynne Keisle.

James Bowers used his computer skills to place my book in proper format. Cover design is a combination of ShutterStock and artist Jeremy Carpenter.

Special thanks go to my talented editor, Angie Mayfield, who had the wisdom of Solomon and the patience of Job.

1
THE CHASE

How could I have done such a dumb thing, Davy wondered? A few ill chosen words, innocently enough spoken and suddenly Davy found himself chased by a hostile juvenile gang, Satan's Little Brothers. *How could I have been so stupid? There are some people you just don't joke around with.*

What Davy did not know was that Dee Dee was trying to make her boyfriend Harold, who led the gang, jealous by making accusations about Davy. "I'm telling you Harold, he was trying to hit on me."

"I see him! He's over here," Davy heard one of them call out. The chase was on again.

With Davy's competitive nature, he might even have experienced some exhilaration by the danger of the chase. He occasionally caught a glimpse of The Tower of the Americas between buildings. What a difference a few hours could make. Just this morning he was horsing around with friends at their favorite hangout, the Little Alamo Cafe, playing video games. He could make a handful of change last all day. Davy smirked with confidence, but he quickly returned his thoughts to the urgency at hand; he was going to need the total focus of his full resources in order to survive. He knew they carried clubs and brass knuckles.

Davy ran fast enough to easily outdistance them, but there were enough of them they could cut him off ahead, like a pack of wolves working as a team to bring down a caribou. He had already avoided one such effort to cut him off. Three of the gang had managed to jump in front of him, and one had actually grabbed him. Davy had shaken the dude off, and with some dazzling footwork, he stiff-armed one in the forehead and left the other one grabbing at nothing but air. He smiled as he remembered the roar of the crowd when he had performed the same maneuver on the football field.

Now he dashed between some office buildings and headed down a back alley toward River Walk, an unkempt alley for this section of town. Perhaps it was a reflection of his present station in life. River Walk was a favorite site of entertainment for Davy. Once before, though it seemed like a lifetime now, he had enjoyed spending money as he strolled about the park. He didn't have much money to spend now, but he had many friends there. He often joined a trio: a guitar, a fiddle or trumpet, and a Mexican base guitar, serenading the dining love couples on the outside patios. He helped his friends serve food. Often, the café owners would sport him a meal in appreciation for the extra customers he seemed to bring in. He loved the friendly people and excitement of River Walk. It didn't look like he was going to enjoy it today though. River walk might as well have been a world away.

Davy knew that, even as he ran, some were circling around in cars to draw the net tighter. *What to do? What to do,* he wondered? He didn't think they would kill him, but who wanted to take the chance? In any event, they sure meant him some serious harm, not to mention the indignity of a beating. *I don't want a darned thing to do with it,* he thought.

Davy saw two F-15s from Camp Randolph, flying high overhead, so high they made no sound, as silent as fence posts. They appeared to be so slow they were standing still in the distant sky, but they left a vapor trail behind. *War Games,* he thought, *just games. The real war is down here on the streets trying to survive.* Davy envied the pilot. He could hear at least six pair of running footsteps echoing in the alley behind him. A rock whizzed by narrowly missing his head, bouncing along the street ahead of him.

His nostrils were flared and he was breathing rapidly. Approaching Crockett Street, Davy grabbed a round post with his right hand and swung himself in a quick arc to his right without breaking speed. He continued running another twenty feet before stopping to get his bearing, much as a wide-eyed rabbit looks for an escape route to lose a pack of dogs. Then he heard, "Davy! Hey, Davy, over here, quickly now!"

Surprised to hear his name called, he looked around and saw a black stretch limousine parked by the curve. It had a brilliant shine and dark tinted windows; the back window was rolled down, and a rich looking dude with a cell phone in his hand and the back door ajar was imploring once again, "Quick Davy, over here. You must act quickly. They will be upon you if you don't hurry."

Davy couldn't believe what he was hearing or seeing. He was thrilled with the prospect of such opportune escape, but he hesitated. His years on the streets, if nothing else, had taught him to be suspicious. After all, getting out of an entrapment was more difficult than getting in, but, he visualized the beating he was sure to receive if he hesitated too long. He darted for the car as the man fully opened the door to receive him. Davy lunged across his feet into a pile on the floor, drawing his legs up after him. He heard the door slam shut, the closing of the window and the clicking of the car's electronic locks.

"Don't worry Davy, you are quite safe now. No need to scrunch down on the floor. The windows are dark tinted so they can't see you. Tinted glass only lets you see out, not in. And, even if they did, they couldn't get in this car, not even with a blow torch and a sack of crow bars," said the well-dressed gentleman with a weak attempt at humor.

Davy rose up slowly and with caution. He saw the boys come running around the corner not fifteen feet from his hiding place and with natural instinct jerked his head down a bit. But rising up again, he reached toward the window and waved his hand slowly back and forth. It was true; they couldn't see him, even though some stared in his direction as they looked around bewildered, wondering where he could ever have disappeared to in such a short time. He was still in a state of high anxiety, but his intensity relaxed as his adrenals began their descent to earth. As the limo pulled away from the curve, he jumped around on his knees in the back seat and exuberantly gave his pursuers the finger with both hands while bouncing up and down and laughing.

As the boys in the rear window grew smaller, he stopped laughing, dropped his head, and bit his lip pensively. Then he turned around in the seat and stared at the wealthy looking gentleman, neither one saying a word, but the stranger was wearing an amused smile. The middle-aged man wore a dark pinstriped suit, red power tie, and a starched white shirt with gold cufflinks. He had a thin neatly trimmed mustache and exuded the confidence of a high roller.

Davy looked around at the interior of the limo and reached out his hand to feel the deep red velvet of the seats and the finely tooled leather on the doors. He caressed the gold-plated doorknobs, and his nostrils flared as he took in the new car smell mingled with the aromatic oil that held the gentleman's wavy dark hair in place. He surveyed the meticulously groomed man who was still grinning.

"Smells rich, doesn't it?" the man asked.

"OK," said Davy, his natural confidence beginning to return. "So, what's this all about?"

"What are you talking about?" A grin lingered on the man's lips.

Davy sported his own cockeyed suspicious grin.

"Don't give me that. You know what I'm talking about. I'm some poor kid running for my life, and you show up in a stretch limo to rescue me? Some rich dude who even knows my name. I don't know rich people like you. So, what's the deal?

"My apologies, Davy. You are right, you don't know me. But I know you. I know all about you. Perhaps I know more about you than do your friends, maybe even more than you know about yourself. And this isn't actually my car, though I do have a fair amount of money. But I'm not nearly as rich as the man who owns this car, the man I work for. You ever hear of a man by the name of Emerald Silverstone?"

Davy's eyes widened in amazement. "Of course, who in Texas hasn't? Everybody knows who that dude is. He's pretty reclusive I understand. He is some kind of international business man or something like that, the richest man in San Antone supposedly. He is mysterious and eccentric, a real hard-ass the way I hear it. I've never seen him, except rarely on television. I do know he lives near The Dominion, just off Interstate 10, a house on top of a hill. Apparently no one sees him, at least not unless he wants them to, a rare moment on a newscast. What does all this have to do with me, and why are you even telling me this?"

"Davy, Mr. Emerald is an international banker and he has taken an interest in you. He thinks you are a remarkable young man and you have the potential for extraordinary achievement. He has decided to bring you into his organization, take you under his wing, so to speak, teach you to operate in the world of wealth and power. He's going to send you to the right schools and place you in a high position within his empire, one that will give you great importance and wealth. You can think of him as your benefactor, a magnificent benefactor.

"My magnificent benefactor? No way!" He laughed with a hint of disdain. "Things like that don't happen in real life." Davy's face hardened in a way that was unusual for his normally effervescent personality. "I've been pretty much on my own for nearly four years. No one's ever yet taken me under their wing, and no rich dude has ever given me as much as a second look. What, do you think I'm stupid or something? Give me a break, man. What's really going on?"

"I must confess to a bit of a surprise. You are more of a skeptic than I anticipated."

"Look, I appreciate what you did for me; I could have been pretty seriously hurt. But, if you don't mind, I'd just as soon you pull over and let me out."

They sat and stared at each other in silence. The man instructed the driver, "Do as he says."

As the car rolled to a stop, Davy opened the door and stuck one leg out, his shoe dragging on the pea gravel.

"I'm telling you the truth, Davy. You have a magnificent benefactor." The grin was gone from the man's face and he appeared quite genuine. He reached out his hand and said, "My name is Martinique. You may call me Marti if you like."

One leg still outside the car, Davy slowly extended his hand and they shook. "Okay, Martinique, so why would Mr. Silverstone show any interest in me? Why would he even know I exist?"

"Long story short, when Emerald was a boy, he was as much a struggling orphan as you are now. He didn't like being poor. He was determined to achieve massive success, and obviously, he did. He played hard and fast with the rules, offending some in the process. He transitioned with achievement from the illegitimate system to the legitimate one."

Davy sported a half grin, part amused and part skeptical. He instinctively understood the art of brinkmanship.

Martinique continued, "As a person gets older he sometimes has regrets about the way he has lived and comes to understand there's more to life than money, power and fame-a spiritual conversion, if you will. He wants to give something back to the world, make amends for some of the things he has done. So, he has people who search the state looking for young people who have unexpectedly lost their parents and are struggling to get by, young people who have a lot of potential, someone like you, Davy. Many are evaluated; few are chosen."

"With all due respect, Mr. Martinique, I find this a little difficult to comprehend. This sounds a lot like Little Orphan Annie and Big Daddy Warbucks. Like, I believe everything I'm told. Why, you could be anybody. I may not have lived as long as you, but I have figured a few things out on my own."

Marti laughed. "What do people your age know about Little Orphan Annie?"

Davy chuckled. "Hey man, I read a lot. I spend time at the library."

"I know."

"Besides, I've seen the film. It was a great story, I loved it. Perhaps you would have liked it better if I had said Harry Potter?"

"Harry Potter, yes, more appropriate than you know. I'm not sure... I don't know exactly what to say. I did save you from a bad situation back there, so you're ahead of the game so far. But, the offer is genuine. I won't hold you against your will. You may leave now if you wish. I'd be glad to drop you off any place you say. Actually, you can leave any time: now, next week, next month, whatever. But think about it. It's the real deal. You'll never have an opportunity like this come your way again, ever, being mentored by Emerald Silverstone. A lot of highly successful businessmen would die for an opportunity like that. It's your call."

The chauffeur sat minding his own business, but Davy supposed he was drinking in every word. He sat in quiet contemplation before saying, "I guess I don't have a lot to lose. Besides, I like adventure, suppose you tell me more."

He pulled his foot back inside and closed the door.

"Good call, Davy, not unlike what we would expect from you. Welcome aboard. This is a real game changer in your life. I came up the hard way also. I accomplished a certain amount of success on my own. As I look back, I'm not always proud of what I did. I had the good fortune to become connected with Emerald. I have risen to become his right hand man, everybody who sees him goes through me. I lay out his schedule, see his plans are communicated, kind of a gilded flunky."

Davy fully understood the importance of recognizing opportunity when it presented itself. He also understood the strategic importance of not appearing too eager. The limo pulled back onto the road. Davy's grin was boyish and sometimes came across as a confident smirk.

"You are the sixth youth he has taken under his wing the way he is going to be doing for you. You'll need to go to college after some personal instruction he will provide for you from some people highly respected in their field. Not just any college, a prestigious college where you will make important contacts. But first, you will receive some invaluable coaching this summer and fall to prepare you; it's important for you to know how to play the role. Perception is everything."

"And what, exactly, is my role?"

"You will be trained to become one of his managers. The role of a successful businessman."

Davy's face now reflected total focus.

"You can expect to rub shoulders with some of the most powerful movers and shakers in the industries. There is no better schooling than at their side watching and learning what happens in the world where decisions are made that really matter. You will meet Senators and leaders from around the world. You will need to know how to conduct yourself to fit in with the famous, and powerful. You are not just going to leapfrog over your classmates and the wealthy of San Antonio, but over many of the great men of the United States, even beyond. The world as you have known it is about to change radically. Emerald will pay all expenses, make all arrangements, and pay you a generous allowance. Financial struggles are a thing of the past."

Marti had his full attention. Davy's mind was racing ahead as he began to consider the possibilities. He had survived well enough on the streets, but he hated being poor. He looked down at his jeans, clean but faded, and his gym shoes were showing wear. Davy fondly remembered when he wore nice clothing.

"In about ten years, Davy, you will be making more money that you ever dreamed possible. From this time forth, you are going to have a very nice life. Also, you will actually meet and socialize with Emerald from time to time. Few people have that privilege. Most people call him Mr. Silverstone. He will want you to call him Emerald."

"What makes you think I'll be any good at this type of thing? That is, assuming all this works out as you are suggesting."

"Ohhhh, Emerald is very astute at understanding people. He doesn't make many mistakes. Besides, he's been tracking you since you were a freshman, fresh out of Junior High, after your family died. He has analyzed you extensively and knows a lot about you."

"You mean to tell me that all during those four years of high school, years when I struggled and wondered how the hell I was going to survive the following week, all that time, someone was looking over my shoulder planning my future, God like, and I didn't even know it? Man, I didn't even have a clue."

"Something like that."

Davy began to feel a tinge of anger. "If you had that kind of interest in me, why would you let me twist in the wind like that? I could have used some help, at least some encouragement. It would have made a big difference if I had known help was on the way."

"Of course, but allow me to apologize. We hated to leave you dangling for so long, but it was absolutely necessary to do so. We had to see how you functioned under stress, how you handle adversity. You may not appreciate that now, but this was such an important decision. You will understand more with time, so just bear with us."

Davy stared, but said nothing. He could feel the vibration of the tires against the pavement.

"At the estate you will meet Travis and Sarah, two other young apprentices much like yourself. It's unusual to have three novices starting out so close together, or even two for that matter, but it just worked out that way. I'm sure you will like them and should get along well with them. They are good kids and will help you get acclimated. I have something for you. Perhaps this will help."

He handed Davy a framed newspaper clipping. Davy's eyes bugged as he saw a picture of three men with Clinton at a reception hosted by the President in honor of the Dallas Cowboys winning Super Bowl XXX in 1996. On the left was Quarterback Troy Aikman and on the right was Deion Sanders, both in their Sunday best. In the middle stood Davy clad in his high school football uniform, number six.

"Man, that is so cool. How did you do that?"

"It's a simple matter to crop a photo, my apologies to Emmitt Smith, but he's out and you are in, and it was just a little more effort to have it printed like a newspaper. You like?"

"Of course. That was my dream at one time, to play for the Dallas football team."

"I know."

Davy once more became quiet and pensive, but that didn't last long. He never stayed quiet for long. Soon, he and Martinique were engaged in light banter, joking back and forth, asking questions; in short they were feeling each other out, both with a natural instinct for doing so. Marti was particularly entertained by Davy's ability to imitate others, including Emerald Silverstone as well as himself. Before long, Davy actually had Marti laughing out loud, no small feat. His ability to mimic people was legendary with his friends and indicated a true talent.

"I guess I was fortunate you came along when you did," said Davy. "I hate to think what would have happened if you hadn't been there to help me out."

"Actually, nothing would have happened. Nothing happens by chance in Emerald's world. There were two other cars in the immediate vicinity with occupants who would have insured that nothing happened to you. You're special now; get used to it."

"You mean you had reinforcements?"

Davy looked around.

"I don't see them. Where are they now?"

"Right where they need to be. You don't see them, but they are there. You'll find that Emerald usually has backup plans of B, C, and sometimes even D. He doesn't leave much to chance."

"That's nice to know, that someone is looking out for you, but also feels a little creepy."

Marti laughed.

As they sped north on Highway 10, Davy said, "This is the exit for The Dominion, the gated community for the rich and powerful. Why doesn't Emerald live there? Not fancy enough, I suppose."

"Not strategic enough."

The limo slowed down and eased around the corner onto Beaumont Drive where it proceeded another quarter of a mile to the top of a tall hill and turned onto a secluded street called Crystal Park.

"Emerald calls it his Mt. Olympus," spoke Marti as he watched Davy who was mesmerized by the luxurious homes he was viewing.

The limo once more slowed down to turn into a private concrete lane and the driver pushed a five digit code into a keypad on the dash that opened a massive set of iron gates. Inside they were confronted by a second set of gates. A tower stood to either side. Davy considered the towers housed armed guards, though he was not able to see through the tower tinted glass. The driver pushed a second set of five digits and those gates swung open also. The gates symbolized the division between the elite and the common masses. Davy knew that in passing through the gates, he was making that rare transition to the other side.

2
A GRAND ESTATE

As the shiny black stretch limo pulled into the driveway from Crystal Park and eased up the concrete drive, Davy could sense his new future coming toward him as though it were the fulfillment of destiny. The huge brick gate posts held a large bronze sign that proclaimed, Welcome to Emerald Manor. The driveway curved smoothly several times as it wound toward the mansion.

The flags on the golf greens waved for someone to come out and play. Davy saw three gardeners diligently attending a well-manicured lawn which seemed in no immediate need for maintenance. High brick walls surrounded the property, and behind the large backyard was a backdrop of woods. Davy wondered whether the walls were for privacy, or to deter low society people such as himself.

Davy deemed there might be fifty acres in the estate, perhaps more. *Beautiful* thought Davy. *I've never seen trees so vibrant and stately for this part of the country.*

Marti read Davy's mind. "Truckloads of topsoil hauled in. A little attention by the gardeners, fertilizer and lots of water makes a huge difference, enormous amounts of water. Emerald refers to his estate as his own personal Babylonian Hanging Gardens. He likes ornate."

Davy's breath was caught short as they approached the manor. In some ways it reminded him of a small castle. The house had a dome with a golden tinge in the center and two additions extending on either side like the Capital Building. The dome reached perhaps fifty feet into the air with two rows of etched and stained glass windows wrapped around the upper portion. The six-car garage had a thatched roof.

The driveway circled around a beautiful white stone fountain in its center spouting water twenty feet into the air and falling upon four sculptured horses. The perimeter was ringed with brilliant red roses. On the outside of the sidewalk banisters, marble statues were strategically placed amongst the flowers. Two large sculpted lions stood, one on either side before the steps, guarding the entry.

As they passed through two massive wood doors, each with a large brass lion's head with a ring through the nose for a knocker, Davy thought of Dorothy and her friends entering the Emerald City. He could not resist thinking how this very moment symbolized the way his life was perhaps about to change. He was afraid he would awaken and find this was just a very nice dream.

Davy found himself in wonderment as he surveyed the scene before him. The foyer, about ten feet square, had a slate floor and the walls dark timbers that curved inward forming a vaulted ceiling. As Davy advanced under the dome, he thought of some cathedrals he had seen, like St. Mary Cathedral when his cousin married in Austin or St Anthony Cathedral when his class took a field trip to Beaumont. The walls were dark paneling that matched the structural timbers tapering to a point high in the apex.

Some large paintings, six by eight feet, hung on the walls. They took his breath away. Davy stopped before one of the paintings and said, "Otto Van Bismarck. I remember seeing that very picture in history class."

"That's right. This is the original portrait. Bismarck was a great leader of Germany. Emerald is descended from both Bismarck and La Rothschild on his paternal side. The next portrait is of Medici, the great financier in Europe. The portraits next to them, of course, are their wives. Emerald comes from the Medici on his maternal line. His illustrious ancestors include Peter the Great and Charlemagne."

"How can he be related to such famous ancestors? I thought Emerald was an orphan."

"Being an orphan means you have no parents. It doesn't mean you have no ancestors."

"I guess that makes sense. So, Emerald is descended from Otto Van Bismarck, Rothschild and Medici? That is incredible. He was related to all those powerful men?" Davy marveled and wondered how it felt to be born into such an illustrious family.

"Oh them and much more, all the names of power you would recognize in world history. The bastards are all related, descended from the original royal family. The ruling class always married within itself, never polluting itself with common blood. There are two classes, the rulers and those unfortunate masses of the world that are manipulated at will. The ruling class is very jealous of its power and its heritage. If you are not already in, you can't get in, a rather exclusive universe. They consider themselves to be gods, and they expect to be worshiped as gods. You can see why America with its democracy would be a threat to them."

"If he had that kind of heritage, how did he end up as a poor orphan?"

"It's an interesting story. Emerald's grandfather, Sir Reginald Bismarck Silverstone, was a man of great wealth and influence. Emerald's father, Reginald Rothschild Bismarck Silverstone, was also powerful in world politics. Emerald was being groomed, even as a child, to inherit this great position of power in preparation for the time when his father and grandfather should both die. He was a brilliant and strong-willed child."

"Sounds good so far. So, what happened?"

"Emerald's cousin Maximilien, having unbridled ambition and a scheming mind, had other ideas. When the old Patriarch died, Maxi-boy conspired with evil allies to have Emerald's father assassinated, along with all cousins, loyal advisers and political friends whom he saw as potential adversaries. He wanted total kill, all on a single night. One hundred twenty eight died that night. The lone exceptions were Emerald and Abner."

"Wow!" exclaimed Davy. "How did Emerald escape?" Davy had never before experienced such intrigue.

"Abner, a faithful and trusted aid of Sir Reginald, was able to escape, taking the lad, aged eight at the time, with him to America. Abner had access to some residual wealth and was able to support Emerald in a manner worthy of the grandson of Sir Reginald. Abner began to train the lad in the art of high finance and power so that someday he could depose the evil ones and regain his position. Emerald was an eager student; he hungered for revenge and to fulfill his destiny."

"Truth really can be more interesting than fiction," said Davy.

"Unfortunately, Abner was killed in a bizarre accident. He died when a drunken thug ran a red light while trying to elude the police. Some have speculated that Maximilien was responsible for the accident, that he tracked Emerald and Abner down. Maximilien had come under the influence of militant radical Muslims."

"Do you think they killed Abner?"

"They could easily have manipulated Abner's death, but I don't think so. If it had been Maximilien and his evil comrades, they would not have stopped until they had also killed Emerald. If he knew about Emerald and failed to eliminate him, that was his poor judgment. Anyway, it was quite a tragedy and had a profound effect on events. Only Abner had access to the residual income, so that all ended. In the blink of an eye, Emerald was as destitute as any street urchin. He was twelve at the time."

"That is sad," said Davy. It had to be difficult for anyone going from wealth to poverty and losing his whole family. That was quite a tragedy for any person, let alone a child."

"It was an incredible struggle, even to survive at times. However, due to his heritage, his dominant nature and the training he received at the hands of Abner, survive he did. He was eventually able to reclaim what was rightfully his."

"So, he regained his great fortune and position of power? I can't wait to hear that story."

"He reclaimed what was rightfully his, and more. He was worthy of his magnificent heritage. His father and grandfather would have been proud. But, we'll talk about his accomplishments later."

"What did Emerald do about his cousin, Maximilien, the one who had them all killed?"

"Retribution is glorious satisfaction, as Emerald says. Justice was served. He cleaned out the whole nest of them. Of course, with radical Muslims, there are always more to take their place, like locusts, like army ants. They just keep coming. That was when Emerald was a young buck with more enthusiasm then sense."

Davy did a quick calculation in his head. Assuming Emerald was eighty or older, which seemed reasonable, could place the assassination around the Second World War. He grinned at the thought of a poor orphan overcoming huge obstacles to achieve massive wealth. Davy pondered the mystery, the excitement of such a person. He wondered how it felt for one so destitute to achieve so much.

A large crystal chandelier about ten feet in diameter hung suspended twenty feet overhead by a golden chain from the apex of the ceiling. Five tiers of lights, perhaps a hundred or so candle-shaped, flickering light bulbs, gave the impression of gazing into a starry sky. Directly below the chandelier, Davy saw a pile of large rocks artfully stacked.

"An altar," said Marti, "like the ones the ancients built, an altar of rocks. That's an Emerald thing. He would like for you to think of the great dome room as your spiritual womb. The key to life he says lies in worship at the altar in the great dome room."

My spiritual womb, the great dome room? Davy thought it strange, but the thought intrigued him. Exacerbating Davy's amazement, he sensed vibrations emanating from the altar, perhaps chemical or electrical, maybe even spiritual. He quickly dismissed such thoughts as coming from an overactive imagination.

Davy felt an increasing level of anxiety. How is it that a young man, not much more than a boy, a boy of the streets, could step from a life of poverty into such a world of opulence, and all within the space of a few hours without feeling some shock to his sensibilities, perhaps even a sense of revulsion as he realized how such a tiny fraction of the wealth could have done so much to relieve the destitution he saw in another world? His discomfort was overcome by the thought he was to become a part of such wealth. He still had difficulty believing this was all happening.

To the left and the right of the dome two large halls provided access to both stories on the wings. Gazing down the halls he could see a beautiful spiral staircase of polished walnut which extended prominently out into each hall, one on the East Wing and one on the West Wing. The stairs curved upward and emptied into a loft where a railing ran across the full length overlooking the great halls. He could envision James Bond with a curvy blond on his arm, or even Prince William and Kate standing at the balcony overlooking their wedding guests. A feeling came upon him of sanctity, as though he was in the presence of that which he was unworthy, in the presence of God's throne room.

It occurred to him *If things don't work out, perhaps I can take something of value with me on the way out. Something of great value to me would be so insignificant, would never be missed by them.* He quickly dismissed the thought. That would be stealing, something his mother would not have approved. He again marveled at the ornate interior. Everything fit together so naturally and so pleasing to the eye, perhaps designed by angels or other divine creatures, surely the handiwork of God.

Davy thought of his mother, his father, and his little sister. How he wished he could share this moment with them. How could he ever fully enjoy such wealth without a feeling of guilt? He assumed a level of comfort would come with time. For him to accept his new lifestyle it would become necessary for him to let go of influences which shackled him to the past.

Davy was bothered by the thought that giving up his past might somehow be disloyal to his family. Maybe that was just negative thinking. He steeled himself; he would not let negative thoughts accumulated over his short lifetime deprive him of the grand opportunity which stood before him now. He would never return to his past, could never return. His·family would want him to move ahead, to grasp the opportunity with both hands. In some strange way he would not only be succeeding for himself, but for them as well, that he would be redeeming their lives in what had seemed to be such senseless deaths. He vividly remembered their funeral and pulled upon his great inner strength.

"Think you could feel comfortable with such wealth?" asked Marti, appearing to perceive his thoughts.

Davy grinned and nodded his head.

Marti could sense some lingering doubt. "You'll adjust to it quicker than you might imagine. Some internal conflict is to be expected. Soon enough you will feel comfortable and know you belong. You will again be with people who care, a family which you have not had for quite a while now. Everyone needs family, particularly young folks. Welcome home, Davy."

Davy could only nod and swallow the lump he felt rising in his throat.

"It's all so hard to comprehend. What will my friends think of my new lifestyle?"

"Well, that's the thing, Davy. You are not allowed to share this moment with your friends, or even your remaining family. Of course you will need to send some letters with a brief explanation, which we will help you compose so you can leave them behind without any loose ends. I already have the list with addresses compiled. We will need to accomplish this by the end of tomorrow. For the first time, Davy was troubled with the thought he was truly leaving his past behind. It was time to cross the Rubicon.

Marti again seemed to perceive his emotions. "But only for a time. When you are comfortably ensconced in your new life position, you will surely want to reconnect with your family and friends."

Marti motioned with his hand. "Let's go out into the kitchen. I'll introduce you to Antoinette."

Marti led and Davy followed. He could only think how ornate everything looked. "So, Antoinette is the cook then?"

"Not exactly. She's Emerald's wife, sexy little thing, French and feisty as hell. Make sure you behave yourself around her. I don't think she means to, but she does come on a little too much sometimes. He's not naturally jealous, but that just might be a problem. So don't be stupid."

"You're suggesting the benefactor might not be so beneficent if someone was messing with Antoinette?"

"Bingo," replied Marty, pointing his finger at Davy."

"Hey man, there's no way I'm going to let that happen," Davy's nervous laugh covered his mild irritation. *Besides*, he thought, *why would I want to mess around with an older woman? I don't care how feisty she is.*

"I know, but it's better to mention it and be safe than not to mention it and be sorry."

"I know that stuff," replied Davy with some annoyance. "I'm not about to do something stupid and watch all this go down the toilet."

"Hey, hey, don't be offended. I just want to help. Don't get your ass out of joint."

"Strange talk you use at times for a man of your position."

"Oh, I can talk blue blood with the best of them. It's refreshing not to have to talk that arrogant crap all the time. Like they say, you can take the boy out of the country, but you can't take the country out of the boy."

They rounded a corner and entered the kitchen area which surprised Davy. He had expected a large industrial style kitchen with stainless steel accessories all over the place. And though there were some stainless steel pans and cutlery, the kitchen was actually quaint and homey, slightly larger than the average kitchen and well-designed, like a picture out of a Good Housekeeping magazine. Davy was also surprised she was seemingly in her thirties, surely much younger than Emerald. She was also quite attractive.

A trophy wife, thought Davy. She was immersed in a cooking project.

"Antoinette, meet Davy, Davy Monday, the newest member of the family."

She responded with an engaging smile. "Davy! It's so good to meet you. I have heard so much about you, I feel like I already know you. Say, you're quite an outstanding young man, handsome too." She shook his hand daintily, but with enthusiasm.

Davy's gaze swept her petite curved body. Her fluffed frosted hair was the work of a master hair dresser and dangling earrings swung violently like miniature pendulums with each sharp movement of her head. *Nice butt,* he thought. *Nice everything. Pretty sexy for an older lady. She can't be all that old.* He had no objection to her low cut white chiffon blouse and short tight black skirt.

"Whatever you do," interjected Marti, "don't call her Annie. She'll bite your head off, with great efficiency, I might add." Marti grinned broadly. Antoinette responded with a chirp of a laugh and rolled her flashing eyes playfully.

"It's a pleasure to meet you, Antoinette." Davy was delighted to shake her hand.

"No, no, no, the pleasure is all mine. You are such an angel."She cupped his face with her fingers with a slight squeeze.

He was pleased and felt affection for Antoinette. "I'm somewhat surprised. I thought people like you would have a cook. You don't exactly look like a cook"

"Merci," exclaimed Antoinette. "We do, we do. Of course we have a cook. You would expect people like us not to have a cook?"

"Antoinette loves to create new exotic recipes. She's pretty good at it too. She was doing quite well for herself before she ever met Emerald, as a consultant to exclusive restaurants and the very wealthy for private consultation."

Of course, thought Davy. *How could anyone so attractive and gifted not be successful? Surely, Emerald would not marry someone who had not achieved great things.*

"She is food editor of "The Chief's Delight" and has several books to her credit, including *The Provocative Relationship between Exotic Cuisine and the Boudoir.* She started by washing dishes in a French restaurant, would you believe? Lucky thing for Julia Child she married Emerald when she did. Can you imagine Julia Child competing with someone good-looking, sexy, vivacious, and a better cook?" Antoinette chirped another laugh and waved her hand.

Marti continued, "The chef works full time, supposedly. Actually, Antoinette runs him out of her kitchen. Romaine probably doesn't put in more than eight hours in any given week; he just sits at home and draws his salary, reads or goes fishing. Nice gig, if you know what I mean. I'll say one thing; we eat very well here, probably better than anyone else on the face of the earth. More food than we could possibly eat. She usually ends up feeding leftovers to Fifi and Mitzi. They feel entitled to such delicacies and just assume that all dogs eat that way. They are spoiled rotten."

"They are good dogs. They are my poodles. I love them, and that's that. Anyway, Romaine gets in my way. I know he means well, and he is a good chef as far as that goes. I love to cook. I'd rather cook than have sex. I even love to wash dishes; it is so sensual. Everything I do is sensual! Her eyes illuminated with excitement.

Davy was hesitant to pursue that avenue of conversation, fearful of being unable to control his rising passion. He retreated into the safety of passive observation as Antoinette and Marti engaged in small talk and repartee. Their conversation flowed freely and seemed natural. Davy instinctively knew that soon he would adapt to the flow every bit as naturally. He looked forward to developing his own friendly relationship with her. Antoinette seemed animated with the conversation, but when she had her fill, she ran them both out, waving her large wooden spoon wildly, and bopping Marti in a show of aggressive playfulness on the back of the head. Marti feigned outrage and fear as he and Davy fled.

Marti was chuckling to himself as they left the kitchen, but rubbed his head and said, "Damn, that kind of hurt a little bit. Like I said, she's one interesting lady."

"I don't want to diss you, but you just got bested by the lady," Davy ribbed in a good nature way."

Just make sure you don't get too friendly with her. If you mess with Emerald's woman, you'll last about as long as a ladybug in a chicken yard."

"I'm sure that is true," said Davy. "Anyway, I'd never do that. A ladybug in a chicken yard? You crack me up." He did his best chicken impersonation. "Man, she kicked your ass." Marti laughed.

They passed the horse fountain once again as Marti began a tour of the grounds. Marti said, "There are eighty acres here. The height of the hill plus the wall gives us great privacy. Irrigation keeps the lawn, bushes, grass and trees incredibly lush. Everything on the outside pales in comparison to Emerald's Babylonian Hanging Gardens, as he refers to his estate. Inside the stone wall is an inner chain link fence providing a twenty foot dog run for the Dobermans."

"Dobermans? Is that like pet Dobermans or protection Dobermans?"

"Guard dogs, definitely not pets. Armed guards are stationed around the property, but pretty much out of sight. You won't even know they are there. Trust me; they know what they are doing. That is all backed up by sophisticated electronic surveillance equipment, the latest and best of course. Keep a tight perimeter, as Emerald says."

"Yes sir," responded Davy. He looked around, but they were no more visible than any he had seen while riding in the limo. It was not lost on Davy that great wealth requires intense security.

"He keeps a low profile as does any power player who's worth his salt. Everyone knows he is a very rich man. They just don't have any idea how rich he is. He has considerable influence in most governments on the face of the earth. Political influence leads to power. To have that much wealth and influence is like looking at an iceberg, nine-tenths of it is underwater. Never let people know what's really going on. Hold your cards close to your vest. Let the world always underestimate you. Control is the key and that leads to power. Politicians understand that concept quite well and nobody understands it better than Emerald."

Davy nodded. He stared at Marti, searching for a clue to all the mysterious information he knew must surely come.

"You will have one week to relax and become acquainted, get comfortable with the house and grounds and with your new family. After one week you will receive your own private tutor. He is just finishing up with Travis and Sarah. They are your new brother and sister in the family. You will meet them soon enough."

Davy wondered how it would feel to have family again, how they would compare to the only family he had known. *No one could ever be as precious to me as my father, my mother and little sister. I would never allow it.*

"Shaheik will school you in such things as how to conduct yourself in proper company, how to project the image of power, how to intimidate when that is your purpose, how to appear ineffective when that is your purpose, and many more things you will never learn in school."

"How is it I have never heard such things before?" asked Davy.

"They don't teach massive success in the schools, Davy. They teach you how to subordinate yourself to the needs of the wealthy and powerful, how to help them to become even more wealthy and powerful. The masses are kept purposely ignorant. The school systems are funded by the insiders, both public and private schools, so why would it not work that way? It is their own private personnel pool and indoctrination camp that provides them with the best and smartest brains that graduate every year."

Davy found the conversation mesmerizing, realizing he had access to privileged information.

"Only by working for the rich and powerful on the inside do you get a real education, learn how to manipulate the system. Common people don't have a chance. They have no idea how things work, not even the professors and college presidents. They are just tools in the hands of the wealthy, as are the churches, the banks, law enforcement, the medical field, the news media, the entertainment industry, even the military."

"I find that a little disconcerting."

"Of course. Politicians are quite adroit at working the system. They give the appearance of serving the public, but usually they are milking the system. Politicians are so easy to manipulate. The most important thing in their world is winning the next election and hanging on to power. We don't care who wins an election. We control them all. The thing you need to understand is The System is God. Remember that and you will do quite well."

"What do you mean by that?"

"He who is most loyal to The System is the one most likely to be anointed by The System. He who does not respect The System is likely to be crushed. People become successful by understanding The System is God. Nobody understands that better than Emerald. He is loyal to The System. He demands absolute loyalty from his associates."

"But, I thought Emerald didn't exactly work within The System, at least in his earlier years."

"Emerald has always understood the value of respecting The System. There is more than one system; for example, there are many isolated local systems: medical, legal, educational, financial, law enforcement, armed services, just to mention a few, and those are just the legal ones. It is possible to rob a bank or commit murder and get off with a relatively light punishment or perhaps none at all. But it would be a terrible mistake to offend the judge or the judiciary system. For that they will hang you high. Some systems are legit and some are not, depends on which arena you choose to play. All such systems are always subordinate to a higher system until you reach the very top. The important thing is, the System is always God. Ignore that at your own peril."

"I've never thought of it like that."

"Few do. They can't figure out why life is so difficult."

Marti didn't take time to introduce him to the three gardeners, who were Hispanic. Davy nodded toward them and said, "Buenos dios, Amigos." Marti ignored them and they kept working with their heads down. Maria, the cleaning lady who also did the laundry and ironing, was also treated with indifference by Marti, though he did take a brief moment to introduce her to Davy, as he would of necessity interact with her occasionally.

Marti continued his instructions. "I know you are a gregarious person by nature and you genuinely like people, all people, regardless of their station in life. That's good, Davy. It can move you rapidly along your purpose in life. Emerald is amazed that as a homeless boy you were elected as senior class president."

"Yes, that did come as quite a surprise. One of my friends, Jimmy Price, wants to major in political science. He made a bet with some friends he could get me elected."

"You were elected class president on a bet?"

Davy laughed. "Sounds crazy doesn't it?"

Marti grinned."Maybe not so crazy as you might think. Focused people can accomplish much. Your ability to mix so freely and effortlessly with people is one of the traits Emerald highly prizes in you, and it will serve you well. You have extraordinary talent. But you need to focus your efforts. There are seven billion people in the world. If you expend your efforts being nice to every single one, there won't be much of you left to help Emerald accomplish his purposes. You might not fulfill your potential. In short, it's not appropriate to fraternize with the service staff."

Davy swallowed with discomfort, wondering why it was not appropriate to be friendly to anyone.

"You now have an image to uphold, a role to play. To be successful, you must play it well. The thing is, you're operating on a whole new level now. You have to decide which side of the fence you wish to play. It will take all of your efforts and skills focusing on people who really matter, people of great power you want to influence. You are entering an exciting world, Davy. You'll have to run hard and become totally committed to your destiny, but it will be worth it.

"You believe I have that kind of ability?"

"If Emerald didn't think you could do that, trust me, you would never have been selected. That's why we watched you closely for four years before bringing you aboard. It will be worth the effort though. Someday you will travel the world in your own private jet. You will have experiences others can only dream of. You will meet the movers and shakers of the world. You will cavort with movie stars, the rich and the famous. It's a wonderful life. You will live like a king. Are you up to the challenge, Davy?"

Cloaking his reservations, Davy said, "Of course. I have confidence in myself and I have the desire and the drive. Emerald thinks I can do it and that's good enough for me."

"Well-spoken, Davy. I can see you will go far. You're going all the way to the top. Would you like to meet your new family?"

"Mr. Silverstone?"

"No, not Emerald, though surely he will want to meet you and he does consider you as family. But Emerald is a busy man and is often gone, conducting his worldwide business. I communicate with Emerald every day. I'm like the traffic controller at La Guardia Airport, only on a larger scale. I facilitate the action, but the real action is out there, in the business world. That is where you will come in. You will become one of the men in charge, out in the business and political world."

It all seemed a bit much for Davy to comprehend. For all his dreams of wealth and power, Davy had never considered the responsibility and personal risks that might attend such glorious positions. Nor had he ever considered the requirement to such a position of realigning his personal values. But those were issues he would deal with later.

Marti continued, "Me, I'm just happy doing what I do, all the perks without the responsibility or risks. You may only see Emerald every few months. When you meet him he will dump more information on you in a short time than you have ever experienced before, so be prepared to absorb as much as possible. You are now family. You are part of a high quality family. You will be expected to perform at a high level. Speaking of family, would you like to meet Travis and Sarah now?"

"Of course."

3
A NEW BROTHER AND SISTER

Returning to the mansion and ascending the spiral staircase in the grand hall to the East, Davy's thoughts returned to his youth when he watched the Disney film of Cinderella with his family. What other comparison could his poor store of memory recall; certainly nothing he had actually experienced himself? He remembered how he had such an awareness of love and comfort, sitting beside his mother, father, and little sister.

The whole movie, the castle, the magnificence all seemed larger than life at the time. He had hungered as a child to experience that kind of life, one of massive luxury. But as much as he longed for the good life, one filled with an abundance of pleasure, rich with experience, one of unlimited opportunity, he now realized that in entering one strange new world, he was leaving another behind, one he had thoroughly loved, even with its limitations, with all of its abrasions. As he climbed higher he knew he could not live in both worlds. He instinctively knew Emerald would never tolerate divided loyalty.

To enter the opportunity of his new life before him would require him to forever close the door on his past. He wondered if he could do so, if he really wanted to. His thoughts returned to his family once more. How he missed them. He would give anything if they could be with him now, to share the moment with him, to experience the beauty and luxury they had never known. What galactic spiritual forces were at work to decide who will live their lives in glorious luxury and who will experience a desperate struggle in an abrading world of despair? In the midst of his glorious wonderment of opportunity, he could not help but feel a tinge of sadness, as though he was deserting his heritage and leaving an important part of himself behind.

Marti continued his instructions. "You will meet remarkable associates in this house. You will have an opportunity to learn great things and to build valuable relationships. Building an intimate network of quality relationships is vital to success. You must do that well.

"I feel I do a reasonable job of building a network of quality relationships."

"Probably not. The last three doors on the left are apartments. You will live in one. They each have a kitchenette complete with a small refrigerator, electric grill, table, chairs and cabinets. Travis and Sarah live in the other two."

"Travis and Sarah, so they are my new brother and sister, recently adopted, the chosen few like me?" He found himself with an increased longing for family which he had before successfully kept stifled. The surging feeling surprised him.

"They are," Marti said with a grin." Let's go find them now. They are in the conference room with Shahiek. He is finishing up his instructions in ballroom dancing and proper etiquette and protocol with the elite. You don't run into a room full of emissaries like you just came in from slopping hogs."

"Slopping the hogs?" Davy laughed. "That is indeed strange talk for someone in your life position. What would you know about slopping hogs?"

"Actually, quite a bit. Back in Arkansas, my old man had twenty acres out in the country a ways, rather secluded. Most of it was in woods, but he had a few acres of crops. Some people considered us as poor trash. He had a moonshine still in the middle of the woods, so whiskey paid the bills. But he had a chicken yard and he kept a few sows and an old boar and raised pigs. Or more accurately, I raised pigs."

"I can't see you raising pigs."

"About the only thing the old man raised was hell. He was better at drinking than he was at working, so it was up to me to keep the family going. My mother died when I was still young, probably from grief. They had a baby when I was about three. I don't know if it was a boy or girl. I don't even know what happened to it. Must have died. I barely remember. They never let me hold it. Anyway, he came home extra drunk one night. I watched him take his heavy leather belt off, staring at me the whole time with glassy eyes. I knew what was coming. I had bruises and blood whelps all over me. I thought I might die. I remember it as clearly as if it were yesterday. I thought about killing him when he went to sleep; perhaps it was necessary if I was going to survive."

"That is sad. I'm sorry for what you went through."

Marti shrugged. "What doesn't kill you makes you stronger. Early the next morning, I packed my bags and left. I cleaned his billfold out, about seven hundred dollars. He always carried around a wad of bills, but he sure as hell never spent any on me. I was fourteen at the time and never looked back. I heard later the old man lost the place. I don't know how he made any money without the still. He probably died drunk in a ditch somewhere. Anyway, I wouldn't have used that analogy about hogs if I were talking with the Queen of England. You're not exactly the Queen of England. You have to tailor your conversation to your audience. That's an important ability, speaking specifically to your audience."

"How did you survive? That's pretty young to be out on your own?"

"I had decent survival instincts, mature for my age. I secured a job at a night club cleaning and running errands. I've always made it a point to do more than I was paid to do. That's how you advance in life. The club was ran by some rather sleazy people, but likable. They were good to me. Some customers would come in flaunting money all over the place, usually high class jerks. After they became inebriated, I would follow them out to the parking lot, rough them up a little bit, and take their money. I had to be careful and not do that too often. The owners would have been pissed if they knew I was the one doing that. I figured out I could hang around other night clubs and do the same thing and not jeopardize my employment. I survived."

Davy didn't respond. He didn't think he could do the same thing, but who knows what you would do if you were in another person's shoes.

"That was then. I don't like to think I was that way at one time. But a kid has to survive. You do what you have to do. At least, I was taking from people who had plenty of money. It's not like I was stealing from people who were as desperate as I was, or from little old ladies. At least that's what I told myself. I quit doing all that when I was able to survive with legitimate employment. I found out I had a lot of talent and became fairly successful on my own. But, my life changed dramatically when I met Emerald."

Davy nodded, unsure how much he should add to the conversation, but letting Marti know he was listening.

Marti knocked on the door and leaned his head in. Davy could hear the mumble of conversational tones, but was unable to discern any meaning. Marti backed away from the door and was followed by a young man Davy guessed to be a couple years his senior.

"Davy, this is Travis Gordon. Travis, say hello to Davy Monday."

The two shook with warm, friendly, firm handshakes and exchanged greetings. Davy eyed his six foot four frame.

"So, you're Davy? "We've been hearing quite a bit about you lately. You must be someone pretty special."

Davy was taken off guard by such generous compliment, but he was pleased.

"I can't say as I'm anything special. But you seem impressive enough."

Travis smiled in approval and Davy instantly liked Travis, who looked sophisticated and commanding with a business appearance. Travis wore an easy smile with his casual, but expensive slacks and sports shirt with a sweater vest. Davy surmised that his wavy blond hair and dark blue eyes did not exactly give a macho impression. His earth-tone clothing matched his complexion, being color coordinated. Travis seemed to respect Davy, which pleased Davy immensely. The thought came to him, *he's quite a bit bigger than I am, but I believe I could whip him if I had to. Probably won't happen. He seems nice enough.*

"Sarah is still inside," continued Marti, interrupting the small talk of new acquaintances which seemed to flow rather easily. "She's finishing up with some final instructions for her assignment from Shaheik for next class.

The door, which was slightly ajar, suddenly swung open and out stepped Sarah Lockhart singing a lively tune of Happy Days Are Here Again, glad to be out of class. Spotting Davy, she broke with a wide grin. Davy was smitten by her beauty. His first attraction was to her eyes- light blue and crystal clear, bright, sparkly, dancing, expressive, and full of life. She had a clean-cut dimple on each cheek, both of which seemed without bottom when she grinned broadly, which she did freely. Her cheeks and lips were reddish without the assistance of cosmetics. She had a natural beauty that bespoke of radiant health. Her beauty was enhanced by an air of innocence and Davy considered that she might be an angel. He gladly reached out and shook her hand and utilizing his best charm said, "I am delighted to meet you."

Even with her appearance of angelic innocence, he noticed an expression of flirty sensuality. Davy made a valiant effort to keep his amorous feelings under control as he did not wish to offend her on any level. Ever since his family had died, he successfully guarded his heart from the perils of love and intimate attachment all through high school. It's not that he didn't enjoy the companionship of girls, no, far from that; it's just that after losing his parents and little sister, he had a deep fear of losing the object of his affections ever again. It was just too painful to lose the one loved so deeply. And while Davy was gregarious and had a wide circle of good friends, he always maintained a wall of emotional defense, never allowing himself to become too emotionally attached to any one person. The power of his attraction for Sarah had caught him somewhat off guard, and he struggled to regain mastery of himself, of all his bodily parts, and to guise his infatuation. He did so in the way most natural to him, with a humorous remark. Getting people to laugh solved numerous problems for Davy.

Shaheik came out and Marti introduced him to Davy. "Hello. I am happy to meet you, but I am in a terrible hurry. I am sure I will see you soon. With that he quickly left. Davy considered perhaps he was from the Far East.

Marti spoke again. "Well guys, I have things to do. Travis, you and Sarah show Davy around, his apartment, the family lounge, whatever you choose. With that he abruptly excused himself, leaving the three young people together in a moment of awkward silence.

It was Sarah who broke the silence. "Okay, so let's show you our family lounge."

They walked to the last door on the right down the hall. Inside was a room furnished with several stuffed couches, some beanbag cushion lounges, and some straight chairs with round and square game tables with a game in progress on one. The lounge was definitely designed with young people in mind.

"Like ping pong?" asked Travis picking up a paddle and laying it back on the table.

"Sure, I like all sports, anything that requires a challenge."

Travis laughed. "I thought so."

In one corner of the room was a built-in bar and kitchenette, and in another corner a large screen television. On the walls hung several nice pictures of Emerald and famous people, including two Popes, both autographed, of course. A pair of medieval swords crossed in front of a large royal crest of arms and a cigar store wooden Indian stood in another corner. Someone had placed a bright red necktie on him, a bow on his hair and lipstick liberally applied. He suspected it was Sarah.

"Sweet," said Davy. "This is really nice."

"We're expected to keep it organized," said Sarah. "You get something out; you put it back, unless it's a game in progress, of course. Marti scolds us if we don't keep it neat. The maid comes in once a week to give the place a deep cleaning. College kids might live in a pigs sty, but we're supposed to reflect our station in life."

"Yes," said Travis. "You ever notice how rich people aren't sloppy. And, if they are, they have someone going around cleaning up after them. Their houses never look lived in, you know, toys and clothing scattered all over the floors and furniture. Their houses always look like they are ready for a photo shoot in *Glitz Magazine*."

"Hey," said Davy with a grin, "I always thought messy and disorganized was what made a home feel so comfy and lived in."

Sarah laughed and her eyes sparkled. "Spoken like a typical teenage boy. I know how you guys are. You pile your clothes in the middle of the room, and the next thing you know, you can't find anything to wear or even your bed."

"That's not true!"chuckled Travis with emphasis. "Girls are much worse."

"They aren't either. I'm not." She was adamant. "Boys are so much worse." She picked up a pillow and threw at him. Travis caught the pillow and placed it carefully on the couch, patting it in place.

"There, did you notice how neatly I did that?"

Davy was amused at their good-natured ribbing."This is really nice, this house, you guys, everything that's happening. Man, you gotta love it."

"You think this is something," said Travis, "wait 'til you see this." He opened the door to an adjoining room. They entered a surround sound theater with a projector at the back and eight padded leather recliner vibrator chairs set in a slight arc around the screen. The screen filled one whole wall.

"Awesome," said Davy, his eyes widening in approval.

"You can access movies just by entering a code. We'll show you all that." She flipped a switch; the screen flickered, came to life, and then appeared Leo DiCaprio with two bombshell supermodels, Danielle Mandabach and Crystal Kiltz, one on each arm. They were larger than life as they swaggered down the red carpet of the Kodiak Theater, the public and press eagerly snapping pictures and calling to the stars. She flipped the switch again and the picture disappeared into a small dot in the center of the screen.

"Awesome."

"Wait until you see sports." Travis spoke with enthusiasm. "Basketball, baseball, the players are life-sized. You feel like you are standing there about ten feet behind the quarterback at the line of scrimmage."

"All right! Go Cowboys!" Davy threw an imaginary football. Sarah rolled her eyes. Travis reached up with one hand and caught the imaginary football, placed it carefully on the table and patted it in place.

"See, nice and neat," he said while eying Sarah.

They returned to the main room where Davy was led to another small room. It contained several full-sized commercial video games.

"Check this out," said Travis. He showed the training simulator for an F-16 fighter plane. "It was sitting in a warehouse somewhere on an air force base, no longer being used. This sucker cost something like eight million dollars when it was new. Emerald was able to get his hands on it for considerably less money. You talk about a blast, sitting in the virtual seat of an F-16."

This time, Davy voiced no expression. He simply climbed in and with some instructions from Travis was soon gaining altitude, turning left and right, flying his jet upside down, doing barrel rolls, firing the 20mm cannon and missiles at enemy jet fighters while simultaneously dodging attacks. Sarah marched, Air Force style, back to the lounge area while belting out "Off we go, into the wild blue yonder."

It was over an hour before he emerged back into the world of Sarah and Travis. They were both sipping on a can of soda as they realized he would not be available company until he had his fill of the F-16. Now, he was back with them, though his heart was still inside the simulator.

They picked up the conversation as though he had not been gone. "If you want to go swimming, bowling," said Travis, "sit in the sauna, exercise, shoot hoops, use the batting cage, play tennis or squash; that's all in the basement level."

"Sweet," responded Davy. "I can't believe this is happening to me."

"Believe it," said Sarah. "Katrina comes in once a month, gives us a manicure and pedicure. She comes in weekly to give us a deep massage. She uses reflexology, kinesiology, color and aroma therapy, and healing oils to keep our skin youthful, from aging. And then, once a month we each receive a colonic."

"What," asked Davy with a quizzical expression? "What's a colonic?"

"You don't know what a colonic is?"

"Wait a minute, I'm not sure. Is it what I think it is? I mean, what it sounds like?"

"It's not that big a deal; it's just like an enema, only a little more thorough. Actually, it's a high colonic if you want the correct terminology."

"No, I don't think so. I have no interest in having someone giving me that, a colonic."

Sarah and Travis were both snickering. "It's not that big a deal. Don't make it into something bigger than it is."

"I don't care what you say; nobody, and I mean nobody is touching that part of my anatomy. That's my own private concern."

By now, Sarah and Travis had broken into full laughter. Sarah replied, "It's to improve your health silly. Antoinette cooking with herbs helps to clean the cells of toxins. The deep message we receive moves the toxins along the lymphatic system. Foot soaks and colonics help eliminate the poisons out of the body entirely. Why do you think Hollywood stars are so beautiful? Only the rich can experience such glorious health and vitality. By getting rid of the toxins in your body, you will feel better, be more alert, and have more energy. It's a wonderful opportunity, Davy. Embrace it."

She laughed as she spun herself around in a swivel chair with her arms and legs outstretched.

"Yeah," added Travis. I definitely feel better. Besides, it's not optional. It's something Emerald requires of us."

"Man," said Davy, "I have to think about that a little."

"That is such a minor thing compared to all our advantages," said Sarah. There are so many neat things. Wait until they host some social events. Those are usually held in the ballroom in the basement. There's an orchestra loft that holds about twenty musicians."

"Yeah," said Travis, "They have a social event about once a quarter. Emerald likes to court people who really matter. You wouldn't believe some of the sports figures and movie stars we've seen, singers, you name it. Of course we've only been here long enough to see one of those, but it was pretty neat."

"It was a wonderful experience," said Sarah, "so exciting." Her eyes sparkled.

Travis laughed. "Sarah loved it. She likes excitement. Actually, she was the center of attention. The movie stars were all hanging around her. She can really turn on when she has an audience."

"So, I happen to like parties." She laughed. "That's who I am."

"Marti tells us not to get all goofy over the rich and famous," said Travis. "They like for people to swoon over them, but it makes them nervous, and then they look down on people who do so."

"You're kidding? Real celebrities?"

"He expects us to act like we were born rubbing shoulders with celebrities. That's not so hard to do sometimes. But some of them are real jerks, small people who made it big. Some of the starlets I've seen are real bitches. But some of them are pretty neat, really down to earth. It's almost like they yearn for someone genuine to mix with. The thing is, it's not that we are lucky to know them. In a few years, they will consider themselves lucky to know us. Marti wants us to get used to playing the role."

Sarah's eyes lit up. "I loved the social thing."

"No kidding,"said Travis. "Talk about someone being in their element."

Sarah laughed with delight. "Can I help it if people enjoy being around me?"

Davy became contemplative. "I can't believe this is all happening. This morning I was as close to being a nobody as you can get. If I had died, a few people would have slowed down a few days, said 'too bad,' and some might even have shed a few tears, but then they would have gone back to their everyday lives, and I would just have been a distant memory. I guess your real friends are those who shed tears with you, or for you. But here I am, suddenly in a whole other world, you know, like you're watching a particular actor on television, and he's playing some poor sap, and then you change the channel, and just like that, the same actor is playing some multimillionaire playboy or a movie star. How do you change so quickly and effortlessly from one person into another, and how do you hold on to that part that is the real you, and not get lost in the process?"

"Oh, you'll make the adjustment fast enough. In a week you'll feel more at home here than where you were, and in six months you will actually feel out of place where you came from. You will eventually begin to feel a sense of entitlement to live this way. That's what Marti says. Change happens quickly. All humans go through metamorphosis, adapting to their environment, whether they want to or not. You become different than you were."

"I'm not so sure how I feel about that."

"It doesn't make any difference how you feel about it, you'll change whether you want to or not. Think about it, if you can't change, you can't become rich."

Sarah spoke up with a mischievous grin. "Travis doesn't believe we are created as free moral agents. He believes we come from monkeys and our character is formed by our environment."

"Here we go again." He sported a half grin.

"Don't pay any attention to him; he's an atheist." Her eyes twinkled.

"Now that's not true. I'm an agnostic. You know that. Atheists are as rigid in their thinking as believers. Their religion is rebellion against some authority. They spend all their time and energy trashing a God they don't believe even exists. Me, I'm indifferent. How can you hate something you don't believe? I'm just saying, what's the use in believing anything you can't know for sure? Just show me something concrete. I'm open to the concept. I just prefer proof over superstition. Otherwise, I'll just ride it out and see what develops."

"But, by then it will be too late."

"She thinks I'm going to hell and get toasted forever."

"Guys, guys," broke in Davy. He felt uncomfortable with the sudden shift in conversation toward religion, especially since they were so animated in their bantering back and forth. Not that they seemed belligerent toward each other, they acted more like brother and sister or friends who were ribbing each other with joviality, though aggressively. Even so, Davy didn't want to get sucked into the conversation, at least until he knew them both better and had established rapport with them. He was fearful his present situation might be too fragile. "So, what about the pool and bowling alley, any chance we could take a look?"

"Sure," responded Sarah and Travis together, their minor skirmish disappearing as quickly as it had arisen. Davy breathed a relieved sigh.

In the basement they bowled one game, which Sarah seemed to enjoy the most even when she threw a gutter ball. There abilities were reasonably well-matched, but Davy managed to win by a comfortable margin.

"Enough of this," was the response of Travis after a brief stint on some exercise equipment. The shower rooms held a fresh change of perfectly fitting clothing.

"Would you look at this," said Davy as he held up a white knit sports shirt had their initials on the left chest in fancy lettering.

Next they visited the ballroom. Davy's impression could be summed up in two words, *awesome* and *incredible*.

"Look," said Sarah wide-eyed. "Isn't it beautiful."

Small round tables with four chairs each surrounded the dance floor. Travis adjusted the special effects controls. The curved ceiling was sky blue and lights flickered giving it the appearance of being outside under the stars. Another knob controlled the sound of rain, thunder and lightning flashes softly in the background.

"Kind of like real life," said Travis, "a lot of special effects with someone behind the scenes operating the controls."

Colored spotlights refracted off a rotating disco ball for a spectacular show of flashing light. When they left, they shut off all switches leaving the cavernous ballroom in silent darkness.

"Kind of like real life," Sarah repeated the words of Travis. "The party ends and somebody turns out the lights."

On the way back to their apartments they stopped by the greenhouse which was filled with stunning flowers, including orchids. Sarah breathed deeply. "I love the fragrance of flowers." The pungent aroma of vegetables and exotic herbs made him think of gourmet cooking.

Sarah said,"Aren't the flowers wonderful?" She tenderly caressed some petals.

Travis explained, "Antoinette uses the herbs in her cooking. She uses natural foods the way physicians use medicines, to heal people, to make them stronger and younger. She seems to receive great satisfaction from cooking."

"She loves it," said Sarah. "It's the combinations of assorted herbs plus the way they are prepared. She actually turns back the clock of aging in some cases. At least, that's what I hear. Rich people use all kinds of exotic treatments to keep them young and healthy."

"You would think the public would be more aware of that."

Sarah continued, "She has been a student of Dr. Roberto for many years. He studies herbology and homeopathic medicines from all cultures from around the world, people known for longevity. He is a medical doctor who has majors in statistics, genetics and chemistry."

"Really now," said Davy.

"Oh yes," she responded without slowing down. "According to Marti, his whole purpose in life is rejuvenation and restoration to youthfulness. My understanding is that he is well over one hundred and is extremely active. I have heard he is one hundred twenty, but I don't believe it. Stories like that tend to be exaggerated. He restricts his services to a small group of wealthy patrons."

"He can't be that old." said Davy in a matter-of-fact tone. "You're suggesting that certain foods, spices and herbs can turn the clock back, actually reverse the aging process?"

"Why do you think Emerald married her?" asked Sarah, "besides the fact that she's pretty darned cute?"

"And sexy," added Travis. "Don't forget sexy."

They all laughed.

"Holy cow!" exclaimed Travis while pointing, apparently startled by something. "Look at that!"

Davy and Sarah were startled and looked where he pointed, asking together, "Where?"

"What?"

"I don't see anything."

"It was a rat! A humongous rat, about the size of a cat! It was a giant rat! Man, that was one ugly looking rodent." Travis looked unnerved. Picking up a rock, he tossed it toward the location of the rat. The rock ricocheted off a wheelbarrow into the air toward the glass wall. Travis cringed, realizing too late his mistake. The rock hit a water pipe with a clink and dropped harmlessly to the ground. They all laughed nervously and with relief.

"You are sooo lucky," said Sarah.

"I find it hard to believe there would be rats running around Silverstone Estate. Have you ever seen one before?" asked Davy.

"Never!" said Travis. "I've never ever seen a rat around here. Not a mouse, not a bug, nothing. That was one ugly creature. He looked downright evil. That's as close as I want to get to that varmint."

Davy charged to the location to check it out followed closely by Sarah, but Travis lingered a comfortable distance behind. They saw neither rodent nor evidence it was ever there.

"Be careful," said Travis. "It could be rabid."

"I don't like mice and rats," said Sarah. "They pee and defecate on food. They make my skin crawl. It's like they are the embodiment of some evil spirit."

"And they eat a large percentage of grain that is supposed to feed the world," added Davy. "But, it's only a rat. My friends and I used to kill them with slingshots as a kid down by some old warehouses."

"It wasn't just a rat!

"Hey man, you see one rat, you've seen them all."

"What I don't like about rats and mice is they remind me of evil and of death," said Travis. They carry germs and disease, like the Bubonic Plague. They make my skin crawl too."

On the way back to the mansion they met the head groundskeeper who was weeding a flower bed.

"There's a rat!" exclaimed Travis with tempered excitement.

"A what?"

"A rat. A monster rat," said Sarah.

The head groundskeeper looked dubious. "I've never seen a rat here. What makes you think it was a rat?"

"I'm telling you, it was a rat! I know what a damned rat looks like! Okay?"

The head groundskeeper studied Travis without revealing any emotion. "Of course, I will take care of it immediately."

Only Davy seemed to value the excitement. They then returned to their family lounge, where they entered into a rather interesting conversation.

4
AN INTIMATE CONVERSATION

When they returned to their family lounge, Travis was still unnerved. "I just don't like rats, never have. But this one looked more sinister than normal. I can't explain it." He paced for a bit before joining the others at the table.

"That reminds me of the spider I saw," said Sarah.

"A spider?" inquired Davy with amusement. "What's that all about?"

"Sarah saw a spider, downstairs in the basement," said Travis. Nobody else saw it, but I can tell you the rat was real."

Sarah was incredulous. "Nobody saw the rat either. You're the only one who saw it, just like I was the only one who saw the spider. No difference."

Davy grinned at Sarah and said, "A spider? You saw a spider?"

"Yes, down in the basement. It was a large black spider with a bright yellow spot on its back It had a huge body and long legs. It was hairy looking and really gave me the creeps." She shivered. "It had this thick intricate spider web on a door frame. Normally, I'd just get a stick and kill a spider, but it scared me. I went to get one of the gardeners, and when we returned, it was gone, no spider, no web, no nothing. Travis thought I was just imagining things, but it was real. It's different when Travis sees something. He just expects us to believe it."

"But, the spider was so out of place. You never see spiders at Emerald Estates."

"So are rats. Have you ever seen a rat here?" She leaned forward pointing with her finger.

"No," admitted Travis, sighing, "but that was in the manor and this was in the greenhouse. I suppose you're right. I'm sorry I doubted you. I guess it's just more real when it happens to you."

"Thanks," she said, her triumph ensconced in joyous appreciation.

Davy shook his head. "Spiders and rats, neither one is a big deal."

Sarah thought and then said, "Maybe it's a sign from God, like a vision or something. Maybe he's warning us about some danger."

"Spiders aren't that uncommon, even in fancy houses. You say it had a bright yellow spot on its back?" asked Davy. "Normally, bright colors in insects and reptiles indicate they are poisonous."

"Emerald Estate is not just another fancy house. Maybe it's a demonic spirit materialized," added Travis.

"What are you talking about?" Sarah gave him a quizzical look.

"Sure, why not? You think angels can materialize, why not evil spirits? Maybe evil spirits were trying to tell us something."

Sarah looked at Davy and said, "Don't pay any attention to him. He likes to mess with your head sometimes."

Travis laughed with subdued amusement. Sarah ignored his mirth.

"If this was a novel," said Davy, "they would mean something: an omen, a harbinger of things to come. There would be secret rooms, trap doors, maybe demons and monsters; all kinds of intrigue."

"Sounds creepy," said Sarah. Travis laughed.

Suddenly Sarah said, "Wait right here, guys. I'll be right back." She quickly left and closed the door quietly behind her.

"She went to get her dog," said Travis.

"Her dog?" asked Davy with amusement. "She has a dog?"

"A small one. She found her shortly after she arrived here. The dog was cold, hungry, and malnourished."

"How in the world did she find a stray dog on the estate?"

"She found it in the city, on one of her rare excursions to the outside with Marti. Sarah nourished her back to good health with her mothering instincts. She loves that dog, so don't disrespect the dog. If she loves some guy someday like she loves her dog, that is going to be one lucky boy."

Davy laughed. "That's cool. Anyone who is kind to animals is a good person in my book."

Sarah quickly returned carrying her dog, a Wiener dog, not as big as a wet cat. "This is my baby, Scarlet. Mommy loves you, yes she does. You're such a cute doggie. You like it when mommy rubs your belly, yes you do." The dog had a bright red ribbon on her tail.

She explained to Davy, "Scarlet has a crooked tail. That means she has a bad back and will become crippled while she's still young, so probably nobody wanted her and just discarded her to die. She was almost dead when I found her shortly after I arrived here, but I nourished her back to good health. Dogs that are imperfect should be loved too."

She set the dog on the couch and sat down with Davy and Travis around a small table to play a card game called slap-jack.

"Watch this," said Travis, motioning toward Scarlet. The dog rooted herself under a blanket on the couch and pulled the blanket around her so only her nose was visible peeking out. They laughed as Scarlet watched them through her little peek hole.

Sarah explained, "She's cold-natured, so she always covers herself. She likes to be around people and is content to lie there quietly as long as we keep her company."

"Cool," said Davy.

Sarah shuffled the cards. "She loves to be around people even though she doesn't require attention. She is sooo loveable."

They began to play slap-jack with the cards being equally divided between the players. Whoever ends up with all the cards is the one who wins. It's a simple game, so simple they could talk freely without concentrating on a lot of detailed attention to the rules. All they had to do was keep focused on being the first to spot a jack that had just been played and then having a faster hand than the others. It allows for an enthusiastic show of aggression to gain the most possession of cards, particularly so when the cards are laid down in rapid succession. No one was more animated than Sarah.

They would sometimes become so engaged in their conversation they would momentarily forget to watch for the jack, allowing someone an easy jackpot by default, much to the chagrin of the others. Usually they were attentive and play was aggressive. It started off easy enough, but the longer they played the more energy flowed until they were laughing and knocking cards on the floor. More than once one of them grabbed the cards out of another's hand, claiming to have slapped the jack first.

Grinning, Davy teased Sarah with his eyes and words. "My daddy told me never to trust an obsessive person, especially one who's obsessed with winning."

"What," responded Sarah? "Me? You think I'm obsessive?" She started laughing. "Look who's talking. You're the one who's obsessed to win."

Davy was snickering. "I've never seen anyone who wants to win as badly as you. You're pretty aggressive."

"What else did your daddy say?" asked Sarah with playful sarcasm.

"My daddy told me to be a magnanimous person, but never trust someone who is unreasonably magnanimous."

"Okay," said Travis, obviously enjoying the chiding, "if that's what your daddy said, then what did your mommy say?"

Without missing a beat, Davy said, "My mommy said that passion comes from God, but compulsion comes from Satan."

"Hmmmm," said Travis, "very interesting. Passion is good; compulsion is bad. I like that."

"Just saying, gotta watch Sarah because she's soooo competitive. She really wants to win."

Sarah laughed and threw some cards in his face. "You are funny, annoying, but funny."

Davy calmly picked up the cards and added to his own hand.

"So, Miss Sarah," said Travis, "did your Grammy ever impart words of wisdom to you?"

An impish grin crossed her face. "My Grammy said that the only thing wrong with cute little boys is that they grow up to be disgusting men."

Both boys chortled and Davy said, half under his breath, "That explains her attitude."

"What did you say?" asked Sarah with feigned incredulity.

"I said, you are a very sweet person. That's what I said, and I'm sticking to it."

Sarah laughed. "You lie. I heard what you said. You are in so much trouble."

Travis was amused with Davy's ability to stir up Sarah's emotions. He was equally amused at Sarah's ability to hold her own with Davy.

"What about you, Travis?" asked Davy. "Your parents ever give you worldly wisdom?"

"My daddy got his wisdom from old beer commercials. He said, 'Go for the gusto'. My mommy got her wisdom from her mommy. She said, 'Always wear clean underwear in case you are in an accident and have to go to the hospital'."

Several times they came close to knocking the table over and once one of them actually fell out of the chair. There was a lot of laughing and accusations of cheating. Such is the play of rowdy teenagers. They were all quick of hand, making for close competition, but Sarah appeared to have a slight advantage, one she enjoyed immensely. The game was an excellent ice-breaker, freeing them from the inhibitions of young people who are new to each other. When Sarah finally won the last card, Davy said, "See, I knew you were obsessed to win."

To which Sarah replied back in sing song fashion, "I won the game. La, la, la, la, la." She danced a small jig to match the song.

Davy noticed her golden brown hair flowed freely about her shoulders and tossed like a mane when she laughed or suddenly turned her head to one side in conversation. He threw some cards toward her face. Travis chuckled. With their loss of interest in cards, they broke to retrieve drinks and moved to the bean bag lounges. Sarah responded to Scarlet's begging eyes and took the dog with them. There they began a deeper level of conversation, sharing with each other their innermost feelings, as young people sometimes do.

"So," inquired Sarah, "what happened to your family?"

"Car accident," replied Davy, "when I was a freshman in high school. We were at the varsity football game. That's when I was given the news."

"If you were in the crowd, how did they find you?" asked Sarah.

"I was on the team, one of the players."

"On the team?" asked Travis. "Freshmen usually don't play varsity. Were you one of those hot shot jocks?"

Actually, I was the starting quarterback. Can you believe that? I was coordinated and tall for my age. It's unusual for a freshman to be starting on the varsity, especially as quarterback. I was lucky. It just so happened they didn't have any good quarterbacks on the team, so I ended up starting. The coach figured if he gave me the experience, I would develop into an outstanding player over the next four years."

"That is unusual, starting quarterback as a freshman," said Travis.

"I liked being quarterback because you get to run things. Everything falls on your shoulders. My teammates called me showboat, but the opponents called me bad ass. We were a young team, and undefeated for the season with only three games left. People were talking about the potential of developing a future state champion. I loved football. Until then it was my whole life. I played pickup games all the time. I had pictures of football stars all over my room. My favorite was an autographed one of Troy Aikman."

Travis and Sarah listened without interrupting.

Davy became more pensive as he continued. "It's funny how what's important in your life can change so radically, in a moment. Mom and Dad left the game at half-time to go pick up my little sister from dancing lessons; she was six at the time. Her name was Ginny. That was the last time I ever saw them, alive anyway. They were hit head-on by a drunk driver on the highway. He was doing eighty and was passing on a double yellow line. All three were killed instantly. They didn't tell me about it until the game was over."

Davy took a deep breath. "It's tough losing the three people you love the most, especially when you're a freshman in high school."

He took another deep breath. "It was like being punched in the stomach so hard you can't breathe. I cried until I couldn't cry any more."

"I'm so sorry," said Sarah with quiet sincerity.

"Yes, me too," added Travis. That's a pretty tough thing to have to go through."

Davy continued, "Naturally, I had to give up football. I hated to do so because I loved the game so much, and I had counted on earning a scholarship. I felt like I let my team mates down; they lost the last three games. One moment, football was the most important thing in my life. After the accident, I think I actually hated it. I guess I blamed their tragedy on football. The coaches tried to talk me into playing, but I couldn't do it. By the time I finally got over all that, it was too late. You become rusty without playing. You lose your edge."

Sarah reached out and patted him with one hand while placing the other on his arm.

"I was just suffering so much grief. My grades suffered. I was lucky to move on to the next class. I think my teachers cut me some slack. Anyway, I bounced back the next year a little bit, but it wasn't easy. By the time I was a junior, I was driven by what my dad had always said, that to succeed you must not make excuses, that obstacles are challenges to overcome."

"That is awesome," said Travis. "Wise words from a dad."

Davy bowed his head quietly before continuing. "I always had a lot of friends at school, even after I lost my family and didn't have much money. It was like everyone wanted to be friends with me, even the ones who came from affluent families. It didn't seem to matter that I didn't have any money. It was during this time when I discovered I had a knack that served me well. Kids in school are always looking for something: a car, a motorcycle, a saddle, electric guitar, whatever."

Davy hesitated before continuing. "I listened to what they wanted, and then I'd keep my eyes open and ask questions. I found out you can find a lot of stuff if you ask the right questions and ask the right people. I had formed a good relationship with some people who owned small businesses and they would try to steer me in the right direction. If they didn't know, they usually knew somebody who did. So, I'd find stuff, bring the seller and buyer together, and charge a commission for doing so. Then I had enough money I could pay for it outright, buy it cheap, and resell it to my classmates for good money. Kids want what they want, and they were happy to pay good money to get it. Of course, I was glad to oblige them. I kind of earned a reputation as a finder. They thought I was the best thing that came along since IPod. People in the community, adults even, began to utilize my finding skills."

"Cool," said Sarah.

"Very cool," said Travis. "That probably helped fill a void and helped you be independent."

"I began to make enough money to live on, and then I started to accumulate some in the bank, about three thousand dollars. I didn't spend much on luxuries because the business I was doing was kind of feast or famine, something big would come along or nothing at all, so I needed a reserve to carry me over. My fear of not having money was pretty strong. But I felt like I was beginning to make a little more money the more experience I gained, and thought when I reached five thousand in savings I would feel a little freer to spend for things I wanted. I don't think I was that far away. I could see my business growing. It seemed like I was getting good enough at it part time while I was still a student, so I thought I could build it into a full-time business after I finished school."

"You can bet that's one of the reasons Emerald took notice of you," said Travis. "You have a natural head for business, kind of a built in sixth sense. He says that is a rare commodity and few people have it."

"No kidding? He believes I have natural business sense? I guess I never thought of it that way."

"Sure. If you had it as a kid in school, he sees you having incredible talent when you enter the business world. That's pretty impressive."

"The funeral was hard, knowing I would never see them again. It was tough having my world of security jerked out from under me. I didn't have any idea how I would survive. There was enough insurance to cover immediate expenses, funeral bills and stuff, but there wasn't much left over, and what there was Aunt Myrtle took over."

"That sucks," said Travis.

"Well, in fairness, there were some expenses. Anyway, Aunt Myrtle, mom's sister, took me in, out of obligation. But, I could tell I was a burden to her; she really didn't want me there. She never married, never had any children of her own. I was what you would call an imposition. Oh, I always had a roof over my head, a place to sleep, even meals, if you could call them that, but that's about it. She wasn't at all like my mother, warm, loving, affectionate. I tried being friendly to her, you know, giving her emotional support, making her feel loved, everybody needs that, even Aunt Myrtle. I figured she especially needed it since she seemed so lonely. But it didn't seem to work so well no matter how hard I tried. I mean it was like the more I tried, the more she resented me."

Sarah reached out and touched his arm.

"I don't know, I just didn't want to be a burden to her, so I began to spend more time with my friends, sleep over with them. Sometimes, I even found places to sleep on the street. I went back less and less. I always knew if I needed to in a pinch, the key to the back door was under the mat, and there was food in the refrigerator if I was desperate. I had a good friend whose dad owned a truck stop. He let me use the shower room every day. I found out that if I laid my clothing under my bed-role, I could get most of the wrinkles out while I slept. I found a recess in the concrete wall under a bridge that made a perfect place to sleep."

"Weren't you afraid?" asked Sarah.

"I never thought about being afraid. If you're having fun, it's more like an adventure."

"That's an interesting concept," said Travis, "sounds like Huckleberry Finn."

"Living under a bridge was when I discovered a passion for writing. When you don't have family, or anyone close enough to share your thoughts and deepest emotions with, it seems like they just get all jumbled up inside. I found by recording my emotions in a journal that life seemed to make sense once more. I felt like I had discovered a new part of me, one I never knew existed before. I began writing every day. I was driven to do so. I found solace in literature class. I think I would sooner have missed a meal than to have missed a day writing in my journal. That helped me through some pretty tough times. It gave me deeper insight into what was happening in my life."

"Interesting," said Travis. "Insight how?"

"Well, for one thing, I came to believe that my life was coming in stages, and that each stage serves a purpose in the overall meaning."

"You believe that each stage serves an overall purpose? That's good."

"The first stage of my life was when I had family. That was where I learned values and developed my character. My parents emphasized good moral values, especially Mom. That's where I developed my competitive nature, especially from Dad. He always urged me to think like a businessman, like a winner. That's where I learned to feel loved and appreciated, where I learned to love and respect myself.

"The next stage was being without family and feeling alone in the world. That was another part of my character development. To survive, I had to learn to rely on myself. If it was going to be, it was up to me. It was adapt or die. I had no one to look out after me. I had to grow up quick. I had to develop a whole new side to my character. I figured it was all right though. I thought perhaps I was being prepared for something else, a higher purpose, and this would all lead somewhere."

"That's awesome," said Travis. "I wish I could have thought like that. I know I would have been much better off. So, what now?"

"Don't you see? Now, I've entered a new and different stage in my life, as an intern for Emerald. But this isn't an end in itself, just living the good life and being happy. I'm being prepared again. I don't believe I came into my present happy circumstances just for my own personal enjoyment and indulgence. Where I am now will lead somewhere else, going out into the business world trained by Emerald, and who knows then where my destiny leads, or how many phases I will go through during my life. I only know it is all a part of my own life story. But that's what makes life an adventure, grabbing a hold of life by the horns, just the way it comes, finding a purpose in both the good and bad of life."

"Wow!" said Travis. "You got all that from writing? That is inspirational, makes me want to start writing."

"I like the way you see the problems of life as great adventure," said Sarah. "Most people can't do that. I wish I could be more like that."

"The way I see it, adventure is an attitude. Everyone wants adventure, but no one wants to be inconvenienced. But that's what adventure is all about. Only the courageous can have an adventurous spirit or can recognize adventure, or enjoy it when it comes along."

"Destiny is an interesting concept," said Travis. "I get the feeling you have sense of destiny in your life."

"That's it. It's all about finding your destiny. If you resist, if you don't follow the path where destiny leads, then how can you ever fulfill your destiny? You have to trust your destiny."

"Having a sense of destiny can be inspiring," Sarah said.

"Besides, that's where I found my passion for writing, underneath the bridge in my bed, all alone, contemplating the meaning of life, writing in my journal."

"What about your journal?" asked Sarah. "If it's so important to you, I mean, do you have it now?"

"Oh yes, it is important to me, very important. It is still there, under the bridge. I didn't have the opportunity to retrieve it. It's concealed pretty well. I don't think anyone will find it, but I surely must retrieve it someday, when the time is right."

"Yes, you must," said Sarah. "You have to retrieve your writings. I'd love to read them."

"Davy laughed. "Well, some of them may be a little personal, but my journal is important to me. I have some precious memories of my parents. My mother read to us every night. She read us the classics, Roman and Greek mythology, biographies of great men, even Shakespeare."

"That is so wonderful," said Sarah.

"My father started a small business from scratch creating prototype models for companies. He was modestly successful early on, so we were comfortable financially. He seemed to be in the process of growing his business, so the future looked promising. And then, you know, they were killed. My dad had spent a lot of time with me, taking time to talk with me and tossing the football. He talked a lot about what it took to run a business. He was coaching me for the future. I got my competitive nature from my dad and my spiritual foundation from my mom. I wrote a lot about my family, but I wrote about other things I found interesting."

Travis and Sarah listened with interest, giving him the gift of long pauses without breaking into the conversation, time to search for words, time to explore his emotions.

Finally, Davy ran out of words. He turned to Sarah and said, "What about you? What happened to your family?"

"My father was a jerk. He ran out on my mother before I was born. I wouldn't even recognize him if I saw him today. Mother died shortly after I was born. She hemorrhaged and they couldn't stop the bleeding. I don't know if my father even knew she died. If he did, he wasn't interested enough to show up for the funeral. At least, that's what my grandmother said. She burned all of his pictures, so I've never seen him. My grandmother never got over losing her only child."

"I'm so sorry."

"Thank you. My grandmother, bless her heart, raised me. I couldn't have asked for a more loving mother. I never knew my parents, so I feel like there's a vast emotional hole in my life. I supposed I could be consumed with depression if I let myself think about it."

"I'd never have guessed that, about you dealing with depression. You seem so cheerful, always. I've never seen anyone who seemed to be so happy. You have a positive effect on people. I can tell, you're the kind of person who's always lifting the spirits of others."

"Oh, she's good," said Travis. "When I'm feeling blue, Sarah is the one person who can cheer me up. She has a special and precious gift. She's always concerned about others."

"I do try to be positive and uplifting to others, but I have my difficult moments, especially when I am alone."

"That is amazing," said Davy, "that you can focus on others when you are feeling down yourself. I just can't imagine never knowing My parents. How does a person deal with never knowing their parents? How did you do that?"

"It wasn't easy. I guess I found solace by turning to the Bible, turning to God. Because I believe, I hope to see them in Heaven someday."

Davy gave a quick glance toward Travis.

"That's all right," said Sarah. "We carry on sometimes, but we give each other a lot of slack. We tease each other some, but we've had some good conversations. Actually, Travis is very supportive of me, even though we see things differently. The trick is to disagree without being disagreeable. We really do love each other. Bless his atheist heart."

They all laughed and then Sarah continued, "Reading scripture has been helpful to me. I don't know how I would ever have survived without it. That was the only way I could deal with the pain. But, I guess it was kind of natural. My grandmother was a devoted Baptist. She read the Word daily and we prayed every meal. I have her Bible, and it is precious to me. I would never be without it."

"Well, I think that's great. I don't see anything wrong with that."

"Actually," said Travis, "I don't see anything wrong with it either. I mean, it's not my cup of tea, but I would never take anything away from somebody who believes it. I wouldn't want Sarah any other way. God bless her holy roller heart."

They all three laughed again, and then Davy added, "Anyway, I really feel for you. I just can't imagine never knowing my parents. That would be devastating to me; it just seems to me to be so sad."

"Thank you," said Sarah. "I appreciate it."

After a moment of silence, Davy turned to Travis and asked, "So, what's your story?"

Travis took a deep breath. "My parents were both killed, shortly after I graduated. I came home from a party with some friends and they were both dead."

Travis took another deep breath. "I walked in and there they were, both tied up and shot in the back of the head. Blood was still dripping to the floor, lots of blood on the floor. It was like I was looking at a couple of dogs that had been killed, only it wasn't. It was my parents. It was horrible, unbearable. The house was messed up, drawers emptied, he took everything of value. I sat down and cried, must have been half an hour or more before I called the police."

"I am so sorry," said Davy.

Travis stuttered a bit before he was able to continue. "The thing that made it so hard for me was we had a bad argument before I left. That just made it so much worse. The guy who did it went to prison, but that wasn't much solace. It didn't bring them back."

"Wow! That's terrible," said Davy. "I guess you've both had it worse than I did. And I thought I had it bad."

"That's hard to say," said Sarah. "How can you say one of us had it better, or worse than the others? Part of the equation is how we are programmed and how we respond to what happens to us."

"So," asked Davy, "how were you able to deal with your situation, Travis, both parents being murdered like that? I mean, that's pretty heavy."

"Probably not all that well. Like you, I had to live with my aunt for awhile. It wasn't pretty; she's pretty intense and dominating. I wasn't quite as noble as you were. I got rather depressed. I started drinking a little more, and then a little more, did some drugs, I became outright rebellious. I got in trouble with authorities a few times. My Aunt wasn't one to mess around, tough as nails, so I ended up in a juvenile institution. I had some time on my hands to do some heavy thinking. I decided if I was going to get it together, I was going to have to do it myself. I knew my parents wouldn't have approved of my lifestyle, the way I was turning out. I didn't want to become a drug addict like the man who killed them."

Davy and Sarah both nodded.

"My friends always accused me of being a math brain. I won the city and state high school math contest, so I started studying math books, accounting, anything in juvenile library I could get my hands on. Actually, I kind of enjoyed it. When I was discharged from juvenile, I didn't do any drinking, except occasionally when socializing, and no drugs. I found a job with an accounting firm. I honest to God knew more about it as a kid than all those older men with a college education.

Sarah laughed out loud. "You just referred to God. I thought you didn't believe in God."

Travis started to respond to her jab, thought better of it and continued. "It was just a job to them, but I was really enjoying myself. Then they started coming to me for advice, relying on me more and more. I was doing the work, but they were making the big bucks, so I thought becoming a certified accountant was my best chance for success in life. I wanted to handle money in a large business, lots of money. I started socking some cash away for college. I knew it was going to be tough putting myself through school, but I was pretty darned determined. I knew my dad would want me to get an education. He was a professor and chairman of the math department. I was going to have to work hard; that I knew. That's when I was contacted by Marti, so here I am."

"So, you come from an intellectual background. The brain is the son of a brain."

"I don't know about that. I was captain of the high school chess team and the debate team. I suppose I was pretty decent in both areas. I was also class valedictorian."

"Wow!"said Davy. "That's awesome. That means Emerald knew

you made a drastic change, that you had to overcome, not only your difficult situation with your parents, but your own personal problems as well."

"I found out they had been watching me, and when I screwed up they took me off the list, but when they found out later what I was doing they became interested in me again. If I hadn't turned it around when I did, I would have missed this wonderful opportunity. No way Emerald would have been interested in me. The way I was going, I might even have been dead by now if I hadn't changed."

"Well, that's no small feat you accomplished," said Davy, "dealing with your parents murder, and then getting yourself together the way you did. I mean that and being a math genius and all. You display such leadership qualities, show so much sophistication, have gravitas and all that. No wonder Emerald was impressed with you."

"I suppose. Who knows what all goes through his head? I'm sure it's much more than we can comprehend."

Davy turned toward Sarah and asked, "So, why are you here? Don't take me wrong, you are obviously a highly qualified person, but I don't see you being the corporate type."

Sarah giggled. "You got that right, doesn't interest me in the least. His interest in me is more philanthropic. I want to be a nurse. When my grandmother went into a nursing home, I developed a desire to help people who had health problems. My heart went out to so many of the residents. I began doing volunteer work in the nursing home and focusing on my grades so I could get into nursing school. I don't know how I expected to pay for it. I didn't think about that. So here I am now. I don't know that I necessarily have to work in a nursing home; I might go to a mission field somewhere. All I know is, I prayed about it for some time and I just know that God wants me to be a nurse and to help people."

Travis rolled his eyes mischievously and grinned. Sarah smacked him on the arm and said, "Stop that." She was laughing. So was Travis. He was holding his arm but refusing to acknowledge the pain.

Davy grinned and said, "So, Travis, you don't believe in God? What exactly do you believe?"

"Well, it's not like I have anything against this God thing. I do get a kick out of stirring up Sarah. But, who knows? I mean, there's nothing concrete. I've never seen God, have you?"

Sarah grinned and ducked her head, allowing him to continue unchecked.

"No, I'm serious. Everybody has a different idea about whom, or what God is, all kinds of denominations, all kinds of religions. You have

Catholics, Mennonites, Scientology, Jehovah's Witnesses, Christian Science, Mormons, Unitarians, Rosicrucian, Muslims, Buddhist, Hindu, even Voodoo, you name it. Who's right? They can't all be right, and if one of them is right, then all the rest of them are wrong. Somebody has to be wrong. I figure ninety percent of all religious people in the world have to be wrong. They just can't all be right. Some of history's worst atrocities, man's inhumanity to man, holy wars and inquisitions, have been committed in the name of religion, religion against religion, all praying to the same God."

Sarah made a disagreeing face.

"If there's a God," continued Travis, "why doesn't he just reveal himself and clean up this confusion, tell us the right thing to do and to believe. If he appeared in person and showed that he was God and I knew the right thing to do, then I would do it. I think most people would, if they knew for sure it was really from God. Why would he expect you to do right, even threaten to send you to hell, and then not even give you definite information so you would know what's the right thing to do. That just strikes me as being really odd, certainly not the thought process of a coherent person, let alone an all-knowing intelligent God."

"Well," said Davy, "you sure seem to know a lot about different religions for someone who professes not to believe."

"Hey, just because I don't believe doesn't mean I'm ignorant. I have an analytical mind, an inquiring mind. At one time, I really wanted to know, I did a lot of searching about religion. I probably know more about religion than most religious people. I just don't get it."

"That's because you are trying to understand God with your head and not your heart," added Sarah.

"Sadly, what you say about ignorant Christians is true," responded Davy. "Some religious people I know are seriously ignorant."

Travis continued, "Most of those evangelists and television ministers, living like kings and movie stars, and scamming people. Religious people will follow anybody, like Jim Jones. I mean, the people that followed him, they all seemed like pretty nice people, probably sincere, but Jones was a real nut. Many Christians are like sheep; they will follow any shyster. They lack intellect. Beware of anyone who manipulates your emotions, that's what I always say."

Davy nodded his head thoughtfully. "What you say is too often true."

Sarah protested. "That's not true. Not all Christians are like that. It's not fair to blame all Christians for the misdeeds of some."

But Travis was on a roll.

"It's all about money. If you send me money, I'll send you a magic trinket. Send me money or God will send you to hell and torture you for eternity. What a racket. Just saying beware of any preacher who manipulates the emotions; there is no one more dangerous. But the biggest thing is, if there is a good God, then why is there so much evil in the world? Why would he allow my parents to be... to be murdered, at a time in my life when I needed them so much? That's what I need to know. So until I can see God, touch him, and ask him some questions, I'll just keep my money thank you. And I do have some questions I would like to ask God, if there really is a God, and if I ever get a chance to talk to him. You can bet I'll give him a piece of my mind."

"You're crazy," said Sarah, smiling.

Travis was laughing. "It's true. You can't dispute it."

Travis' demeanor changed in an instant, like when a solitary black cloud suddenly passes before the bright sun. Tears came to his eyes and he suddenly buried his head in his hands. Sarah and Davy rushed to hold and comfort him. For several minutes, no one said a word, letting silence and compassion serve as an effective healing balm. Finally, Travis raised his head with a brave smile and resumed his former self. Sarah and Davy drew back to their previous positions in respectful silence.

"What did your parents believe," asked Sarah? "Did they believe?"

Travis stared at the floor before responding. "Yes, they did. They belonged to a rather prestigious church, a large one, well respected. They donated their time and money. I think you might call them nominal Christians. I miss my parents, badly at times, and I respect them, at least I try to. But what good did it do them? If there was a God, then where was he when they needed him so desperately? If there is no God, then they were foolish. I admired my parents, want to be like them in a lot of ways. But I don't want to be a fool either. I think they were."

Davy laid his hand on Travis' shoulder and squeezed with reassurance.

Travis wiped the remaining tear from his eye. "What about you Davy, do you believe in this God thing?"

"Well sure, of course. I just took it for granted. It never occurred to me some people didn't believe in God at all. I mean, I've always known there were people that didn't believe, but that didn't seem real to me. I always thought most people believed on some level, but, I've never known anyone who was adamant about believing there is no God."

Travis and Sarah listened quietly as Davy continued.

"I probably have a little different view of God than Sarah does. My dad wasn't very religious, but he seemed to believe in his own quiet way. He wasn't much for organized religion. He mainly went to church to please Mom. She studied the Bible pretty regularly, and met with others in a study group every week. She usually took me along, so I was exposed to it, but of course, I was more interested in playing with the other children, or thinking about football, stuff young people do. I guess I did learn quite a bit, more than I realized at the time, and I've always had a spiritual foundation, but after mom and dad died and I was struggling to survive, I guess you don't have a lot of spare time to participate in organized worship so it becomes kind of a luxury. I've always had a sense of faith though, and there were a few times when I was so desperate, I felt the only thing left to do was to pray, so I guess I have to say that I do believe in God. Yes, I must if I prayed. Maybe it was just the influence of my mother."

"There you go," said Travis as he threw a fresh Coke can to Davy. "Your mother taught you one thing and that's what you believe and Sarah's grandmother taught her something else, so that's what she believes, so most people believe what they're taught, either that or they are honked off because of something in their life they hate, so their religious belief comes from rebellion against something. People don't really believe what they believe because they searched it out in a meaningful way for themselves. "

Sarah said, "I just don't believe this is all there is, that it all ends with death. Most people don't get a chance to enjoy life. Look at all the people who have been murdered, or lived in squalid poverty, so poor they never had access to even some of the basics of life. What about all those who lived in Nazi concentration camps, or were enslaved in the Deep South before the Civil War. They worked long bitter days every day of the year, received meager meals and a minimum of sleep. They were literally worked to death. Even young healthy people only lasted a few years under those conditions. They experienced nothing but misery. It just doesn't seem right."

She put her fingers of one hand to her mouth and said, "It is a dear hope of mine to see my mother and grandmother again someday, and Bessie too."

"Who's Bessie," asked Davy.

"She's my cousin. She was my best friend. She died when I was young."

Davy suspected that soon they would be talking about death on a deeper level. His previous experience with friends had taught him that when they talked that way about religion, they usually ended in serious conversation. Death seemed to be an ever-present specter for young people who had lost their parents. His assumptions on the direction of their conversation would be justified.

5

RUMINATIONS ON DEATH

"Dang," said Sarah. "Sam died."

She got up and walked to the aquarium followed by Davy and Travis, where Sam was floating upside down. She scooped him up, walked to the bathroom, said a quick prayer, and flushed him down the toilet.

"Short eulogy," said Travis.

"Well, there's not much you can say about a goldfish."

They all went to the kitchen, fixed themselves some drinks and popped some corn. Scarlet timidly licked her tongue and begged with her eyes and raised eyebrows. Sarah rewarded her with a piece of cold hotdog. With the smell of buttered popcorn in the air, they returned to the bean bags.

Sarah continued their previous conversation. "So, Davy, what do you believe exactly about religion? Are you a Christian?"

"Well, that's kind of a loaded question; it means different things to different people. Certainly I believe in God, only I call him Elohim. I believe he has a name. His name is Yahweh so that's what I call him. I use his name. I also believe the whole Bible is relevant so I probably place more emphasis on the Old Testament than you do."

"You think God's name is Yahweh? Strange. Do you believe in Jesus?"

"Sure, he's the Messiah. But his real name is Yeshua."

"What!" asked Sarah? Her tone was incredulous. "Yaw-shoo-wah?"

"That's close enough. "

"Why would you call him that?"

"That was his original Hebrew name. It was changed to Jesus hundreds of years after he died. Jesus is a Greek name."

"That's crazy. Why do people always have to mess with things? His name is Jesus, and that's the way it is. Besides, what difference does it make what you call him? The important thing is we are talking about the same person. It doesn't matter what you call him."

"Well, I don't know. The scripture does say there is only one name under heaven where men may be saved. Maybe it is important to get it right."

Sarah responded sharply, "That's crazy, just crazy. Where did you learn all that stuff? Have you, like, gone to divinity school or something?"

"No, as a kid growing up. For instance, you know about Adam and Eve in the Garden of Eden and the serpent?"

"Of course."

And you know stories about Abraham, Moses, Samson and David. You know all those stories?"

"Of course."

"Did you go to some kind of school of divinity?"

"No," she said with exasperation. "I just learned them from Sunday School. Most kids just know them."

"So there you go; that's the same way I learned what I know, as a kid growing up. It's just second nature with me. That's the world I grew up in."

"The things that you say seem so strange. What else do you believe?" asked Sarah.

"I don't believe in Hell, at least not in Dante's version of Hell. But you're probably not going to like that answer either."

"Do you believe in Heaven?"

"Yes, but you don't go there when you die."

You don't believe you go to Heaven when you die?"

"Not the way it's taught by most churches."

"What do you think happens to you when you die then, if there is no Heaven or Hell?"

"I didn't say there was no heaven or hell, but you just die, like an animal. You will be resurrected, into the Kingdom of Elohim. I believe that we will inherit the earth. We will see our parents again; my little sister will finish growing up. All the babies that died will have an opportunity to live out their lives. It will be different than this world, no evil. It will be like the Garden of Eden with a worldwide government ruled by Yeshua. No corruption, no sickness, no death. Can you imagine seeing your parents right here on this earth? The Bible calls it the resurrection."

Travis just listened, resisting the urge to jump into the middle of the conversation.

Sarah responded, "Well, the resurrection is the same as the rapture. That's when Christians go to Heaven."

"The resurrection is a return to physical life, like Lazarus raising from the dead, like Ezekiel's Valley of Dry Bones. The rapture is not actually mentioned in the Bible, but the resurrection is mentioned hundreds of times."

"But the Bible says you go to heaven when you die."

"No it doesn't."

"It does too." She was adamant. "I've heard ministers say that lots of times; it's in the Bible or they certainly wouldn't say it."

"It never comes right out and says anywhere that you go to heaven when you die."

"I'm pretty sure it's in there."

"No it's not."

"Yes it is."

"No it's not."

"Yes it is."

Travis said, "Stop it children. You sound like a couple of five year olds arguing."

Davy and Sarah responded together, "Are not."

Travis shot back, "Are too."

"Are not."

"Are too."

They all three broke out giggling.

"See, that's what I mean," said Travis. "Religious people can't agree on anything. They can't even agree what's in the Bible. I might go for something like Davy is saying; now that might make sense. I wouldn't mind coming back and having another shot at it if I mess up in this life. But there's still no way of knowing for sure. It's still just a belief, nothing concrete to go on."

"Oh, shush up," said Sarah with impatience. "Go on, what else do you believe?"

"Well, the point is, I think the most important question we could ever ask is, if we die, will we live again? I mean, isn't that what it's all about, wanting to know what happens to me when I die."

Travis nodded his head in thoughtful consideration.

"I think we can all agree on that," said Sarah."

"I also believe Saturday is the Sabbath."

"But the New Testament changed that, from Saturday to Sunday."

"No it didn't." Davy was a little more animated. "You can't show me anyplace in the Bible that authorizes changing the Sabbath from Saturday to Sunday."

"Yes it did."

"No it didn't."

"Here we go again," added Travis.

"Are you Seventh Day Adventist then?"

"No,"

"Are you Jewish?"

"No."

"So, what are you then? You have to be something. Who else believes that? Nobody else I know believes Saturday is still the Sabbath. That's just a Jewish custom."

"There are other people who believe in the Sabbath and the Feast Days. I prefer to think of my religious inclinations as Messianic Renewal. It's just that I think a lot of modern Christian beliefs started with Constantine. He was a pagan, you know. Modern organized religions believe a lot of things the original disciples didn't teach."

"But Constantine converted to Christianity."

"No he didn't. He remained a pagan his entire life."

"Yes he did. I've read in history books that he did."

"Depends on which history book you read."

Travis rolled his eyes.

Sarah found Davy's comments almost as annoying as Travis's.

"Why does any of this even matter?" broke in Travis. "Who cares? When it comes to religion, it's all just theory anyway. The only time it matters is when you are in church, and then it only matters to you, not to anyone else. Everybody believes what they believe and that's okay. Why should anybody care about what anybody else believes?"

Sarah was getting her hackles up a bit and was about to come back in a stout defense, but Davy spoke first.

"It matters because what you believe about religion affects how you think and act in everyday life, so it does impact your life, and everyone around you. Take politics for instance. I have noticed that liberals and conservatives tend to have different core religious beliefs. That explains why they have the political views they hold. Just notice when you hear them talk. It's also true in a lot of other areas of your life, like in business and in sports."

"Liberals and conservatives have different core religious beliefs and that impacts their political views? That's interesting," replied Travis. "I never really thought about it like that before. I'll keep that thought in mind when I watch the evening newscast."

"Well," added Sarah, "I just think it's more of a personal thing."

The three of them sat in quiet contemplation for a while. Sarah stared at the empty aquarium and said, "I'm sad that Sam died. I hate to see anything die."

"So do I," said Davy. Just think, some day we'll all die, just like Sam."

"I hope I don't get flushed down the pot," said Travis.

"Do you ever think about death?" asked Sarah, "and what it will be like when you die?"

"The experience of dying?" asked Davy. "Sure, I've thought about it."

"What do you think it will be like?"

"Well, I guess everybody thinks about dying at times? At least, if you've experienced it the way we have. It's such a radical change in a kid's life. I mean my mother, father, and sister died, so they've all experienced it. But death is such an experience of solitude. It only happens to every person once, and then they can't share how it feels with anyone else, not even their closest friend. Death is a wall of separation that cannot be breached by the living. I know that at some point in time there will come a moment, a point of death that will be as real to me as this conversation we are having now. Life and death have always seemed such a mystery. I can't help but wonder what it feels like to die, you know, the actual process, when you come to that place in your life, and you are aware that life is slipping away from you. What do you think death is like?"

Sarah gave it some thought. "When I was a little girl, about six, my cousin Bessie drowned in a family boating outing one weekend on the river. We were close in age and she was my best friend. It was my first experience with death. I was devastated. I thought about how horrified she must have been when she realized she was drowning. I remember my Aunt took my hand and walked with me to the casket. With all my heart, I wanted Bessie to sit up and climb out. She lay so still – I knew she wouldn't, but I leaned close anyway and whispered, 'Please get up, Bessie.' Of course, she didn't."

She paused before continuing, "I was horrified to see the casket closed over her face. For a long time, I pictured Bessie, quiet and still, lying in the ground with dirt all around her. I thought of her lying there day after day, forever, never moving again. I was horrified of death. One day, I saw a picture of Jesus surrounded by little children and always after, in my mind, Bessie was part of that picture. Now, I think death is like some of the dreams I have had, you know, like where you feel your soul is leaving your body. You just float away and you see God and feel loved. I think it's going to be a nice experience and you are going to see all your loved ones who have died and are waiting for you in heaven."

Davy nodded with empathy. "That would be nice." Travis expressed facial skepticism.

She continued, "I would like to believe that is what happened to my cousin. I want to believe that about my mother and my grandmother. That's the way I want it to be for me. Maybe that's why I'm attracted to the Bible. It gives me hope. Jesus promised to overcome death and that we would see each other in heaven. That's important to me, to see Bessie and my grandmother again, to meet my mother for the first time. Maybe I'd even like to see my dad, see for myself what he was really like. The thing is I want to live. I desperately want to live. I don't believe we get a chance to live to our fullest potential here in this life, not the way we are supposed to. It's like we all get cheated out of life. Life seems so unfair; there has to be more. I believe that someday we will really get to experience the fullness of life that God intended for us to live. "

"I don't know about that," added Travis, being more respectful to Sarah's feelings and proceeding cautiously. "I've seen animals die and I don't think it's all that pleasant. I remember when my grandmother died. She just lay there gasping for breath. I witnessed her dying. It was awful. I remember when they were ready to close the casket at the end of the funeral and the family was all gathered around; my father told me to take a good look, because that would be the last time I would ever see her. I was crushed by the thought."

"That was pretty heavy for a child," said Davy.

Travis continued. "I remember thinking at the time that I didn't ever want to die, but I had some comfort in knowing that my parents would die first, and that death was a long ways off, so as long as they were alive, I didn't have to deal with it. I felt pretty guilty remembering that after my parents died, but it sure gave me comfort at the time. Here we are now, and my parents are gone, and suddenly death doesn't seem all that far removed. I mean, if the next sixty years go by as fast as the last fifteen years of my life, I'll be there plenty soon enough. I could die sooner than that."

He looked at Davy and then Sarah. "Any one of us could be dead in a few years. It's kind of scary when you think about it, the certainty of death. I want to get as much living in as I can before that happens. What if you're wrong about going to heaven when you die? Then you just wasted your whole life. I want to experience all the good stuff now, just in case. I want to squeeze enjoyment out of every single day."

"But what if you're wrong, and there really is a heaven, and then you miss out?"

"I guess that's the chance I'm willing to take. I have a problem with a good God who tortures people in hell forever because they don't agree with him or they just don't understand what he expects from them. If I was going to believe something, it would probably be the way Native Americans believe. I like the way their worship is incorporated with nature. But, there is no way of really knowing."

There was a moment of silent reflection and then Sarah said, "Of all the good times I had with Bessie, you know what I remember most? I stayed overnight with her several days the week before she died. Every night her mother read to us before we went to bed. One night she read to us *Rapunzel*, and when she got to the part where the man said, 'Rapunzel, Rapunzel, throw down your hair,' Bessie jumped out of her chair with enthusiasm and broke in before her mother, Aunt Molly, could finish and said, 'I know what he said, Rapunzel throw down your rabbit.' Aunt Molly and I looked at her like what in the world are you talking about? She said, 'Well, he said throw down your hair, and a rabbit is a hare, right? So he was saying, throw down your rabbit.' Bessie and I broke out laughing and we started saying nonsense stuff, like throw down your head of lettuce, and all kinds of crazy things. Aunt Molly was annoyed, but then she started laughing too, and we all laughed until Aunt Molly made us be quiet so she could finish the story."

Sarah had a distant look in her eyes.

"It's kind of funny how, with all the good memories we had, that one just kind of sticks out. For those few days, one of us would say Rapunzel, Rapunzel, and the other one would say throw down your rabbit. And then we would break out giggling. Who knew it would be our last good memory together? I don't ever remember seeing Aunt Molly laugh again after that."

Davy said, "That is a precious story. It's sad, but I like it. Those are the kind of memories, the little things that are an important part of a person's life. I'm glad you shared that with us. I remember the good times I spent with my cousin Harold in Arkansas and my other cousin Carlos in Mexico. Those were my closest cousins. I haven't seen either one since my family died. Harold moved to the high woods of Montana a few years ago; he wants me to come see him, but Carlos still lives where he did in Escondero. Many summers together we had great times. It's been several years since I've seen either one of them. I really miss that. I'd love to see them again."

A contemplative smile broke his face. "I am going to see them as soon as possible."

"That is something I can't exactly relate to," said Travis. "I didn't have any cousins. You make it sound like I really missed something."

"Cousins are wonderful," continued Davy, playing in the village with Carlos and hunting on the farm with Harold. "Those were some of my best memories. I've had good times, and I've had bad times. I've had some really bad times. You know what kept me going through all the hard times, the sad times, the bad times? It was the precious memories of Harold and Carlos. It also helped when I thought that the most glorious human achievement is victory over adversity, the essence of divinity. Mom used to say that a lot. That gives me strength, helped me through some tough times."

"That is so awesome," said Travis, "Another of Davy's profound thoughts."

"Your mother sounds like she was a wonderful person," said Sarah.

"Oh, she was. I just wish you could have met her. The thing I most remember her saying was that life is precious. She said we could never really fully appreciate how precious life is until after we lose it. That didn't mean all that much to me at the time, but now I understand, since they are gone. I just wish I could have been more appreciative of them when they were still here. Now, it's too late. Life is funny that way. You can't understand until it is too late."

And so they talked, late into the night, losing all concept of time, as only young people are inclined to do when they are bonding and sharing themselves in conversation, gazing into each other's soul. They covered a wide range of subjects, from government fraud and political stupidity, to their favorite and worst teacher, to Armageddon and the ending of the world. Young people are fearful of the thought of the world ending in a holocaust.

At one time, the apocalypse had been the exclusive domain of the Christian denomination, but now the Mayan calendar, New Agers, Hindu mystics and Hopi Indians seem to have formed their own popular following. Nostradamus and other doomsday prognosticators, including Bible code enthusiasts, have received ever more time on television and in the news. Even secular politicians and scientists are now using a doomsday clock to predict the end of the world in a nuclear holocaust. Young people just want to know they will have an opportunity to live the fullness of their lives. Armageddon is something best left for future young people to deal with, let someone else have their lives cut short.

In addition they shared past friends and sweethearts, their favorite movies, favorite dancers, singers, movie stars, sports heroes, and how their world would be so much different had their parents lived. They talked about some of the difficulties they had experienced.

"There was a time," said Davy, "I was in such a financial bind I actually sold some of my blood. Lucky for me that type AB negative is rare. They paid for it."

"No kidding?" said Travis with a grin. "You have AB negative type blood? I do too. Talk about coincidence."

"Hey, that is a coincidence," said Davy

"I sold some blood a couple of times when I needed money," said Travis. "When you are desperate enough you will do anything. Now I feel like we are blood brothers."

"You shouldn't give blood if you are using drugs," said Sarah. "It's not fair to the person receiving it."

"I know, I would never do so now. But, like I said, when you are desperate, you do some things you shouldn't do. What about you? Don't tell me you have AB negative also?"

"That would be a coincidence, but no, sorry to be the odd ball out. I just have regular O blood, like most people have. I guess I'm not exotic like you guys. I wonder what blood type Jesus had. I've never thought about that before. I bet it was type O, the universal donor."

Travis smirked his amused grin. Sarah ignored him.

Then Davy asked, "What about this Emerald, have you ever met him?

Sarah and Travis looked at each other and studied. She answered, "About two months ago. He came one day and left the next. Travis and I met him separately, about an hour each. That's the only time we have ever seen him."

"What kind of a fellow is he?"

"He's kind of strange," said Sarah. "Different than anyone I ever knew. But he's okay. He seems like a pretty nice guy, certainly very professional. He kind of reminds me of a robot, without much emotion, just focused, like he doesn't want to reveal himself, very controlled. It's like any emotion he shows is programmed for effect."

"Oh, he's focused all right. He's focused on his financial empire," added Travis. "He knows his stuff, let me tell you that. He has a brilliant mind, like the Michelangelo of the business world. He speaks five foreign languages fluently. In a way it's like talking to a computer; he hardly shows any emotion at all, except maybe intensity. But he reads you like a book; you can just feel it. You get the feeling he knows more about you than you know yourself. I think he has a great amount of passion; it's just that he keeps it focused on his purpose like a laser beam."

"Of course, said Davy. "Successful people tend to be focused."

"It's an interesting experience," said Sarah, "talking with Emerald. He pontificates a lot."

"Well," added Travis, "that may be a little unfair. He has such wonderful wisdom, and I think he just wants to share it as effectively and efficiently as possible, especially since we'll only see him about an hour every few months. It's like he wants to download his vast knowledge, make it available to others. Consider how much you learned in school in a month or a semester and then think about absorbing all that in an hour."

"Radical," said Davy.

"I thought he was a little strange," said Sarah again, "but he seemed nice enough. I don't mean strange in a negative way. I realize what all he's doing for me, and I deeply appreciate it. It's just that I think that he's just – well, you know, strange." She laughed. Travis rolled his eyes.

"Maybe you should be careful what you say. How do you know you aren't being recorded?" asked Davy.

Sarah laughed. "If we were being recorded, we would have been kicked out a long time ago."

"Well, at least Sarah would have," added Travis. "She tends to speak her mind."

"Hey," said Sarah, "that's who I am."

Davy inquired about Marti and Antoinette. Travis and Sarah looked at each other and she laughed.

"What?" asked Davy,

"Oh, Sarah thinks they're a little too friendly. She thinks there's something going on. I don't think so. There's too much to lose for Marti, Antoinette too as far as that goes. They are quite friendly, but I don't think it's that."

"Trust me," said Sarah, "Women are much more intuitive than men are."

And so, they chewed on that gossip rag for a while.

"Sarah sometimes calls Marti the Chameleon," added Travis.

"I don't either! Besides, I only said it one time. And, you call him Mr. Velvet."

"No I don't. I just did that one time."

"See. See," said Sarah, pointing her finger and laughing.

Travis smirked, knowing he had been caught.

By now they were so deep into the night they had all three become giddy, laughing at every small thing, the most innocent remark, that which was least intended for humor leading to frivolous laughter, particularly so when Davy began to mimic prominent people and cartoon characters. His specialty was The Three Stooges, "whoop, whoop, whoop," and Yosemite Sam, "Great horny toads, I hates rabbits." But even that stage passed, and they sat around the table, dead tired, too exhausted to speak.

It was Davy who broke the silence. "I feel comfortable with both of you in a way I have with no one else since my family died. I'm just now realizing how much of an emotional wall I have built around myself. I've resisted getting too close to anybody. It's like I never again wanted to risk having so much pain from losing the one you loved. But in doing so, I have been missing something very important in my life. Everyone needs family.

Sarah and Travis nodded.

"Emotionally, deep within, we all desperately need family. Avoiding the risk of pain is to avoid life. In order to love someone, I have to be willing to become vulnerable again. Refusing to do so means I can not experience love. That's what I have been doing. I can no longer do that. You two have become my new family, my brother and sister. You give me inspiration to live fully and deeply once more. I feel a sense of love I have not felt since my family was killed. It is a risk I must take. I think it would be wonderful for us to develop the love of family."

"Amen," said Sarah.

"Here, here" added Travis.

They sat in a close circle about the round table. Davy noticed they all had their arms leaning on the table with their wrists crossed, so that their hands were only inches from each other. He took his right hand and clasped Sarah's left hand, and then he took his left hand and clasped Travis's right hand. They did likewise with their free hand so that the linkage was complete.

Davy said, "Look what we have done. We have formed our own star. Maybe this can be a symbol of our new relationship. Someday, when I am a great businessman, I will have a brass plaque, no, make that a golden plaque, a very expensive one of course, made to sit on my desk with the three corner star, formed by three pair of hands, and I will have it on all my stationary. People will ask me what it means and I will tell them it is a secret, personal and precious. Only three people in the entire world will know what it means. Both of you will always be close to my heart no matter where else in the world you might be, as long as it sits on my desk. We will always be dear family, for as long as we live."

Davy hesitated before continuing, "There is only one thing I would ask of you."

Sarah and Travis both gave Davy a quizzical look which implored, "Go on."

"Promise you will never leave me, never abandon me. I don't think I could stand losing my family again. I think I would die."

"Never," stated Sarah emphatically.

"We would never leave you," added Travis. "Just remember though, you are as important to us as we are to you. Just don't you ever leave us."

"I can promise you that will never happen."

It was a meaningful and intimate moment. Finally Sarah said, "I am so tired. I can't hold my head up."

The other two nodded their agreement and they each, reluctantly, retired to their apartment. Davy fell into a deep sleep, but toward morning he grew restless. He pondered his changed circumstances. Just the previous night he had slept on the street under a bridge. Tonight he was sleeping in a luxurious bedroom of one of the richest men in Texas. He had a new future, a new family.

Davy had fitful sleep that night and two dreams. The first was a fearful dream and left him badly shaken. He saw the light fade, the night sky darken and turn into oppressive darkness. Davy sensed evil within the blackness bearing down on him. Then came tornadoes, a multitude, sinister and menacing, threatening to destroy everything in their path. There was lightning, fierce and frightening, striking the ground as though the earth was receiving the wrath of God. Thunder roared like the cannons of war.

He saw an angel appear bearing a great golden trumpet, and when the angel raised the trumpet to blow, it was not a shrill trump that came forth as he expected, but a grave voice spoke as one would hear from a loudspeaker. The trumpet said, "Now is the wrath of God kindled against America. The nation God favored has profaned her benefactor, and great is her destruction. Woe is America, for she is destroyed as fine crystal is shattered by the black smith hammer. Her destruction is total and foreigners will plunder her. Woe to her inhabitants. Let the brave men howl and their loins turn to water. Let the women weep and wail. Great and dreadful is the judgment of God."

Davy was tormented and tried to awaken, but was unable to do so. When he finally did awaken, he was sweating profusely and his hands were shaking. *What was that all about,* he wondered? *That made no sense at all.* Some fears defy explanation, but lightning reminded him of spiritual warfare.

He was unable to return to his slumber until close to dawn. Then came his second dream. It was a wonderful dream about Sarah, and upon awakening, he was more than a little ashamed.

6
MARTI'S REVELATIONS

In the days that followed, Davy began to feel more comfortable with his new environment as he developed his new friendships. Davy, Sarah, and Travis usually ate lunch together in their family room, choosing from an abundance of fresh fruits and grocery in their refrigerator. They ate dinner with Marti and Antoinette in the formal setting of the downstairs dining room. The good china and crystal goblets were used, the room illuminated by half a dozen candles. The butler kept them well-served.

It was a friendly and joyful occasion. Sometimes Antoinette and Marti talked concerning Emerald, but usually not. Periodically a special guest, most of whom were mysterious and interesting, brought tales from distant lands and from the world of high finance and deep intrigue. Davy perceived that he rarely heard the real story, the story behind the story, that which was reserved for more worthy ears. Davy marveled and took in everything he heard and observed. He found that by feigning lack of active interest he was able to learn even more as the guests were less guarded.

Davy also marveled at Antoinette's culinary skills; her meals were delicious. "You know, I think I would enjoy learning to cook. I never really thought about that before, but I'm sure that's something I would like. I enjoyed helping my mom in the kitchen. That brings back great memories."

"Really now? You want to learn to cook, I will teach you. I love teaching people to cook, especially those who express a genuine interest. It will be satisfying."

So began trips to the kitchen area twice a week for Davy's appointed cooking lesson. There was never a dull moment when he was in Antoinette's kitchen.

"Always use stainless steel pots and pans to cook in, never anything else, only the best. Never aluminum, never cast iron, never copper. Why would you want to poison yourself? Only one tablespoon of water in the pan for vegetables and keep the heat on low. Over cooking destroys the nutrition and ruins the taste. You want everything to be gourmet quality. Good food should be good medicine for you. It should heal you. If you cook it right, you can add fifty years to your life, even more. I will teach you everything you need to know, and then some." She laughed. She usually laughed after she spoke.

Davy was always amazed at her feisty abundant energy. Her rapid fire conversation somehow reminded him of a Gatling gun. He felt guilty at times when he found himself becoming aroused when he was around her, but he was careful to set a bridle on his passions. He thought to himself, *the last thing I need is to get tied up with Potifar's wife, sorry Joseph, no offense.*

However, Davy didn't feel overly guilty. After all, he was a typical red blooded American boy and that was to be expected. Besides, he enjoyed it. He wondered if Antoinette knew how aroused he occasionally became around her. He suspected her of teasing him at times, but he was never quite sure. Davy prided himself on the art of brinkmanship.

Another of Davy's unexpected pleasures was learning to play golf with Marti. Twice a week on Tuesday and Thursday, without fail, Marti would be on the golf course, and often Davy would join him. It was there they talked freely and formed a casual relationship. Davy enjoyed interjecting spunk into the game. He did his share of the talking.

"What a grand day to be playing golf," said Davy as he addressed the ball. "The sun is bright and warm, not too hot. The breeze is soft and dry."

He took a deep breath enjoying the sweet aroma of flowers. "Listen to the birds serenade us cheerfully. What a beautiful day to be alive."

"Oh, yes, life is sweet indeed," replied Marti, "certainly for the upper crust."

"Where might I find a journal?"

"What might you want with a journal?"

"I like to write. I've always written a journal, at least since my family died."

"Of course, I know you like to write. I'm not sure that's a good idea, keeping a journal."

"Why not?"

"I don't think Emerald would want someone with inside information writing things down."

"Oh, it wouldn't be like that. I would never reveal anything about Emerald or his operation. He could trust me. It's just that writing is my passion."

"That's not the point. The point is that people who are stealth operators are suspicious of people who write. Not a good idea. I'd be careful if I were you."

"I hadn't thought about that."

"You play fairly decent golf," inquired Marti. "Where did you learn to play?"

"I played some when I was in Junior High golf league. Some of the freshmen on the school golf team invited me to play occasionally and I played in a summer camp. I enjoyed golf, but not as much as football; not aggressive enough."

Marti laughed. "Yes, you do have an aggressive streak."

"The rest of the players used to be so serious; they were all quiet when someone was getting ready to hit the ball. Not me. I was having fun, telling jokes, laughing, carrying on. You wouldn't think school kids would get so annoyed. Let me know if I'm too loud for you."

"Not a problem, I have nerves of steel, the focus of a steel trap."

"I don't know; I can be pretty annoying sometimes. You are certainly good at the game. I think you are about as good as I've seen. And I've seen some good players."

"I used to play on the PGA tour."

"No way! You have to be pretty darned good to play the PGA tour."

"I sure did. When I was young I used to caddy at the local golf course. That's the best way for a young man in a hurry to develop acquaintances that are important enough to help him get where he's going. Some of the players I caddied for were hustlers, made their money from what they considered as rich suckers. You might say I was hustling the hustlers."

"You, hustling the hustlers? That is funny."

"I became proficient at sizing up my marks. I'd wait until they had won a wad of dough from some clubhouse gentry through the day, and then I'd start acting like a real jerk, and they would start trying to teach me a lesson, and the next thing was I had all the money they had hustled over several days."

Davy laughed. "So how do you hustle hustlers?"

"I could really irritate them and get on their nerves, start mouthing off about how much better I was then they were. The important thing was to make them believe I had just come into a wad of dough. I would act like I was stupid, and as I lost let them think that I was struggling and that I was in over my head; that's the secret. Keep raising the stakes and make them feel like they are sure to win the final wad. The greedy bastards couldn't stop until they had all of what they thought I had. I hate to brag, but I was the best. My wealthy mentors knew what I was doing and they got a kick out of it. They didn't mind losing money, but they did mind feeling like they had been cheated by hustlers, so they saw what I was doing as a sort of revenge on their behalf. I made a lot of great contacts that way. That's the name of the game, making contacts."

"You actually played the PGA tour?"

"You don't believe me?"

"Actually, I do. I've not been around golf a lot, but I have been around it enough to know you play a pretty awesome game. It's just that it's hard for me to believe I know someone who's actually played the tour. Did you ever win any of the big ones?"

"No, I never did. I was never good enough to make the big money. I did play well enough to scare some of the top players a few times. They knew I was good enough to beat them on any given day. It's hard to win consistently, day after day."

"I enjoyed playing golf. That's one of the things I had to give up after my family died. I'd give anything to play like you do."

"Maybe you can. You are a talented athlete. I am not only a great golfer, but a great teacher as well. Continue to be here every Tuesday and Thursday and I'll have you playing great golf within a month."

"Alright big guy, count on me being there."

Davy teed up on the next hole, a par three as Marti instructed.

"All your power comes from your left shoulder and down through your arm. Relax your right hand so it is barely holding the grip on the back-swing. When you start the downswing, release your right hand so you are swinging the club entirely with your left arm when you tee off. Starting from your right knee, over your hip, up your large back muscle cross to your large left shoulder muscle, over your left shoulder and feel the power magnifying from your shoulder, down your arm, like some great spring pulling your left hand."

"You've got to be kidding. You want me to tee off with just one hand."

"Trust me, when you are pulling the club from your left shoulder, without putting your right arm into it, you will hit the ball farther than you are now with both hands on the club. It may feel a little awkward at first, but you will begin to feel comfortable with it after a few swings. You will gain confidence, and trust. You will hit the ball farther with one hand than you can now with two. And don't push the swing with your wrists. Pull down with your left wrist, like you are going to drive the tip of the club handle right straight down through the ball. Let the club snap itself around and unleash its own power through the ball."

Davy shanked the first swing. The next swing sent the ball to the green. "Wow! I can't believe I did that, with just one arm."

"I told you; I know what I'm talking about. I know enough tricks of the trade to teach you how to play real golf. I'll have you starring on your college golf team. You'll be setting school records."

Davy smiled with satisfaction. He noticed that Marti seemed more comfortable with him than he had seen him with anyone else. Davy was imitating Marti's method of finding key people, developing relationships, and becoming a confidante. As they walked to the green they chatted easily.

Suddenly Marti asked, for no apparent reason, "Were you ever molested as a boy?"

"No, never anything like that. Why do you ask?"

"I have. Do you have any idea what it is like to be molested as a child?"

"No sir, it must be awful."

"It is, when you're just a helpless kid and can't do anything about it." His face began to harden.

"Was it your father?"

"No. At least he never did that. It was my uncle. He was worse than my old man."

Marti's face grew even harder as he continued. "I hated that bastard, more than I ever hated anyone else, ever. He only visited us a few times that I remember. Those were the only times I ever saw him, about five times. Maybe it was more. Maybe I blocked some of it out. But I soon learned what to expect when he came. He seldom visited, but I lived in fear that he would. The son-of-a-bitch got his just reward though."

"Did you kill him?"

"No, but I didn't save him either. That was just as good."

There was a long moment of silence before Marti continued. "The last time he visited, I ran out into the woods. I stayed there all day – without anything to eat or drink. Late in the afternoon, I ended up by the river and there he was in a boat fishing. I knew he had been drinking, so I prayed he would fall in and drown."

Marti laughed an empty laugh. "I think that's the only time I have ever prayed. I could hardly believe it, but after a while, he actually stood up and began to organize his equipment. He wasn't very steady on his feet. I just knew he was going to fall in, and he did. There he was struggling in the water and I knew he was going to drown. I stepped out from behind the trees and said, 'You're going to drown you bastard.' That's what I said. "

Davy could feel the hatred in his voice. They stared at each other, and Marti continued.

"He called out for me to save him. I said, 'You damned old man, I'm going to watch you drown and go to hell, and I'll be glad for it.' He went under several times, but he kept struggling. Every time he called out for help, he swallowed more water. And then he was gone. The thing I remember afterward was how everything was still and quiet, just like he had never been there. The river was slow, peaceful and still. I wondered if what I had seen was real, if it had actually happened. I knew it had happened. I mean there was the boat and he wasn't in it, even though he had been there only moments earlier, so I knew he had to be at the bottom of the river. But emotionally, I still couldn't believe it was real. It's kind of funny how I can still see the grass and the leaves on the trees that day, all so green, still etched in my memory. It's like I was seeing the world in color for the first time."

"You must have been happy he was gone."

"I don't know that happy is the right word. I was glad he was gone. I knew I would be safe from then on."

"Did you ever feel guilty about that, you know, letting him drown?"

"I don't think I ever felt guilty about letting him drown. Maybe I felt guilty about not feeling guilty, perhaps. I suppose that sounds kind of crazy."

"No, I don't think it does. Maybe you did the right thing."

"Really now? Is that what you would have done?"

"I don't know. I think I would have done the same thing, who knows? The thing you have to think about is someone like that needs to be stopped. Who knows who else he was molesting. Who knows what innocent child you might have saved in the future? Sometimes, life is a trade off and there are no easy answers, but you have to decide anyway."

"That's what I thought, but I guess I just needed to hear someone else say it. I never fully believed it when I told myself. Thanks. The thing is I have never told this to anyone else before. You are the first person, the only person who knows."

"No kidding? Why me?"

"I guess I had to tell someone. It feels like a great burden has been lifted. Maybe you are the first person I felt comfortable enough with to share it."

"That's a terrible thing to happen to any child. It could be debilitating to a person. You seem to have overcome the situation, to have moved beyond. That's good."

"Well, you do what you have to do. It's the struggle that makes you strong, isn't that what they say? You get tough or die. I chose to move on."

"Good for you."

"I hated my uncle. I hated my old man. The only thing they ever gave me was a loathing for myself. Maybe I should be grateful in a way. It was my loathing of myself, my hatred of those two that drove me to succeed. If I hadn't succeeded to the level I have, I think I would have shriveled up and died. I had to succeed. But by God, I did succeed, on a large scale. I am somebody."

Davy felt great compassion, placed his hand on Marti's shoulder and said, "You did it, probably more than you can appreciate. It's not your level of success that matters; what is important are the obstacles you overcame. I think you have succeeded on a greater level than you give yourself credit. You have done extraordinarily well."

Marti patted Davy's hand, still on his shoulder and said, "Thanks. I guess I really needed that." For the moment they had an instant of bonding, intense bonding, and then like all moments, it was over.

They finished the hole in silence. Davy noticed that Marti's face began to relax a bit. Marti teed up on the next par three and hit a perfect swing that sent his ball close to the flag. As they arrived on the green, they found Davy's ball, but Marti's was nowhere to be found. After a short search, Davy found it, nestled safely in the cup. "Looks like you made a hole in one."

Marti gave a thunderous happy shout and threw his club over his head as far as he could throw. It disappeared over a tree.

"Say, that's pretty good distance on that swing. But it is a swing, so that's going to cost you one stroke, so there goes your hole in one."

Marti started laughing. "I don't think so."

"Sure. A swing is a stroke. Goodbye hole in one."

"You don't even want to go there. I'm just fortunate you were here to witness it. This is my third hole in one, and I was lucky enough each time to have a witness."

"Hey man, I'm going to deny it. There's no way I'm going to be your witness. Goodbye hole in one."

Marti was too professional to display annoyance, though he wore a sharp grin.

Now Davy was laughing. "Tsk tsk. Too bad. Bye, bye hole in one.

They searched behind the tree for the club, and then around the next tree. The club was nowhere to be found.

"You had good distance for sure, but I don't think you cleared that next tree. I'd be willing to bet your club is up in the tree somewhere."

Marti stared with his hand cupped to his chin and an amused smile on his lips. "You're probably right. It has to be up there somewhere."

"So, Mr. Genius, golf man, how do you intend to get it down?"

"Who wants to get it down? Leave the son-of-a-bitch up there."

"Leave it up there? You've got to be kidding. Knowing your taste, I'll bet that is one expensive golf club."

"It is, of course it would be expensive. I wouldn't have one that wasn't. But it all depends on how you look at it. My time is too valuable to be climbing around in a tree looking for a golf club. It is cheaper for me to buy a new one than to find it. Would you believe that's the second club I've lost in a tree? They are both still up there. I suppose they will come down someday when they get good and ready."

"I can't believe this. You rich people think differently. I'd climb that tree in a heartbeat if it was mine."

"Tell you what. You climb that tree and retrieve my club, and I'll give you double price for what I paid for. I'll mount it on a plaque with the ball and hang it in my office like I did the other two times I hit a hole in one."

"I'll climb the tree and find it, and I expect to be paid for it, but I'm still going to deny I saw you hit a hole in one."

Marti started laughing. "You're a son-of-a-bitch, you know that?"

Their conversation was interrupted by the roar of four jets flying above in close wingtip formation. Both men watched with one hand shading their eyes from the brightness of the blue summer Texas skies.

"War games," said Davy.

"War games, indeed," repeated Marti.

"That sounds like such a contradiction, war and games in the same sentence. Today it's just games, but tomorrow, it could be for real. People could die in massive numbers, millions of people. Nations; even groups of nations, perhaps the whole of humanity could just disappear overnight. It's hard to fathom," said Davy.

"That's life, kid. Sometimes there is only a hair's breath between games and disaster. Welcome to the grownup world. That is what makes life exciting."

As Marti was teeing off on the next hole, Davy said, "This is a long par three. Are you sure you can throw your club that far?"

Marti addressed the ball, looked quite serious, wiggled his butt enough to loosen himself up a bit, but then started laughing as he teed off. "You son-of-a bitch. Now, look what you've done, my worst shot of the day."

"You sure curse a lot."

Marti grinned as he focused on his pending swing. "I have developed my own special vocabulary. However, I've seen you use a few choice words occasionally."

"I know. I guess I'm trying to clean my vocabulary up a bit. I'm trying hard not to use profanity in front of Sarah."

"She doesn't use many of those words, does she?"

"I've never heard her use any."

Marti slapped his hand on Davy's shoulder and grinned. "Tell you what, for you I'll watch my language. At least, I will try. Don't get upset if I mess up once in a while."

Davy was pleased. "Thanks man, I appreciate that."

He felt the gentle wind on his face as his gaze swept the opulence of the estate, thought a moment and then said, "There is so much wealth in this vicinity. It almost seems profane on some level. However, I have to tell you, it is wonderful to be in the midst of so much wealth."

"That is true. How wondrous are the joys of wealth? But, like everything, wealth can be heavy at times."

"How so?"

You have competitors, Davy, billions of competitors, all driven by greed and arrogance. The game is not over until one of them owns it all, every single dollar. Creates a lot of tension, it does. From the world rulers, to great generals, to great capitalists, to the slime-bag druggies on the street, they all want one thing; they want it all. It's all about dominion, total domination. They all want to be God. That explains a lot of problems in the world."

"Do you want it all?"

"No. I just want to live with someone who has it all. I want the good life without the risks."

As they walked toward the next tee, Davy inquired, "So, do you mind if I ask what was it like when you first began to make lots of money and what were you doing when you made your first big score?"

"Voodoo."

7
THE PROPHECY

"Voodoo?" Davy was incredulous. "Are you talking about black magic, like in Haiti?"

Marti chuckled. "I had several involvements that were interesting, but I suppose my first really big score came when I started selling armaments."

"Armaments?"

"The Canadian 101 Voodoo supersonic jet fighter to be exact. They decided to retire the old Air Force workhorse, so they sold them off, the way you would get rid of your old car so you could buy a new one. At that time, you could buy a bunch of them cheap, well, relatively speaking. Of course, they weren't cheap if you didn't have that kind of money, which I didn't."

"You actually bought fighter jets? How does that work, exactly? How does a common citizen, one without money, buy fighter jets from a foreign country, and what did you do with them?"

"Well now, that's the interesting part. Rogue nations around the world- the Mid East, South America, Asia, North Korea- they were all looking for military hardware. When I found all this out, seeing I didn't actually have the money, I had to bait the Canadian government, pretend I had access to cash and bring them to the point of sale. At the same time I had to bait the militant countries and lead them to believe I already had the fighters in my possession, and then I had to raise the money, a lot of money, at exactly the right time, rapid fire transactions with an incredibly short turnaround time."

Davy grinned with approval.

"It wasn't easy, but I managed to do all that. I made it happen. I raised enough money to prime the pump, start the action, collect payment, hurry back to make another payment, deliver more jets, and hurry back to buy some more. It wasn't long before I had made enough money that I no longer had to operate on borrowed money. It was plenty risky. Looking back, I'm amazed I was even able to make it work. It's a wonder it didn't blow up in my face."

"That was impressive."

"Thank God it went smoothly. If I hadn't been able to repay the cash I had originally borrowed, I would have ended up dead. I had to do business with some unsavory characters."

"That sounds risky, all right. So, how long did you traffic in fighter jets?"

"A little over a year. I became a multimillionaire in that short time."

"That's incredible. What happened? Why did you quit?"

"One day I was sitting in my office, feet propped up on my desk, reflecting on my fine business acumen and my fortuitous prosperity, when in walked two men well-dressed in business suits. They presented me with their FBI identification and asked if I was the one called Martinique. I informed them I was and asked how I could help them. They asked if I was buying Canadian military jets and reselling them to foreign countries. I said I was, and asked if it was against the law. They said, no, it actually wasn't, not the way I had it structured; it's just that they thought it was a terrible idea. I told them if they thought it was a bad idea, so did I, and I would close my operation that very day. One of them said he was very glad to hear that, it solves some major problems for everyone involved, so they turned around and walked out without so much as a smile or a pat on the ass. That's how it happened."

"So, what you were doing was legal and you were making lots of money, why did you quit?"

"One of the lessons I learned early in life is never get into a pissing contest with the mafia or the government. Actually, the government is worse. You will always end up being the pissee, the one pissed on, never the pisser. They win every time. David Koresh and the Branch Davidians at Waco found this out. So did Randy Weaver at Ruby Ridge. Bonnie and Clyde found out the hard way. So did Johnny Dillinger and Baby Faced Nelson, Machine Gun Kelly, even Saddam Hussein and Osama Bin Laden. As long as they were just killing citizens, it wasn't any big deal, but when they started to screw with the government, made them look bad, the government placed them in their cross-hairs, and they were dead men walking."

"Of course, the government has to keep things legal."

"Has nothing to do with being legal. It's all about powerful people staying in control. If the FBI doesn't get you the CIA will. If the CIA doesn't get you the IRS will. That's what got Capone, you know. The purpose of the IRS is to steal money from private citizens and transfer it to corrupt politicians. It is a terrorist organization, the most feared terrorist organization on earth."

"The most feared? More so than Al Qaeda?

"Oh yes. The I.R.S. Has destroyed more lives than Al Qaeda. All governments need a terrorist organization to control the masses by fear. The Internal Revenue Service has operated in stealth up til now, but that is about to change. When you see the IRS going after political enemies, the next step is for the public to feel the boot-heel heavy on their neck. Never interfere with the Mafia or government when it comes to money, at least if you value your life. It is the job of the IRS to put the fear of God into our citizens."

"You don't like the IRS? I guess most people don't."

"And with good reason. The IRS is the agent of fear that will destroy America. Anyway, I went on to bigger and better things."

"What could be bigger than selling fighter jets to foreign countries? And weren't you afraid of getting on the bad side of the government again?"

"You have to understand I was operating in the shadows. When the government found me out, I was agreeable and instantly quit. I went back into the shadows again. This time, it was nuclear warheads."

"Nuclear war heads. You have got to be kidding me."

Marti laughed. "I'm serious. When the Soviet Empire broke up, chaos resulted. Adequate security was nonexistent. Corruption was rampant. Militant countries with depraved dictators were willing to spend a fortune to get their hands on nuclear warheads. You wouldn't believe some of the countries that now secretly have the bomb. It's more than anyone would ever suspect. People would be scared silly if they knew."

"That is scary. So you made good money then, more money than before?"

"The money I made in nuclear trade dwarfed the money I made on fighter jets; it made that look like peanuts."

"How long did you do that?"

"A little less than a year."

"Out of curiosity, how does a common citizen get into business selling fighter jets and then nuclear armaments to foreign countries? I'm guessing you don't see that sort of thing advertised in the local want ads."

"Contacts, that's what it's all about. If you know the right people, you know things that other people don't know. You know things before other people know them, when opportunities are ripe. It's all about having informants on the inside. That's why I strongly emphasized for you to make the right connections with the people you meet in Emerald's empire. I know you didn't fully understand the importance of contacts; people never seem able to grasp it. Without inside resources you are going nowhere, so inscribe that indelibly on the inside of your mind, it's all about contacts."

Davy brushed a bug out of his hair that had become entangled. "So, why did you get out, if you were making that kind of money? Did the government find you out again?"

"No, my secret was well kept this time. I bailed out when I decided what I was doing was crazy."

Marti teed up and whacked the ball.

"Crazy?"

"I realized right away that I was working with some really mean bastards and they were playing for high stakes. I figured I was lucky not to have been killed in that short time. Several of the major nuke players ended up dead. What's the use of having wealth if you are not alive to enjoy it? Besides, if they brought on a nuclear holocaust, that affects me. With that realization, I got out as quickly as possible."

"Seems like you had some information that would have been vital to our government."

"I passed some of the information to the CIA, clandestinely of course, but they ignored most of it, the ignorant bastards. I had become quite wealthy by the time I quit. That's when I had the opportunity to begin working with Emerald. My dealing in armaments and atomic war heads turned out to be excellent preparation for working with Mr. Silverstone. I was then living the good life, but without the risk. Emerald takes all of that, relishes it even."

Davy laughed. "And I thought I liked to live on the edge. You really lived on the edge. I thought this stuff only happened in James Bond movies."

"Yeah, I suppose so, but I came to my senses. That's why I like my position here with Emerald. I enjoy life, but I don't have to worry about getting a bullet in the back of the head. But don't get me wrong, just because I'm pragmatic doesn't mean I run scared. I'm not afraid of any son-of-a-bitch on the face of the earth. I might get killed tomorrow and if I do, I don't give a damn, but, I'll tell you this, it's going to take somebody pretty damned good to bring me down. Uh, pardon my French."

Davy laughed. "Sure, this one time."

Marti broadened into his cool half grin. "It's a hard habit to break, especially when I get animated. I'll try to do better."

"Thanks. I appreciate it."

Davy furrowed his brow and then asked, "So, can you tell me a little about Emerald. I have been here a while, and I still have never seen him. He is larger than life, but he seems like a mystery, like a phantom. It's almost like he doesn't even exist."

"Oh, he exists all right. That you will find out soon enough."

"I'm looking forward to meeting him."

"For starters, he is responsible for the Georgia Guide Stones."

"What's that?"

"Never mind. Okay, what can I tell you? You will never find a man who is more committed to his purpose in life."

"His purpose in life? And what might that be?"

"He believes it is his purpose in life to rule the world."

"He believes it is his purpose to rule the world? Why would he believe that?"

"Somebody has to do it, to save an insane world from itself. Besides, he believes it is his destiny, indeed that his role in world events has been prophesied."

"No kidding? There is prophesy concerning Emerald, prophecy like the Oracles of Delphi, or like you see in the Bible? Are you serious?"

"Three weeks before he was born, his mother had a dream. She dreamed a messenger came to her and told her to name the expected child Emerald. She considered the messenger to be an angel sent from God. Her dream was the source of no small amount of conflict with her husband and he made life miserable for her during this time. Emerald's father, Alexander, believed the child would someday rule the world, so he wanted the name to be Bismarck Medici Silverstone, so named after his ancestors, a name worthy of a great world leader."

Davy listened, intrigued.

"Three days before his birth, Emerald's father also had a dream, one he would claim later was as real as any waking moment of his life. He dreamed he saw a messenger come to him, one with snowy white hair that he wore like a mane, and his eyes shone a radiant green that shined with all the focus of a laser beam. The messenger showed him a scroll of parchment, and Alexander was so enthralled with the message that he got up and wrote it down."

Davy listened silently without interrupting, intrigued by the story. It was like a fantastical scene out of The Arabian Nights.

"The next day, Alexander arose early to deal with a crisis. After the crisis passed, he went busily about his labor until he remembered later in the day the strange dream that had impacted him so, only by then he couldn't recall the dream. But he did remember writing something down, so he went and looked and saw his message. It read simply Daniel 2:35. Then he looked it up in a Bible, and the verse said *but the rock that struck the statue became a huge mountain and filled the whole earth."*

"Yes, I know that verse."

"This perplexed him greatly. He then inquired of his advisers and they informed him that the rock referred to one who would destroy the governments of this world and set up his own kingdom, one who would rule, for the first time ever, the entire world. He then recalled the entire dream. He saw the rock strike the statue and become a huge mountain that consumed the world. The statue was totally destroyed. It was an intense dream. At that time he realized it was indeed prophetic, the radiant green, the stone, his son Emerald, prophesied to rule the earth."

"Wow! That's pretty amazing. Do you believe the prophesy?"

"Who knows? The important thing is Emerald believes it. That's what energizes his whole personality."

Marti stopped talking and stared at Davy. "When you do finally meet Emerald, he is going to give you more information, in just a short time, than you have ever received before. He will share with you the wealth of his life experiences. This knowledge is privileged and few there are who have received it. It's not like you will have the opportunity for him to keep repeating himself. You have to get it the first time you hear it. You understand?"

For the first time since arriving at the manor, Davy was feeling some serious self doubt.

As they were walking back toward the mansion, their game of golf completed, they passed what looked like a huge set of binoculars on an iron pipe base set in the ground. "What's that," inquired Davy?

"An electronic pair of binoculars. Very powerful indeed."

"What's if for?"

"I can look down on the golf course and observe world players at The Dominion. It's so powerful I can even read their score cards if I want to focus in that tightly. I also have a set of head phones that can pick up their conversation if I focus that in also. You'd be surprised at some of the things I've learned."

"Wow. Those could be pretty powerful tools in the world of high finance."

"You have no idea. It's interesting what powerful people from around the world talk about when they think no one is listening."

"Could I use them?"

"Eventually, yes, of course."

Davy thought for a moment and then asked, "So, have you ever been married?"

"No, I never have."

"Why not?"

"Well, the way I've got it figured, women are crazy and men are stupid, so it's a volatile situation. Besides, every wife is a prostitute and every husband is her john. I guess the way I've got it figured is that it is easier to just pay for it up front. Besides, you don't have someone nagging you in the middle of a Spurs basketball game."

"That sounds kind of cynical. But, you do take orders from Emerald."

"Yes, but that is different. He doesn't nag. Besides he pays me very well. That makes a big difference."

"That's true. What about growing old without someone to love you?"

Marti grinned slowly and with coyness. "In my opinion, love is vastly over rated. The way I've got it figured, as long as I've got money, I'll always have someone to love me."

"Still sounds cynical."

Marti chortled.

They were engaging in easy conversation when Davy heard the growling of a dog, ferocious enough to set the hair on his neck. He and Marti turned around and saw a large male Doberman rapidly approaching them, one trained in vicious attack with full intention of serious bodily harm. Davy froze. A lone high-powered rifle shot rang out and the dog collapsed into a rolling ball, stopping a short distance from their feet.

A man, tall, lean and mysterious with intense focus, emerged from beyond the trees and spoke. His eyes were like flint, the rifle he carried casually. "I apologize, Mr. Martinique. The dog managed to break through the restraining fence. The dog was unusually aggressive and his training was a work still in process, so I was unable to recall him. I will see to it that our maintenance man is adequately chastised. I assure you, it will not happen again."

"It's quite all right. It is your extraordinary talent that has prevented it from turning into a tragedy. I have full confidence in you."

"Thank you, sir. I will send someone right over to dispose of the carcass." He turned smartly and disappeared beyond the trees.

"What was that all about?" asked Davy, badly shaken.

"That is Davenport. He is in charge of security."

"I've never seen him before."

"And neither will you in the future, not if he's doing his job right.

He was a Navy Seal and worked once for Israeli elite security forces, the Mossad. He is very good at what he does. He is the one man in this world you do not want mad at you. He has the ability to kill anybody on the face of the earth, and he would do it so cleanly that no one would ever know who did it. He likes to live on the edge though; he's tough to keep under control at times. Not many men would know how to control him, but I do. I know exactly how to handle him."

"Why would you have someone like that, who might get out of control, who could be so dangerous?"

"Because I want the best working for us. Besides, I would rather have him on the inside of the tent pissing out than on the outside pissing in."

Davy laughed. "That makes sense. I guess working with those kinds of people certainly makes for an interesting lifestyle."

The next day Davy had an opportunity to meet the chef, Romaine, and gradually came to know him a little better. Usually, he showed up on days that Antoinette was gone and prepared dinner for the household. Romaine was a fine-boned man of medium build, had an easy going manner, and spoke with a heavy Italian accent. His subtle humor was low keyed and sometimes you had to think a moment before you realized how funny his last comment was. The trait most notable about Romaine was the bad limp of his left leg.

"I injured it during the war, thought I was going to lose it. Some days I think I would have been better off if I had lost it. Maybe I should take a meat cleaver and just whack it off. I could perhaps get a robotic leg. I could run farther and faster than ever before, like the bionic man. Of course, that was before your time, TV show. Besides, you don't need two legs to cook; it's not like I use my feet to stir the batter. The point is I am a very good chef. At least everyone thinks so, everyone except for Antoinette. She gets on my nerves, but I get under her skin. That is a satisfactory tradeoff. She doesn't have much tolerance."

Davy and Romaine got along well and enjoyed each other. He enjoyed his humorous conversation and he learned altogether different cooking techniques than from Antoinette, more practical culinary for Davy's interests. It was during one of these times that Davy remarked upon his enjoyment of writing. He shared about his hidden journal upon which he had written daily, enjoyed so immensely, and missed so dearly.

"You like to write? That is wonderful. Writers are interesting people. They are more interesting than any others I know."

"You know some writers? Neat. How do you know writers?"

"I am one. I belong to a writer's group. We meet once a week. That is my favorite personal time. I would rather visit with writers than any other group of people. Besides, I have published some books, three to be exact. I am working on number four and expect to be sending it to a publisher shortly. I now make as much money in royalties as I receive from Mr. Silverstone. My bestselling book is *Magic Foods and Secret Exercises that can Increase the Male Libido.*"

"That's funny. So, you published three books. That's great. How do you find time to write so many books?"

Romaine laughed. "It's easy. I get paid for being a full-time chef, but Antoinette runs me out and sends me home. I get paid to sit at home and write. It is very sweet."

"I had my heart set on writing at one time. Writing and football were my two life passions. Neither one is likely to happen now. College didn't work out at the time, and now that I will be going to college, I'm not sure they are going to fit in."

"You don't need college to be a great writer. It helps of course. But, if you're good enough, no one cares about your education. But you do need to expose yourself to interesting writers. That and read a lot."

"I do. I am a voracious reader. They all know me at the library."

Romaine, out of his passion for writing, began to mentor Davy's writing interests, staying over a few hours as they discussed writing technique. Romaine casually mentioned that he was Hindu.

"Hindu? I thought you were Italian. I never thought of an Italian being a Hindu."

"My father was a devout Catholic. Italy is where the Pope... but you know all that. He married my mother, from India, when he was there on a covert mission for our government. My father insisted I was raised in the Catholic faith, and so my mother acquiesced. The thing is I was raised at my mother's knee, and what she taught me my father did not know. So when he died in a tragic accident when I was twenty, I adopted the Hindu faith. It has served me well over the years. My mother, of course, was very pleased. She then married a man from India who is also Hindu. We no longer have dissension in our family."

"I am interested to know more about the Hindu religion."

"What do you wish to know?"

"The whole idea of Sati seems pretty strange for me. Why would a woman wish to die on her husband's funeral pier?"

Romaine laughed. "That now only happens in isolated incidents It's kind of like Christians who handle rattlesnakes. Sati has ceased to be an issue in this modern age. It is now against the law you know, but it still happens occasionally."

"Well yeah, now that you mention it, I guess churches that handle snakes are kind of strange."

"Most people know little about the Hindu religion. It is an old and venerable religion, passed down by the masters, the gurus, the swami and others. The Hindu religion did not originate from one great teacher like most religions. Its knowledge was revealed from the mystery of the universe to maharishi of old."

"What does it do for you?"

"It gives me a sense of peace. People don't upset me. Hindu is a religion of inner peace."

"What about Gandhi? Wasn't he killed by a Hindu?"

"Why do people always ask such hard questions when it comes to religion? There are different kinds of Hindu, just like there are many kinds of Christians. Some Christians kill other Christians. Did you never read about the time of Great Inquisition that took place in Europe, Catholics and Protestants killing and torturing each other in the most vicious manner? Look at Irish Protestants and Catholics even today carrying out atrocities against each other. In Islam, you have the Sunni and the Shiites, both of the same religion, carrying out savage war against each other. Religion has always spawned violence. But, that is too much to discuss now. Maybe next time we can discuss my religion more. I will tell you all you want to know about the Hindu religion."

But there was to be no next time. A few days later Davy approached the kitchen and heard an ensuing argument between Romaine and Antoinette. She was getting in at least three words to his every one. As Romaine passed Davy in the hallway, he said angrily, "She could annoy the dead. She has the attitude of a grisly with a jalapeno stuck up its ass. I don't need this, I just quit."

Davy was deeply disappointed to know his writing lessons were ending before they had hardly been started. *Why is it that when things seem to be going my way, they suddenly turn to ashes. Why do opportunities just disappear? It's like some antagonistic spiritual force is toying with me.*

True to Davy's nature, he formed other acquaintances. Being discreet concerning Marti's previous admonitions, he from time to time would slip into the domestic staff lounge, and there he formed an easy relationship with the three Latino grounds keepers. In many ways they were more like friends he had known in his earlier life.

Romero was middle age, though he looked a little older, the result of hard living. He was a quiet and gentle man, but a hard worker, a natural leader of the grounds crew, and clearly the most dependable of the three. He lived in a small house with his wife, three children and his elderly mother. He was saving his money to assist his brother and family to afford the move from Mexico. Davy was pleased to find he had lived in Escondero and knew his aunt and uncle. They shared much in their recollections.

Diego was younger, perhaps mid-twenties, and projected a harder look, even appeared to be somewhat of a rebel. He had copious tattoos on his neck and both arms. Even so, he was intelligent, focused, and the source of interesting conversation. He was also a hard worker and at times seemed to be driven by anger.

The one they called Nick was much younger, perhaps still in his teens. He was a shy boy who stuttered some and said little. When he did contribute to the conversation, it was usually in response to a direct question and in such a timid voice that required concentrated listening to understand him. He was a good kid, and like the others, a hard worker. They had to be productive in their employment. They needed the money to survive.

Considering their English was broken and difficult to understand, Davy usually conversed with them in Spanish. He was proficient enough for comfortable conversation, but occasionally would mispronounce a word and the three would break out in laughter. Sometimes the butler, named Dane, would join them, but he rarely spoke. More than the butler, they were joined by Maria the housekeeper. She usually mostly listened, laughed often at their comments, but when they touched on a subject that animated her, she could take over the conversation. Because Davy respected them all, he was quickly accepted into their group. Therefore, Davy continued to expand his own world of experience. Marti appeared to be unaware that Davy was socializing with the domestic staff.

8
THE PATRIARCH

Davy adjusted easily into his new lifestyle and the bonding with his new brother and sister grew ever stronger, ever deeper. He was able to control his amorous inclinations toward Sarah, at least reasonably so, and with some effort began to see her more with respect as he might have for his mother or little sister, which seemed to him the safest course to take. After all, if their love were to bloom romantically, then how much better it should be grounded in the friendship of respect. Besides, he felt unworthy of her. In any event, his love for them both grew steadily, particularly so for Sarah. They were the brother and sister he so longed for, but until now was denied.

Davy had an older brother, one who had died at six months of age two years before he was born. The death of their oldest son had been devastating for his parents, but their sorrow was turned to joy with the arrival of Davy. He occasionally thought of Doug, his older brother, particularly when they visited the cemetery, adorning the small stone with fresh flowers, but from Davy's perspective he might as well have been born two hundred years sooner, such is the impenetrable wall of death.

His parents had held Doug in their hands and had gazed into his eyes. He had gazed into theirs; they had loved and experienced him. Davy had only heard of Doug, though separated by a mere two years. He experienced Doug vicariously, through his parents. Even so, he had always felt a connection with Doug. As a small child he had tenderly touched the engraved writing on the small tombstone and had carried on his own private conversation with his unknown brother.

His little sister, Ginny, experienced the same lack of familiarity to Davy's first six years prior to her birth, almost as if she had walked into a theater after the movie had started. *That is the way with us all,* thought Davy. *We come into life in the middle of some story, our parents, our grandparents, the community and the larger world.* Sarah and Travis were filling with love the great hole he felt in his young life, the need for family.

It was ten o'clock in the morning when he ran into Sarah. "Did you know he is here?" she asked excitedly.

"Who is here?"

"Emerald," she said with excitement as though he should have known.

"Emerald? Here? You are kidding me? I had no idea he was coming."

"Well that's the way it is with Emerald. He just shows up; you usually don't know ahead of time. He moves at the speed of light sometimes. I just finished talking to him. He always has a meeting with us when he's home. He wants to see you now. He asked me to send you right up."

"Me? Right now?"

"Yes, right now."

"In his office?"

"Yes, silly, of course in his office, where else? It's at the top of the west spiral stairs."

Davy stood staring, working up the courage to move.

"Go, go," she said, feigning bossiness and waving him on with her hands.

Davy walked with heavy feet toward Emerald's spiral stairway and then upward. He had never climbed the stairs to Emerald's wing before and he carried a burden of intimidation. At the top of the stairs Davy saw that the hall was similar to the one he, Sarah, and Travis lived on. He knew the doors on the left side emptied into Emerald's suite of rooms, his personal living quarters. On the right was Emerald's office, which was without any door for a barrier.

The doorway was about four feet in width. The bottom wall was only about three feet in height with flower boxes sitting on each running about six feet in either direction away from the doorway. On the upper cut of wall hung some more flower boxes suspended by fine cables, and they were all filled with flowers and vines so they draped down and intermingled with flowers in the lower boxes. The effect was to provide openness and accessibility while also providing a barrier for a semblance of privacy.

The decor of three walls each had their own theme. The wall facing Davy had several large pictures of Greek and Roman ancient architectural buildings: the Parthian, the Pantheon, the Coliseum, the Circus Maximus. On shelves were larger than life marble busts of Caesars, gods and goddesses, as well as bronze statues of mythological creatures such as the Cyclops, a minotaur, a centaur, Medusa, Cerberus, a chimaur, the Phoenix and Pegasus.

The theme of the wall to his right was Egyptian with pictures of the Great Pyramid, the Sphinx, Cleopatra, Ramses and King Tut's golden esophagus. They were accompanied by statues of Egyptian gods and goddesses: Isis, Osiris, Ra, Horus, Seth and Anubis. Propped against the wall was an Egyptian mummy, or possibly an imitation mummy. The third wall was an amalgam of ancient temples from around the world, including Africa, Asia and South America. There were several full colored pictures of Priests and Kings dressed in full ceremonial regalia and a large bronze dragon statue that was fine and intricate in its artistry and fearsome to behold.

Emerald was sitting at his desk working on papers as Davy entered and cleared his throat. Noticing Davy, Emerald briskly stood with a smile and hurried around the desk to greet him, his hand extended. They shook hands firmly and warmly with Emerald holding onto Davy's arm above the elbow with his left hand. Emerald was a small man, perhaps five foot four and of slender build.

Davy was a bit surprised. "I thought you were taller." He laughed nervously. "You always seemed much larger on television."

Emerald laughed. "Well, I am taller than Napoleon. The thing is it's not how big you are on the outside; it's how big you are on the inside that counts. Of one you are limited, but the other is without limitation, only that which is self imposed. You can be as big as your imagination, your commitment and your grit."

"Yeah, that makes sense." His calm appearance betrayed the anxiety of standing before such a powerful person. "I guess I was expecting you to be twelve feet tall."

Emerald laughed with amusement. He was obviously a man of high intensity and he radiated energy, but in a calm relaxed manner which suggested an abundance of self confidence. He had dark penetrating eyes and wavy thinning hair held meticulously in place by fragrant scented hair oil. His suit was pressed and he himself appeared as fresh as though he was showered and dressed the previous hour. *How do some people do that, stay fresh looking all day,* Davy wondered? His knees felt weak and he worried his voice might quiver.

"Davy, I am so excited to finally meet you in person. I have been looking forward to this for some time. This is really a pleasure. You are one special person."

Davy was embarrassed by the generous praise, even intimidated. But he sucked his gut up and said, "Yes sir, I have to confess I have been looking forward to it with great anticipation myself. I am pleased to meet you, and honored. I feel somewhat unworthy to be in the presence of one with your record of success and achievement."

"Nonsense. I'm just like any other man you meet coming down the street, not that much different than your own father might have been. We are family here, Davy. We treat each other like family. If your father had been rich and famous, would he have been any less of a father to you, or would you have had less affection for him? Would your mother have been less loving if she had been rich and famous?"

"Of course not. My relationship with my parents would be more important to me than fame and fortune. I'd give anything to see them once more."

Davy looked about the room before commenting, "The Egyptian Pharaohs, many of them have a golden cobra coiled about their head. I've always wondered about that."

"Yes," said Emerald. "The Egyptian Pharaohs believed that the gods could materialize into the form of a snake, falcons, jackals and other animals."

"How about rodents, rats and spiders?"

"Well yes, now that you mention it, they are also a part of the legend."

Davy looked around, surprised by his level of discomfort. He wondered at the lack of security for such an influential person. "I am surprised you don't have security devises in your office. I don't believe I've seen any video cameras inside the house, only outside."

"Ah yes, of course. They are excellent security devises, but surely you are aware they can work against you the same as they can for you. Technology brought down the presidency of Richard Nixon; they have sent others to prison. I have excellent security around the perimeter and only those I trust are allowed inside of Silverstone Manor. I don't need security cameras inside."

"But what about privacy? If you are having private conversation, anybody in the hall could see and hear you. I would think there would be times when you would want your conversation to remain private."

"Yes, quite so. Electronics. Technology gives us an audible impenetrable wall."

"Electronics?"

"Yes, electronics. Sounds inside the office are filtered electronically. It's kind of like an electronic wall. Keeps private conversation safe inside and eliminates noise from outside. Same thing with vision; the ability to see inside can be controlled electronically. It's like looking into the window of a dark room when it's bright and sunny outside. There might be plenty of light to see on the inside, but you can't see a damned thing from outside."

"Interesting."

"It's all done electronically. I operate the controls from a panel inside my desk."

Davy now wrestled for the appropriate words. "I don't know exactly what to say. Marti kept talking about... about me becoming a part of the family, but I thought that was just generous speech on his part. Not until this moment has it dawned on me that he was talking about a real, honest to goodness family. You do make me feel like family, but I am so unworthy. I'm just at such a loss to know what to say, other than I am appreciative, deeply appreciative."

Emerald laughed, motioned Davy to a chair in front of the desk and returned to his own chair behind it. "How have you found Silverstone Estates? Have you enjoyed yourself?"

"Oh, absolutely. It' been a wonderful experience. I am fortunate to share in this kind of opportunity."

"That's good. I'm glad, and how about Travis and Sarah? Are you getting along with them okay?"

"Yes sir, very much sir. I really like both of them. They are so cool. We seem to feel connected, like we've been friends for a long time. It's hard to imagine you can feel so close to someone in such a short time."

"Good, good. I am pleased. Quality people tend to relate well with each other. I like to associate with quality people. It pays to do so." Emerald paused and then continued, "There's something I'd like to ask you."

Davy swallowed, not knowing what to expect.

"I understand you do a pretty nice job of imitating people."

Davy grinned, feeling self-conscious. "I sometimes mimic people. I enjoy making people laugh."

"So I hear, so I hear. I understand you have an interesting imitation of Marti and of me."

Davy's grin turned to one of embarrassment and he swallowed again. "Yes, I've done both of you, but I do just about everybody. I didn't mean any offense."

"None taken. Would you mind doing that for me? I'd love to hear it."

"I'd really rather not, if you don't mind?"

"Nonsense. I insist. Marti says it's priceless. I'd dearly love to hear it."

Davy took a deep breath and began to mimic first Marti and then Emerald, carrying on a humorous conversation between the two, incorporating their particular idiosyncrasies. Emerald was soon laughing, and then he was laughing so hard he was wiping tears from his eyes.

"God, I love it. It's been a while since I've laughed that hard. Most of the people I associate with are pretty intense. They don't fully appreciate the value of humor. Perhaps I am too much like that myself. Your humor is good. Like all great mimics, you slightly exaggerate people's identifying traits. That's what makes you so good and so humorous. And you are obviously quite perceptive which allows you to notice how people act. That's an excellent trait. You do a wonderful job of putting people at ease. Very good."

Davy was relieved it went well. He hadn't been so sure when he had begun. There was a pause in the conversation, one that allowed Emerald to change its tone.

"Davy, there's something I would like to say to you. My heart goes out to you for losing your family the way you did, and what all you've been through. I know it had to be incredibly tough for you. I can relate, because I went through some rather harrowing experiences myself before I achieved some success."

"Yes, I have heard that; Marti told me some."

"My boy, you have proven yourself well during the last four years. You have a remarkable and resilient manner. You have extraordinary character. A man shows his character by how he handles adversity. You will notice I only have two things on top of my desk, other than my immediate project, The Prince by Machiavelli and this gold plated plaque that says Greatness is conceived in adversity, genius in travail."

Davy read the plaque. "Yes, I believe that, very much. My mother used to say the most glorious human experience was victory over adversity. That gave me strength to carry on at times when I needed it. She often told me life was precious."

"The most glorious human experience is victory over adversity," repeated Emerald. "That's good. I like that. I like it a lot. I may have another plaque made for my desk, giving you credit for the quote, of course. He again repeated, "The most glorious human experience is victory over adversity," this time in a barely audible whisper.

"Very good. Your mother had a lot of wisdom, your father too. They were good people. They helped make you the person you are today."

Davy beamed. Imagine hearing that about yourself and your parents from one such as Emerald.

"You are a remarkable person with unlimited potential, of that I am sure. The success of the son is a compliment to the parents."

"The quote was my mother's. She should receive the credit."

"Of course, it will be attributed to Davy's mother."

Emerald leaned back in his chair and said, "I can't tell you how excited I am to finally have you here. I have watched films of you playing football, from the time you were a freshman. In addition to all your game films, I have watched every practice film. I have studied them carefully. It seems like you always find a way to move the ball down the field. That's what life is all about, Davy, people who are determined to move the ball down the field. Do you know why I enjoy watching your films so much?"

"No sir."

"Call me Emerald," he said, waving Davy off with his hand. "My family calls me Emerald. Everyone else calls me Mr. Silverstone. I want you to call me Emerald."

Davy found his voice soothing and reassuring. "Yes sir, I mean Emerald."

"There you go!" said Emerald with emphasis. "That's much better. The reason I enjoy watching the films, in addition to your great athletic prowess, is because of the effect you have on the rest of the team. You definitely run the team. You lift them up."

Emerald used hand gestures to accent his words, punctuating the air with exclamation marks.

"You inspire them. They will fight to the death to please you. They believe in you. They believe in themselves when you're leading them. Every person on the team is a better player because of you. You give them greatness of heart. How many times did I see you snatch victory out of what seemed certain defeat at the very last minute. Your intangible qualities of leadership far outweigh your athletic abilities, great as they are."

Emerald's eyes gleamed as he asked the next question. "Do you have any idea how rare that quality is?"

"No sir, I mean Emerald. I don't know what to say. I was just basically enjoying myself, trying to win. I really like winning. It just made sense to encourage the others. It seemed like we played better when I did that. I inherited my competitiveness from my dad."

"I am sure you did, more than you know. Something else that impressed me was the way you seemed to know what the defense was up to; you always sensed how best to counteract their defensive posture."

Davy laughed. "You'd be surprised how much you can know about your opponent's intentions just by looking at their eyes." This he said though he had been able to discern precious little information from Emerald's eyes.

"I know. It's called reading body language, and you are naturally extraordinarily talented in doing so. That is more important than you can conceive. Just imagine how good you could be if you were actually trained in the technique and knew what the hell you were doing."

Emerald's comments gave Davy a sense of pleasure to know that Emerald was seeing talent in him which no one else seemed aware of, not even himself.

"And you were only a freshman, amazing. The energy of Emerald's next spontaneous response startled Davy. "You have more leadership capacity than you realize. You have no idea, certainly too much to waste on high school football. It's like a toddler playing inside the cockpit of a B-2 Spirit stealth bomber carrying nuclear warheads. He would have no concept of the immense potential power surrounding him. He would need to grow, to mature, to be trained by someone who knew and could show him the way, then he could accomplish great things with the awesome power at his fingertips. It's all been a game with you thus far, life wasted without focus. That's about to change."

The phone buzzed and Emerald picked it up. "Adiniah, how are you doing? What's happening? That's very interesting, what does he have in mind? I know he's a brilliant person, but I've never dealt with him before. Give me a little more information."

Emerald listened for perhaps ten minutes before responding, "Wow, that is remarkable. Who would ever have thought of such a thing? Absolutely, we are interested in financing him. How much does he need to make it happen? One hundred million dollars! That's a lot of money, my friend."

There was a pause. "Okay, here's what we do; it's his idea so he gets to develop it and be in charge from beginning to end, as long as he doesn't screw it up. The one hundred million will be delivered in equal divisions each quarter for the first year. There should be some income generated by six months, so that should all work out. If it works like I believe it will, he will become rich beyond what even he can comprehend. I know what I'm talking about. However, make sure he understands we own it since we will be financing it. But, he will be the guy in charge. He gets to run it as long as he runs hard and produces."

There was another pause. "Right, right, make sure he understands this has to work. I would not be happy losing that much money. You know that, of course. If he screws up, he's going to think he has a red hot poker stuck up his ass. Let him know he's playing in the big leagues now. Success is awesome; failure is not an option. I would never tolerate failure on this scale. The monkey is on his back. Make sure he understands that. Make damned sure he understands that." Emerald was drumming his fingers on the desk, but he wore a poker face.

Emerald listened some more before responding, "It's a remarkable idea. I'm surprised I haven't thought of it myself. I believe that it will work; it should if it's done right. Then we can all be happy, especially me. I'm good to live with when I'm happy. You know how I think, so get it in play. Thanks, Adiniah. Good job. Bye now."

Emerald hung up the phone and sat staring a full minute, deep in thought, before saying, "Where were we? Oh, yes. You are about to enter The System. The System is God. Remember that, Davy. There are many systems in the world and The System is always God. To do well in life, you have to understand that. My system is interconnected to many systems. To do well in life, you have to understand the concept. Most people don't have a clue. Most people don't do so well. The ones who understand The System is God are the ones who rise to the top."

"Marti told me some about The System."

"Good, he is supposed to. The System does not exist to serve the people. No, the people exist to serve The System. Ancient natives understood that when they sacrificed young maidens to the gods of the volcanoes and the sun gods. They didn't sacrifice volcanoes to the maidens. That's what religion is all about, giving your soul to The System. Egyptians slaves were expendable when building the pyramids. It was the greatness of the pyramids that was important, not the individuals. It was the Pharaoh god who was important."

Emerald's statement offended Davy's natural sense of decency. "But people are important too, right?"

"You are talking about moral principles which are not all that simple. Sometimes, in order to be good, you have to be ruthless. If Lincoln, Grant and Sherman had not been ruthless, the evil of slavery would still exist. If Patton had not been ruthless, the Nazi regime might well have prevailed. Every American president has understood the concept that individual soldiers are expendable in battle for the good of the nation. So you see, sometimes you have to be ruthless to be good."

Emerald hesitated long enough to allow Davy an opportunity to digest what he was hearing. "People want to be a part of a great nation, a great civilization. In order for a nation to be great, the individual must become expendable. In great civilizations the lives of individuals cease to have value. Not, mind you, because I have determined it to be so. It's just the way it is. It doesn't matter what you or I think. That's the way it has always been for the Sumerians, Babylonians, the Greeks, the Romans, all of them. You can never fight The System. It will always break you. You have to learn how to manipulate The System. When you accomplish that successfully, when you control The System, when your system controls the other systems, then you will be God."

Davy listened in awe, wrestling with conflicting voices within his head, but he was hesitant to interrupt. He was totally unprepared for what was to come next.

9
THE ANOINTED ONE

Emerald continued in a low, dramatic voice. "That's why I am so impressed with you. You instinctively understand how to work The System. I became so excited, Davy, when we discovered you. I scrutinized you more than any of the five who came before you. I was more personally involved in the decision to bring you aboard, the whole process. I had to be. You reminded me so much of myself when I was your age. Oh, life placed us in different circumstances, but similar in so many ways. You have touched me like no one else ever has. You are the one I have long searched for. If you are willing to become my son, Davy, I will make you my heir.

Davy felt like he had just been struck by a thunderbolt. Nothing that had happened so far would have indicated this was what Emerald had in mind. He wasn't just talking about making him a part of the family as he had done for the others; he was talking about becoming his legitimate son, his heir. Could he be ruthless enough to satisfy Emerald? Perhaps he would be in a position to change the way some things were done. Davy was truly stunned by what he had heard, or at least thought he had heard, but he was hesitant to ask Emerald to repeat himself. Even so, he said, "Excuse me sir, I mean Emerald, but I'm not... I'm not sure I understood you?"

"You heard me correctly. I said I am going to make you my heir. All I own is going to be yours. I'm getting on in years now, over one hundred years old, one hundred and seven to be exact. Very few people know I am that old; it's none of their business."

"Did you say one hundred and seven? That is impossible. You are surely much younger than that."

Emerald laughed. "Believe it. I am that old. There are reasons why I have lived as long as I have, why I don't look my age, but we will talk more about that later. The point is, I'm not going to live forever, and I need someone to carry on the work when I am gone. I knew you were the one as soon as I saw those films of you, as a freshman shortly after your parents died."

"But when... how did you see my game films? I just assumed all those old films were stored away in a dust covered box somewhere."

"Oh no, I have purchased every single one. I have analyzed them in most minute detail. I know what your teachers, your friends, and your extended family feel about you and how they react to you. You will find that I am detail-oriented and take great pains to see that things are done right, nothing left to chance. I would have loved to have brought you aboard immediately, but it takes time to work through these things. I had to know what you were made of, and that takes time. I had to observe you in your most desperate struggle. You had to be baptized in fire to prove your metal. But, it was worth it. You are everything I hoped you would be, and more. You are worthy to be my heir."

"I am just so astounded. What about your wife? Surely she should come first." He wondered if she might become vindictive when she found out.

"My wife will be very well taken care of. She will have more wealth than she will know what to do with, more than she could ever need. But she is not the one to carry on my work, my great mission. Hell, give her a gold-plated skillet, a fancy stove, and a dildo and she will be quite satisfied."

"What about Travis, Sarah, Marti, all the others, the ones who came into the family before me? What about your generals, your lieutenants, the ones who have served you faithfully over the years? Shouldn't one of them be your heir?" Davy searched for words. "I feel so unworthy. I haven't accomplished anything of substance yet. I may have some potential, and I think I do, but I haven't proven anything yet. I just don't know what to say."

"You don't have to say anything. You just have to accept what is, the benevolence of providence. You are the son I never had. A man has a right to put his son ahead of everyone else. And besides, all the ones I brought into the family, all of my generals and lieutenants under them, they have done very well for themselves under me, better than they could have ever done by themselves. I suppose some will be pissed; such is human nature. Still, if I wish to give what is mine to my son, what is that to them?"

"I'm so... well... just speechless. I do know I should express my gratitude, and I am grateful, deeply grateful, more than I can express at the moment. I only hope I can live up to your expectations of me. I don't want to disappoint you."

Emerald laughed a satisfied laugh. "I have no doubt you will live up to our expectations of you, and more. I am a remarkable judge of character. I have spent my lifetime studying personality types. That's how I know you are the one. Most authorities divide personality types into four groups, but that is woefully inadequate. I have made a lifetime study of how different personalities think and act. If you want to be as rich and as powerful as I am, you have to know what motivates people and what they are going to do. You will need to know more about what they are going to do than they do themselves."

Davy squirmed a bit in his chair with discomfort as he realized the magnitude of the verbal deluge of which both Travis and Marti had forewarned him. Emerald continued, "You happen to have an extremely rare combination of personality characteristics. Your primary type is as a Sensation Type, which is a Choleric, which makes you quite dominant. You are Sensation Volcanic to be exact. You are extremely competitive and driven to win. You have a magnetic personality. People will follow you into combat without questioning you. You also like to be in charge of things, to shake things up, to make things happen. They have the ambition of power. The name Stalin meant "man of iron;" he understood. You are tough-minded and strong-willed. The Choleric personality is both idolized and feared. Many great generals were Choleric."

Davy grinned. "I do like to make things happen." Emerald continued.

"Your secondary personality type is as Melancholy, or an Intuitor, which means you are intellectually creative in a way that implies spiritual access to the gods. Many prophets and visionaries were Melancholy personality types. As were many great leaders. Napoleon Bonaparte used to say that imagination rules the world. You can ascertain future trends before others. You have a great mind for strategy at chess or at war games. This is a rare combination, the Choleric and the Melancholic combination of personality types. Hitler had it. So did Vince Lombardi, Bobby Knight, Leonardo Divinci and Michelangelo. It is your remarkable strength in both these areas that makes you so unique."

Davy could scarcely contain all he was hearing.

"But that's not all. You are also remarkably strong even in your third area; whereas, most people show weakness in their third trait. That is quite unusual. Your third trait is as a Sanguine, or as Feeler, which means you enjoy entertaining people and are sensitive to social situations. People love being around you. You provide energy, ebullience, excitement and flair. You relate to other people's feelings. You are cheerful and brighten the room. People genuinely like you and are drawn to you. Sarah and Antoinette are both Sanguine.

"And then your fourth personality type as Phlegmatic or as a Thinker Type is still remarkably strong. Think of Albert Einstein and Thomas Edison. You examine the details and plan out an agenda that reaches far into the future. You would expect a person to be exceedingly weak in their fourth area. But your weakest area is stronger than for many who have it as their primary personality type. So there you have it, the strength of four people in one, such an unusual combination of personality types that comes along once in a century, if that often."

Emerald clinched his fist for emphasis.

"Haven't you ever wondered at how easily you went through life as an orphan in what should have been devastating circumstances? Not since I was born has one of such outstanding quality come forth. You were born to be a world ruler. It is your destiny."

Again, Davy was stunned. "To be honest, I didn't even know there was such a thing as personality types. If I was born to be a world ruler, why would I be so clueless?"

"Of course, you are ignorant in many areas. You need to be schooled. But, you need to know personality types. You will be taught this, of course, one of your many subjects, subjects you would never get in college. From now on you may think of me as your psychological father, your source of understanding this complex subject."

"Far out," said Davy with an unsure grin.

"You will also be taught body types and how that affects personality. Form and function are related, you know. Body type greatly influences our personality. You will also be taught to read body language. It is a science. You will be able to dissect others thinking, ascertain their motives and extrapolate their intentions. When I send you to Harvard, you will know more about how life works than your professors. They don't know anything. They think they do. They have never lived in the real world. If they know so much, why aren't they in my position and I in theirs?"

Emerald squinted his eyes in narrow focus. "No, they are fools. But, you have to play the game, let them believe they are smarter than you. It is only an inconvenience, nothing more. You will pass them all in a few years."

Davy felt overwhelmed. The information was flowing faster than he could absorb. Sarah, Travis and Marti had warned him of the verbal deluge that should come. Pontification seemed like such a tame word.

Emerald rose from his chair and motioned for Davy to follow. They walked to a table that sat along the wall behind Emerald's desk. On the table sat an antique wooden chest covered with intricate hand carvings. It reminded him of India. Emerald opened the lid of the box and Davy was startled to see crisp new bills, lots of bills wrapped into tight little bundles. They were hundred dollar bills, all in neat tight bundles, wrapped with bands straight from the bank.

"There is a million dollars in this box. It's yours, if you want it. All you have to do is pick it up and take it, any of it, part of it, all of it, whatever you want. It's yours. There's only one stipulation. When you take it, no matter how much or how little, you are done with the Silverstone Empire. You are out! This is a test, Davy, a test of character. I must know I can trust you absolutely, that you can control your impulse for immediate gratification for long-term gain."

Davy gulped as his eyes coveted the box of money.

"A million dollars may seem like a lot of money, but only to those who don't have it. It's not actually that much money. It always runs out. If you stay with me, you will earn more than that every week. In the meantime, you will get a salary of one thousand dollars a month while you are in your internship and going to college. That probably doesn't sound like much, only twelve thousand dollars a year, but it's a hell of a lot more than you are currently making, and it is much when you consider you really have no expenses, no clothing, no shelter, no groceries, transportation and no school supplies or tuition. It's yours to spend frivolously or to invest, whatever you see fit. But when you are fully trained and plugged into my empire, you will live like a king. So don't help yourself to the money in a moment of weakness. You would lose your grand opportunity. You must persevere in the face of temptation to prove you are worthy to be my heir. It will take great inner strength."

"Trust me sir... Emerald, I will not. You can depend on that."

"I know that, Davy. That's the thing about personality types; they always behave a certain way. We are pre-programmed to think and act the way we do. We have less choice than you might imagine. People think they make their own decisions, about who they are, what they think. Take religion for instance." Emerald watched Davy to see if he was following. "People don't really have as much choice about their religious convictions as they might suppose."

"You are saying people don't choose what they believe about religion? Why would you say that?"

"Absolutely not. Most people believe what they believe determined by their DNA. It has been shown that people who have similar religious perspectives, or analogous political beliefs, usually also have similar chemical physical patterns which can be demonstrated in the laboratory. I have seen empirical evidences that prove it so, chemical and DNA results from the lab."

He is suggesting that chemistry defines us spiritually. Maybe our spirituality defines us chemically. "I have never heard of such a thing." Davy's words did not reflect his resistance to such a thought. They both returned to their chairs.

"Probably not, few people have. Most people are happily ensconced in their ignorance. What little self determination of free will they have is quickly overpowered by massive propaganda campaigns by various self-serving political, financial, and religious organizations."

"That is not quite the way I have always envisioned it."

"Yet, it is true. Very few people have the ability to sort out for themselves what they truly believe about religion. They are programmed, controlled, manipulated."

Davy shifted in his chair. "I see."

"Anyway, now where were we? Oh yes, personality types. You have to understand your own physical and emotional make up before you can ever begin to have control over your own religious and political decisions, before you can exert control over others. That is why it's so important to be schooled in personality types. Study hard, Davy, and learn well. When you understand personality types, you will know what a person is going to do before they know it themselves."

"Yes, of course."

"That and body language. When you understand body language in detail, you will be able to read a person like a book. Most people lie some, some lie a lot, but body language never lies, not if you are well taught."

"That is powerful."

"As if that were not enough, and it actually is enough in itself, but we now have the technology to fit a small electronic instrument into my pocket that acts like a lie detector machine. It picks the brainwaves out of the air and tells you whether others are being truthful or not. You can monitor people with it as you walk down the street, without them being aware they are being monitored. All this gives you an unsporting advantage. Everything is fair in love and war, as they say, and high finance as well, I might add. And is there really anything else beside love, war, and money?"

"Am I being monitored right now, by your electronic device?"

Emerald smiled. "I don't need it for you, Davy. I already know everything I need to know. We have done an intensive search on you and your background, going back to your prenatal records. We have even searched out your DNA information. Another thing, you never let the other person know everything that is going on, never. Always keep others partially in the dark, and work that to your advantage. In any event, you will be taught all of this, in time. Have patience, Davy. Everything will come in time."

Davy thought for a minute and then asked, "My prenatal records? My DNA? Wow, that is a pretty intensive background research! How did you do that? I thought medical records were confidential."

"For most people, yes, but remember what I said, whoever controls The System is God."

Davy was a little unnerved by the thought that a stranger could search so freely through his personal records, his personal life, and his family's privacy. That seemed somewhat profane on one level, yet Davy could not help admire the ability to do so, an ability that would someday be his. To be connected to one with such power gave Davy a sense of self importance that tended to more than balance out his concerns.

Davy suddenly jumped as they were interrupted by a thunderclap. They both started laughing at his reaction. "Sonic boom said Emerald."

He reached for the phone and dialed.

"I'd like to speak to General Abernathy please."

There was a bit of silence and then Emerald repeated again, "Could you connect me to General Abernathy please... No, I'd prefer to speak to the General... This is Emerald Silverstone. You must be running some kind of war games, and your pilots are making sonic booms over my estate. I'm engaged in some conferencing and would like for the General to cancel the flights for the next couple of days... Sure he can, just tell him Emerald Silverstone called and made the request... Look, I'm telling you, do what you want, but if General Abernathy has to cancel the flights because he receives an order from the Pentagon, he's going to be plenty pissed... and you're the one he's going to pissed about... so you just do what the hell you want to." He slammed the phone down in its cradle."

He grinned at Davy. "Junior Officer, but he's no fool. I'm pretty sure we're not going to be hearing anymore sonic booms."

There were a hundred different questions going through Davy's mind, none of which he dared to ask. At such a guarded moment it is to be expected that the most unexpected question would slip out. "I've never heard of anyone being one-hundred seven. Are you *really* that old? I have a hard time believing that."

Emerald laughed again, the easy low level laugh of one who is comfortable with whom he is. "The world doesn't know. The world doesn't have a clue. Antoinette does magic with her culinary skills. She has studied the mysteries of the ancient texts. Only a few of the rich and powerful who have access to information that can help them remain so youthful in their older age and live for so long."

"I didn't realize there was that kind of knowledge."

"Of course. As you eat her meals, you will build new cells, stronger cells, cast off disease causing toxins; you will find yourself getting stronger, younger, and more clear thinking as you age. The biggest thing Einstein had going for him was a brain free of toxins. That was the only difference between him and the average Charlie Lunch Pail. When all your former friends are debilitated with disease and dying off, you'll just be hitting your health and financial stride. You will be at your strongest when they are at their worst. Just think of the difference an extra fifty years, perhaps a hundred of your best years would make, tacked on to the end of your productive life."

Davy felt lost. Usually he processed information rather well, but what he was hearing was so foreign to him. Emerald continued.

"What if Alexander the Great had lived to be one-hundred and thirty? What could he have done with his full life? Leonardo Di Vinci and Michelangelo were both well over one hundred and fifty years old when they died. How do you think they became so wise and accomplished so much? They each had to assume two separate identities to keep their ages secret. Their biographies are bogus. Originally, man was designed to live to be a thousand years old. If the world is going to avoid Armageddon, if we are going to avoid letting the doomsday clock expire, then we must somehow recapture that ability."

"You believe man was designed to live to be one thousand years of age?"

"Of course. It says so in ancient sacred writings. Anyway, if you are going to be wealthy and powerful, there are some things you need to understand. To have power means you must control people. That is the definition of power. To control people means you have to know how to control people. It is an art and a science, an ability that needs to be developed. You have to manipulate the schools, the churches, the news media, entertainment, banking, medical field, armed forces and government so they all work for you. If you learn how to control these areas, you can control the masses. When you have them by the balls, their hearts will follow."

Emerald's discourse was interrupted by the phone. Picking up the receiver, Emerald exchanged greetings with someone named Jamar. "That will be fine. That would be a good time to present some of the subjects we discussed at our last meeting. Give the Queen Mother my regards. Thanks. Bye."

"Queen Mother? Like in the Queen of England?"

"Yes, yes, of course."

He thought for a moment and said, "Let's see now, where were we? Oh, yes, think about it! He who controls the schools shapes the developing minds that will control the future of nations. Control all the weapons and you have absolute control of the people. Control what the churches teach and people will do whatever you want for the salvation of their souls. The Church in the Middle Ages certainly knew this and used it effectively. Entertainment molds the values of people. The news media controls the information that is fed to the people, a vast propaganda machine. Banking controls the money. Those who have financial access become wealthy. Those who control the wealth are gods. Those who issue professional licenses are gods; they can destroy your ability to earn a living simply by pulling your license."

Davy liked the peace of mind he had before he was exposed to such power and control. Life was simpler when he didn't know such information, but he realized he would have to make some concessions to access the wealth. "I thought the process of giving professional license was for the protection of the public."

"That's nonsense, of course. The ruse is the government issues professional license for the protection of the public. There must always be a ruse. But, the real issue is power and prestige, for the profession and absolute power for the government. This will all make more sense to you as you learn more."

Davy listened in awe.

Emerald continued, "People will do anything to regain their health after they have lost it, when it is too late. They are fools. They believe whatever the doctors tell them. Doctors are gods to the masses. Control agriculture by government regulation and you decide who eats quality food and who eats junk food. Only the wealthy have access to life-rejuvenating foods. You decide who eats in abundance and who gets no food at all. You reward your friends; you punish your enemies. That's just the way it works."

Davy was hesitant to respond. "I... I... I don't know that I agree with that. I think it takes more character to respond with compassion to your enemies. That just seems to be nobler. Kindness and compassion, I think, would make the world better."

"Oh, really now? You think being nice to your enemies is good? If you don't destroy your enemy when you have the opportunity, he will return when he can and will destroy you. The thing is, as long as there are enemies, there will be wars. It is true that war is hell. Ask anyone who has ever lived through one. Vast national resources are lost, used to destroy one's enemies, resulting in worldwide poverty, famine, and pestilence."

Emerald waved his hand in the air as if pulling up his next thought. "It never ends; there are always more enemies, one war following another, always somewhere in the world. people who want to annihilate you, your family, your race. Of course, you want to do the same to them. Exterminate your enemies; that is the name of the game."

Emerald laughed and continued, "That's the problem with a Democracy; enemies are allowed to exist side by side. Only when all enemies, the evil ones, are eliminated will there be true peace. Only then will war become a thing of the past Only then will poverty, hunger, and disease be eliminated. That can only happen when one man rules the entire world, when I come to fullness of power. It may not be a perfect government or society, but it will still be preferable by far than having the world continually torn asunder by everlasting wars. I will bring that peace, and when I do, the world will be grateful. Therefore Davy, if you are going to run with the big dogs, it's imperative you get your priorities right."

Davy laughed nervously. "You want to bring world peace and prosperity to the whole world? That's admirable, it really is. You want to rule the world? I'll say one thing; you are not one for small goals."

Emerald stared and Davy was cautious as he continued. "I still am inclined to believe it virtuous to be loving and forgiving." He hoped he hadn't been too forward.

"Very well, you have the confidence to defend your position. I respect that. You probably won't understand what I am saying until you have experienced the horror of war, seen for yourself the misery of people living in abject poverty all around the world. You have lived a rather sheltered life by way of comparison, even considering all you have gone through. You think you have been through a lot of adversity, but not really. Many have suffered far more than you have. All I ask is that you keep an open mind. I believe eventually you will see that I am right."

Davy smiled a sigh of relief. He had been true to his principles and apparently had not offended Emerald in the process. Perhaps he had even impressed him.

"Of course," said Davy, "if I am wrong I will be man enough to admit it."

Emerald was satisfied, even pleased, with Davy's response.

"Have you ever noticed how much the government dislikes monopolies? The reason is because the government is itself a monopoly, the largest, most devious monopoly of them all. It is the nature of monopolies to hate competition, and other monopolies are the biggest threat to government. So, all other monopolies must be destroyed. People believe the government destroys monopolies because it is protecting the public, has their best interests at heart. The people are fools, damned fools."

Where is this going, thought Davy? *This all has to be leading somewhere.*

"To understand government, you need to understand that government operates like the mafia, doesn't make any different whether it's a democracy, dictatorship, or whatever. It's not the system that is defective, though some are worse than others; it is the heart of man that is evil, desperately wicked. That is the problem. Evil men always end up in control. Like scum, they always rise to the top regardless of the political system. The goal is always absolute power."

Davy started to speak, but thought better of it.

"The trick is to make people believe you have their best interest at heart. Every dictator has come under the guise of being a savior. The masses are such fools. Right now, at this very moment, there are some who are attempting to create an absolute monopoly on public and private air and water. Once this happens there will be no way out. The slavery of mankind will be absolute. It is up to people like you and me to oppose such evil. You are assuming a great load upon your shoulders. It is your destiny."

"My destiny?"

"Indeed, this is your destiny. The problem is, every single person on the face of the earth wants to be God. They want to enslave their neighbors. That is our great challenge. When you think about it, it is a spiritual problem."

"'I' don't think that... I'm not like that. I don't want to enslave anybody. I know a lot of people who don't want to dominate their neighbor."

"Really now? Why do you think so many people are obsessed with sports, tracing all the way back to the Roman gladiators in the Coliseum, even back into antiquity? What do you think competition on the football field is all about? It is the need to dominate others, the competition. Being quarterback is all about dominating your own team-mates. The sports hero is a god; he wants to dominate the audience, the crowds. That's why so many fights break out at sporting events. That's what the pursuit of wealth and power is all about. It's all about dominating others. That's why you love football so much. It's all about dominating others. There is a fine line, often invisible, between winning at sports and victory on the battlefield. It's only a difference of degrees."

Davy laughed nervously.

"You may not feel comfortable acknowledging that revelation, but, if you peel your good guy image all the way to the bone, you will find the desire to dominate others. You have to know that. You have buried inside of you a darker side. We have to control that emotion, of course, to channel it in a way that is productive. The thing is you are incredibly competitive. That's what I like about you."

Davy sensed that to express a strongly felt dissenting opinion risked compromising his position; he squelched the thought. *What other surprises can he possibly have?*

10
THE PROBLEM WITH POLITICIANS

Emerald continued, "Actually, I am wealthier and more powerful than you imagine, more than anyone imagines. The secret to great wealth and power is a campaign of stealth; never let people know how much power you have. You should know I am the wealthiest, the most powerful man in the world today. The world does not know that, fools that they are."

Again, Davy was amazed at what he was hearing. "You are the wealthiest, most powerful man in the world? I've never heard of that before. If you are that powerful and rich, why is it nobody knows?"

"Deception has its merits and deceit is appropriate at times. I have carefully concealed my influence, but believe me, I tell you the truth."

"Can I ask how you became so wealthy, so powerful?"

"Wealth and power go together; they feed each other. There is a story about a boy who went to a wealthy gentleman and asked how to become wealthy. The man led him to a lake and they waded in until it was to the boy's chest. The man then grabbed the boy and held his head under water. The boy thrashed desperately trying to get his head above water so he could breathe. Just as he thought he was ready to drown, the man lifted his head up. The boy asked, gasping for breath, why he did that. The wealthy man then told him when he wanted wealth as much as he wanted to breathe, he would become wealthy."

"The way you tell it, with such... such intensity, it sounds like a true story."

"I was that boy. I learned the lesson quite well. I call it my grand obsession."

Davy replied, "I don't know if I could ever want extravagant wealth as badly as you apparently wanted it, what you call the grand obsession."

"It doesn't really matter. I needed the grand obsession because I'm the one who created the wealth, who put it all together, from nothing. All you have to do is become an administrator of the Silverstone Empire. The grand obsession is only necessary for the accumulation of wealth, or in some cases, the takeover of wealth."

"Do you really own all that, such great wealth? It is incredible one person could have such power and wealth and no one knows."

"I own massive wealth, more than anyone suspects. However, it doesn't matter who owns it; what matters is who controls it. I control most of the wealth in the world, one way or another; taxes, regulations, permits, zoning, public opinion, intimidation, et cetera, et cetera. Control is the path to great wealth and power."

"I see." Davy's eyes were fixed on Emerald. He wasn't sure how much more he wanted to hear at this time. He felt he was nearing information overload.

"Just remember, Davy, if the world thinks you are powerful, than you are not, not really. Real power comes from operating below the radar, always, at least until such time as you have reached the pinnacle of wealth and power. Deception is no longer necessary after you have achieved the fullness of power. We have an obligation to be powerful for the salvation of the world. There have always been men like Hitler, Stalin, Hussein, evil men who want to rule the world. I am troubled by the thought that mankind is capable of destroying itself, the whole world, and it will eventually do so."

"That is pretty sobering."

"During World War Two man achieved that dubious ability for the first time, at Hiroshima and then at Nagasaki. They unleashed a terrible power of annihilation, an uncontrollable genie that can never be put back in a bottle. Since that time, the nations have accumulated enough nuclear weapons to destroy the world many times over. And that is speaking only of nuclear weapons. There are also biological and chemical weapons which have the potential to be much worse."

Emerald again leaned back in his chair and swept his hand sideways, palm down against the desk.

"There are even more diabolical weapons now on the drawing boards; death rays and anti-matter bombs. There are radio waves that can interrupt the flow of electrons in the cells of your body. They have gasses that will turn your skin to liquids in a matter of minutes. You don't live very long without skin, yes, very painful indeed. There are other gasses that turn your eyes into black tar and then follow your optic nerves to your brain. They will be emerging soon enough. These are weapons of such horror that all before will pale by comparison. The public has no idea of the terrible weapons soon to come. The masses will be helpless before the ruling class."

"That is truly scary. I'm not sure I want to know that kind of information."

"It is the nature of man to have an obsession with war; they lust for the glory of victory on the battlefield. They will gladly die to fulfill that lust, and they are certainly willing to kill for it. And what is war but murder and thievery on a large scale. Let one lone individual murder, steal, and rape and they are reviled, imprisoned by society. But the generals and kings that kill, rape, and steal the most are regarded as our greatest heroes. Humanity idolizes them as gods. In reality, they are vile and despicable men. They are a cancer on humanity. They must be eliminated."

"That would be an impossible task."

"It wasn't so bad as long as sane men, evil perhaps but sane, ruled the nations. We were kept safe by MAD, or mutually assured destruction. But now, those weapons are so abundant that the crazies are able to access them. Hitler was crazy. He carried the blood of Nimrod, which explains why the Axis powers supported him, but he was crazy. He would have destroyed the world in a heartbeat if he had the capacity at the time of his death. He would have destroyed all life and perhaps the earth itself. Thank God he was defeated. There will always be crazies who operate outside of the system. You have radical Muslims, crazy suicide bombers running around today wanting to destroy everything. It's only a matter of time. I figure we have less than two years to save our country, maybe five years if we are going to save the world. Time is of the essence."

Davy listened without responding, a bridle on his tongue. What young man would dare to interrupt the elucidation of one so great, not that Emerald gave him an opportunity to break in even if he had desired.

"America was a grand experiment, but the grand experiment is dead. We have become the most corrupt government on the face of the earth. The American voter has sold his soul for a mess of pottage. No big surprises there. The average voter is illiterate and has no moral values. When ex-convicts, imbeciles, acid heads, perverts, criminals, and immigrants who are hostile to our values make up fifty one percent of our electorate, all hell will break loose. It's over. There is no way back. The swing voters are prostitutes, selling their votes to the highest bidder, selling their souls into slavery. The politicians are prostitutes selling their souls to the prostitutes who vote. It's insanity. The American dream is dead. It just hasn't collapsed yet. Democracy is subject to manipulation by the criminal element and their corrupt political cohorts. Democracy at its best, is total participation with everyone sharing in opportunities. At its worse, democracy is exploitation by mob rule, violent and without mercy.

Davy placed his hand thoughtfully on his mouth. "You don't approve of democracy?"

"One of the problems with democracy is if the people are evil, the government shall be evil. If the voters are ignorant, the government will implode. Sixty percent of the voting public is dumber than hell. When the number of voters on the government dole outnumbers the voters who are the producers of society, the country will go to hell; the system will collapse in a night. The ignorant voters control the board room of American Government. Can you imagine any business being prosperous that had such idiots sitting on the corporate board choosing the C.E.O.? They would run those corporations into the ground. Democracy as America has known it, as we have valued it, no longer exists. It has become a system of extortion by respectable political thugs."

Davy shook his head agreeably having no idea what he should contribute to the conversation.

"Remember that the pirates of the seventeenth century operated as democracies, and they were quite evil. In Russia, democracy is the possession of the Russian Mafia, ex KGB agents. When one side owns all the guns, democracy is a farce. It was a democracy that demanded the crucifixion of the Christ. Democracy at its worst is mob rule. That is what we are seeing more and more, right here in our very country. Think of it, drug addicts, criminals, imbeciles have the same voting power as you and I. The dumb bastards couldn't run a lemonade stand in the heat of summer, let alone a country. It's insanity."

Davy nodded, if only to indicate that he was following the conversation.

"They will have to be eliminated."

"What?" Davy was startled. "Who will?

"Why, the drug addicts, the criminals, those who are a drain on society; all those with radical ideas that destroy society. They are a cancer that must be cut out before they destroy us all."

"But, what about morality?"

"Morality," stated Emerald with force. "It's all about morality. If you will bother to look at the Book of Exodus you will see that God commanded Joshua to liquidate all the tribes of Canaan, including women and children. Yes, God understood the necessity of eliminating all of the cancer."

"But, what about ... I don't think... It's just that I... the Supreme Court would never allow it."

There was a moment of silence as Emerald waited for Davy to continue. Finally, he continued himself. "Beside all that, the Supreme Court will have to be shut down."

"The Supreme Court? How could you do that? Wouldn't that be unconstitutional?"

Emerald laughed with disdain. "The Supreme Court is a joke. The whole purpose of The Court is to protect the integrity of the Constitution itself. Over the years they have eroded the power of the Constitution until it is no longer inviolable. The idiots have destroyed their only source of authority, which is the Constitution. When I come to power, I will tear off their black robes and kick their naked butts out on the streets."

"But, won't they rule that unconstitutional?"

"It won't make any difference. They will no longer be judges. Besides, they have no ability to enforce their ruling, no guns, no police force, and no army."

Before Davy could respond, Emerald abruptly changed the subject, as though he was in mid thought.

"People claim to believe in the theory of evolution, which is a religion as well as political theory that is as old as Babylon. The dumb bastards believe in the survival of the fittest, and then they try to save from extinction some insignificant garter snail that no one cares about. The welfare state is totally contrary to the theory of evolution. Society progresses with the survival of the strongest. The weak are parasites that drag society backwards. The weak should not be fed, they should be eliminated. The Spartans and the Romans knew that. That is sad, of course, but necessary for our higher good. That is the way humanity is constantly reaching new heights. As cruel as it might seem now, evolution will eventually lead to a utopian society. That is our great hope. But, if we continue the welfare state, we will revert to the dark ages for everyone. That is even crueler. We will experience a great plague, greater than any known by Medieval Europe. The flower of humanity will die."

Davy was not comfortable with all he was hearing. He wasn't sure he had the stomach his new position required, but you don't just walk away from the position as heir to world ruler-ship.

"Another of the serious problems with a Democracy is its ineptness. Major problems can never be handled effectively; everything gets bogged down in politics and corruption. The American Government is incompetent. They can't even solve simple problems. White collar crime is rampant. When people are productive, the economy prospers, always. When schemers, swindlers, and politicians try to get rich by sucking money out of the economy with their crooked schemes, without being productive, the economy always tanks."

"Are you saying that dishonesty and corruption are the causes of financial meltdown that our nation experiences from time to time?"

"Dishonesty and deceit are always behind economic crisis, always. A roaring economy and depressions are manipulated as a way of transferring wealth to financial insiders. You can measure the state of the economy by the level of honesty or dishonesty in the country. The problem is corruption. The wealthy elite of society are corrupt. The politicians are corrupt, and so are the masses that elect them. How else could corrupt politicians get elected? The masses are corrupt and so are Union thugs that lead them. The whole system is corrupt. That is why the country now is trillions of dollars in debt; there has never been more greed. Greed is the fuel that drives most people to succeed."

Davy nodded his head, glad for a chance to show agreement.

"People like Madoff, the Keating Five, ad nausea, are worse than people like Jack the Ripper, Bundy or Manson. They have destroyed the lives of millions and have destroyed our country financially. They have delivered a mortal wound to our nation. Politicians make a big deal about cleaning corruption up, but it is all a show. Scum always rises back to the top. Governments are always run by the criminal element."

Davy again nodded, his way of staying engaged in the conversation without committing himself.

"When you count up all the debts the country owes, including future commitments for pensions, Medicaid and Medicare, every man, woman, child and newly born babe, every elderly nursing home resident, everyone in the country owes about two hundred and fifty thousand dollars each. That is more than all our national resources put together. There is no way that can ever be paid off. When our government collapses, soon now, we will experience economic Armageddon. That is what evil men have done to our country."

The thing that scared Davy was all he was hearing made sense.

"When I am ready to exert control, I will solve these problems easily. Evil men will have their expedited day in court and such as are guilty will receive a bullet in the back of the head the next day. We will stop such nonsense. People prosper under a great leader and they will keep their hard earned money. They will rejoice and be grateful. People hunger for a worthy leader. Effective leaders are treated like gods, rightly so."

The phone buzzed so their conversation was placed on hold as he picked up the receiver. He exchanged brief greetings and then listened a bit before saying, "This sounds pretty serious. Give me a brief summary and your recommendation."

After listening some more, he said, "Excellent analysis. This is not exactly what we were hoping for, but neither was it totally unexpected. Implement plan Mother Goose as we discussed last week. The Generals should have the details worked out by now."

Emerald listened some more and said, "Right. Don't let the bastards escape. Have three back up squadrons ready to go in case they are needed, but don't reveal their presence unless absolutely necessary. Also, have some nuclear warheads ready, just in case, but absolutely do not use them except as a last resort. The bit about the nuclear weapons is to be classified as top secret, of course, on a need-to-know bases only. If the press inquires, you are to absolutely deny it."

He listened some more and said, "Right, good. You have my full confidence. Keep me informed."

Hanging up the phone, he sat in deep thought for a full minute before returning to Davy.

"Threat of hostilities in Bangladesh," he explained. "The bad guys are being stirred up by outside interests. You'll read about it in tomorrow's papers, or at least part of it, what we want them to know. It won't be a big story if we manage it properly. Of course, my name won't be mentioned. We will win this skirmish. One of my rules of life is never fight a battle you know you are going to lose, unless it is a strategic loss. The outcome of most battles is determined before they are ever engaged. Losing destroys troop morale. War is a game of the mind with fear being the determining factor. He who loses the most battles loses the war, so never fight a battle unless you know you are going to win."

Emerald smiled as if pleased with himself. "In my world there is always something going on, some crisis that needs my immediate attention. Sometimes I feel like I'm standing on the seat of a unicycle on a high-wire over an active volcano juggling a live hand grenade, a poison-tipped knife, a bowling ball, and a wild-eyed alley cat with turpentine smeared on its ass, all at the same time. It keeps me on my toes. Actually, it's kind of exhilarating. God, I love it." He slapped his hand, palm down, on the desk for emphasis.

Emerald paused. "Where was I? Oh, yes, the state of our country. The greatness of America is behind her. She is no longer able to hold her financial head above water. She is a house of cards waiting to collapse. The grand experiment is dead. The voters shall receive what they deserve. It will be my responsibility to rule over her demise.

"If I fail, evil men will lead Americans away with a hook in their jaw, treated the same way we treated the Indians in the Trail of Tears and the Trail of Death. American sons will be sold into the most evil form of slavery and their daughters will be sold into prostitution, to a population that hates us. We will be treated the way the Nazis treated the Jews, the way blacks were treated in the Deep South before the Civil War, and even after so called emancipation for many years, the Klan and all that. It will be Dachau, Buchenwald, and Auschwitz all over again, except we will be the victims. In other words, it will be a policy of destruction and extermination. Who can say which is worse, slavery or forced prostitution? In either case, it would be better to be dead. Only I stand between our people and the great evil that shall come from the East."

By now Davy was so stunned he no longer even nodded.

"The big question, then, is who shall rule? Will it be politicians, the military, religion, or big finance? These four always rule together, but one usually dominates the others. Let us hope it is not the politicians. Decent people will not have a chance before this soon coming unholy alliance if they are led by politicians. Government leaders are damned blood-sucking parasites whose sole purpose in life is the accumulation of power, at least most of them are. They are the most deceitful of the four. I know this from firsthand experience. The only way they can accumulate power is by taking it from others.

"The definition of a successful politician is one who has stolen the most money and has enslaved the most people. Democratically elected tyrants are no different than any other vile tyrant of history. Their unctuous rhetoric of serving the public's welfare and having their best interest at heart is always intellectual dishonesty, or worse, outright deceit. Never forget that, ever. Politicians are the ultimate con artists. Whenever politicians talk, they lie. When they open their mouths, they lie. When they even think about talking, they lie. When they are sleeping, they are dreaming about lying. If you hear a politician say he has the public interest at heart and he is concerned about you as a person, you should immediately grab your billfold with one hand and cover your rectum with the other; they will both be under assault. I would call that a double indignity."

Davy smirked nervously at Emerald's analogy.

"The salvation of the world rests with men like you and me, men who are willing to dedicate their lives for the protection of the world. The irony is that we have to subjugate the world, to rule the world with an iron fist in order to save it." Emerald clinched his fist for emphasis.

"People don't have enough sense to save themselves. They always, in their ignorance and stupidity, turn the reins of power over to evil men like Hitler, or to the Communists. We must save them from that. A great responsibility rests upon my shoulders, upon our shoulders. So, you see why I need an heir to take over, someone I can trust to get the job done right, someone who has the guts to get it done but will not become a part of the evil when they rise to wealth and power."

"I was always under the impression that democracy and political parties were good, that freedom depended on having a two party system," said Davy. "Isn't the competition between parties what keeps everyone honest, without one party ever gaining a monopoly on power? The two party political system is what gives us freedom. Isn't that the American way?"

Emerald laughed as though he had heard that statement many times before. "Welcome to the inner circle. The thing about political parties, each political party wants absolute control; they seek total power, the same as any tyrant. They would like to destroy all opposition, including the other party. You can't pay any attention to what they say."

Emerald stood grinning at Davy, allowing him to grasp what he was hearing. He continued, "What you say is understandable. But, the thing is, what you believe is what you have been taught at school and by The System. You are the product of The System. And who controls the schools and The System? Those who have the power to manipulate The System are people you don't even know about. People like me. I helped shape your parents' values, which was the right thing at the time. It is likely you will eventually accept my values as your own. Who knows, we shall see."

Davy stared blankly, no longer sure he was capable of understanding what is right and good.

"The thing you need to remember is that our political, financial, and labor leaders are all corrupt. The way I see it, liberals are crazy; they have no brains, just a bunch of lemmings following some demagogue off a cliff. Conservatives are led by greedy bastards, and besides, conservatives are stupid; they don't know how to manipulate the masses."

Once more they were interrupted by the phone and Emerald picked up the receiver. After some small talk he said, "Maybe the best thing to do is to form a new government. Dissolve the Parliament and see if you can forge a new coalition. That young politician that everyone is so impressed with, what's his name, Ahijiah, that's it, let's makes him Prime Minister and make sure it appears to be the will of the people. His selection should please just about everyone, and I think he's someone we can work with. At least he will if he's as smart as we think he is. Do it and keep me informed. Thanks. Bye."

Emerald laughed again and said, "That's the problem with talking to me, lots of interruptions. I do confess that I live a rather intense lifestyle. Now, back to our conversation. Unfortunately, evil men always gain control. In reality, dictators who rise to power by exploiting the masses are the greater evil. The way it ends up is that evil men exploit the good people, those with high ideals in both parties. The masses are such fools. In any event, the nation will become ever more polarized, the anger more accelerated until violence terrorizes the country."

Davy was fumbling with the change in his pants pocket.

"Our political parties will engage in ever increasingly acrimonious accusations about each other. Our country will break out in armed revolt. Bullets will replace ballots. Demonstrators will take to the streets in protests, and stirred by agitators, our country will become dominated by mob rule. Blood will run in the streets. There will be a civil war even more vicious than the one under Lincoln. Not a civil war with two factions; no, it will be a multicultural war. Modern weapons will make Lincoln's war seem like a powder-puff by comparison. So, beware of any politician who manipulates the masses through their emotions."

"A civil war more destructive than Lincoln's? That would be hard to fathom."

"The land will become ruled by war lords like in Afghanistan and outlaw gangs such as Hell's Angels and the Vice Lords, financed by the mafia and the drug cartel, by oil cartels from the East. They will have modern weapons of war, but no restraint. Our armed forces will be controlled by war lords, one military faction fighting against another. And that is before violence explodes from militant Muslims. They will raise the concept of evil to a whole new meaning. Families will live in fear in their own homes, never knowing when some group will come in and butcher the entire family or even the entire community. They will have no way to defend themselves, because of unconstitutional gun laws."

He increased his volume of voice. "I'm talking about the arrival of Armageddon. There will be no place to hide. This is quite common in other countries. America has not yet experienced such a thing, but it shall. The Persians and the Babylonians vied for world power at one time. They will do so again, perhaps in an end of the world scenario. They are the modern nations of Iran and Iraq. It is up to us, Davy, to save our country from all this. The coming nuclear conflagration, trust me it will come, will not be won by those with the most nukes. It will be won by those most able to hack into the military computer network of those who have the most nukes. Imagine our country caught with their nuclear dobber down. We would be unable to detonate, to deliver, or even get them off the ground."

"That would be bad all right."

"Nuclear Weapons and sophisticated war machinery are our only defense against the hoards of the Far East. If they are disabled, eastern combatants would swarm our military outposts around the world like army ants, the way they would bring down a dog or a bear. They will come, millions upon millions, flooding our country, decimating everything in their path. They will stack decapitated heads like so much cord-wood in giant mounds by our city gates. The way I have it figured, using the doomsday clock developed by our great scientific minds, we have almost thirty seconds to Armageddon. I am the only one who can prevent that from happening."

Davy was stunned. Thoughtful consideration was no longer even possible. "You believe we have much to fear from Muslims, then. You're talking about militant Muslims, of course, not moderate ones."

"I am also including moderate Muslims. I have seen with my own eyes this great evil."

Emerald rose from his desk, walked to the window and stared out. "My cousin Maximilian was one, a radical Muslim leading a large evil band of men. They slaughtered my entire family, including women, children and servants, all the advisers. They killed my mother and father, two brothers and seven sisters. They even killed the pets and the livestock, so great is the evil they harbor."

Davy could see the veins tighten in Emerald's neck. Emerald was silent for some time before he returned to his chair having regained his composure, man of steel.

Emerald continued. "I can honestly say that Muslims are the only people I hate, really hate. My hatred for them is one of the powerful emotions that drives me. I will not rest until every single Muslin is dead. The entire population of Muslims must be exterminated, wiped off the face of the earth."

"But there is a big difference between moderate Muslims and the radical militants, the crazies as you call them. I had some good friends, classmates, who were Muslims. They were very nice, good people. I understand how you would feel about those who did that horrible thing to your family. But, don't you think there is a difference between the moderate and the radical militant Muslims?"

Emerald glared at Davy. "Absolutely not! Islam is a religion of hate."

"Your anger seems great. However, didn't Muslims endue such evil at the hands of Christians during the Crusades? Shouldn't the Islam religion be brought into your vision of bringing all religions together?"

"If that were possible, yes. But it is the nature of Islam to either rule or die. Either they will kill all of us or we will kill all of them. There can be no compromise. It is by their own choice they must be exterminated. As I say, you may believe as you will, but eventually you will come to understand I am right. I am confident of that."

Davy was experiencing an increase in anxiety, too much information. He was learning more than he wanted to hear, more than he was capable of receiving. He desired to retreat to the seclusion and safety of his apartment.

Emerald looked thoughtfully at Davy. "Moderate Muslims? A good Muslim, you say, much more kind and committed to living in peace with those of us who are infidels, enemies to Allah? You think they are moved by the goodness of the Koran and that American Muslims are loyal to our country? Let me tell you, they are America's Trojan Horse. When the time is right, the militant Muslims, along with the moderate ones, shall rise up as one to impose their vengeance on us. The purpose of the moderate Muslim is one of great deception, to lull us into a state of weakness. There is no real difference between the two. When the time comes, as it soon will, the moderate Muslim will cut out your guts as quickly as the militant radicals. In reality, one is as evil as the other. They must all be exterminated."

Davy was hesitant, but put his thoughts to words.

"I'm not sure I could ever fully agree with that. I believe there are good people in all races, in all religions."

Emerald grinned and said, "You don't agree. That is all right, perfectly acceptable. You don't have to believe something just because I believe it. You must draw your own conclusions. Eventually, I will send you on assignments into Muslim counties. There you will see for yourself how they treat women, children and infidels, meaning you and me, of course. Infidels," he repeated, "they have some interesting plans for you and me, Infidels. What if your family had been killed by Muslims, not just your immediate family, but all your cousins, your entire family wiped off the face of the earth. I have full confidence you will eventually accept reality. But draw your own conclusions and do so in your own sweet time."

Davy struggled to take in everything he was hearing. Emerald was suggesting that an entire culture should be exterminated. It almost seemed as if Emerald was saying the American way was not sufficient enough, that somehow it must be replaced, which was contrary to everything he had ever believed, and yet, what Emerald was saying made so much sense. Davy was uncomfortable with some that Emerald expounded, but who was he to question such a great mind? His mind was full of questions and doubts; if only he had the foggiest idea what he should ask. Certainly, he was ecstatic at the thought of becoming the wealthiest, most powerful man in the world after Emerald was gone, of course. Who is there among us so sluggish of soul who would not be so moved? He fully appreciated the idea of all people of the world looking up to him they way he did his sports and Hollywood idols. But, most of all, he thought of how impressed Sarah and Travis would be.

And yet, he didn't know if he could work as Emerald did, sixteen hour days, seven days a week for months, for years on end, or if he wanted the fate of nations on his shoulders; who would want such a responsibility? He clearly did not share the same obsession as Emerald. What kind of life would he have? What kind of marriage relationship would he have? He thought of Sarah. At least he knew he would be worthy to be married to someone like Sarah, if she didn't marry someone else before all this took place. And if they did marry, what would this do to their marital relationship? No, he could never do this to her. But Davy could not linger with a single thought. He had to hustle to keep up with the rapid fire of Emerald's intense revelations. But Emerald's tone suddenly changed. He was clearly going in another direction now.

11

THE LEGACY OF NIMROD

Emerald paused for a considerable time and his words came more slowly now, spoken more meaningful for emphasis. "I tell you, Davy, I am a very religious man, certainly in my later years, though not as the world views religion. No, I have much more insight. I have studied the influence of religion on the history of mankind. It has been great; sometimes for good, and sometimes for evil. There was a time when all of the great religions of the world were one, but that all changed after the Great Flood. Actually, the seeds of division began even before the flood. But then there was a great division into two branches, one branch from Noah's son Shem, passed down through Abraham, and then divided even further between Isaac and Ishmael, and again between Jacob and Esau."

"Yes, I know some of this, but I never thought of it like that before."

"Today you have all the nations of the Far East, the Turks, the Arabians, Israelites, Jews, Muslims, Shiites, Sunnis, plus all the myriad Christian denominations all fighting like squabbling children, which they are, all descendents of Shem. There is no worse kind of fighting than the infighting that takes place within families, particularly when done in the name of religion. Tyrants use religion to control people. These modern nations still carry on those ancient feuds, but they are all of one great branch, divided then into many branches."

"I have never even considered such."

"The other great branch, the greater branch, covert in nature, came down through Noah's son Ham, to his son Cush, to his son Nimrod, who was the greatest and most powerful man who ever lived and left a legacy that greatly influences us still today. No man ever had a more profound impact on our present day world. He built the first great civilization. Then he developed a universal religion that was considered as pagan, and apostate by the early descendents of Abraham. This became known as Babylon the Mystery Religion, so powerful it engulfed the world."

"I think most people have heard of the Babylonian Mystery Religion, but I've never really thought much about it."

"The ancient religions and governments of the world; Sumerian, Egyptian, Persian, Roman, Greek, Chinese, India, Africa, Viking, Aztec, Incas, Mayan, Druids, even the Illuminati; all the great mystical religions of the world that worshiped the sun god and moon god, adherents to astrology, descended, then, from the Great Babylonian Mystery Religion. The Mystery Religion of Nimrod also subdivided into many of the great religions of the world. He created civilization as we know it, from the Great Flood until the birth of the Messiah, with the only exception being the Hebrew Children. Like I said, no man has had a greater influence on civilization down to our very day. If you understand that, then a lot of mysteries begin to make sense. Even Christianity has come under his influence."

"You don't hear much about that, do you?"

"No, no, you do not, and that is no coincidence."

"Okay, now, that is interesting." Interesting was a word that allowed Davy to appear engaged while being noncommittal.

"Nimrod became the great god of this world, along with his wife Semiramis, or Ishtar, Isis, Aphrodite, Venus, Diana, or one of her many other names in the religions around the world. He accomplished this through a massive propaganda campaign, using considerable deception, I might add. Their widespread system of temple worship utilized sex orgies in their ceremonies with the priestesses ministering to the needs of the men. These women were treated the same way Hollywood sex gods are today. Sex was the very core of their worship."

"The sex urge can be pretty darned powerful."

"Powerful indeed. Sex is a contributing factor to ninety percent of the evil in the world. The resulting undesired abundance of babies was handled by sacrificing them to their gods and entombing their bones in clay jars in the temple walls. Older children were made to pass through the fire in sacrificial ceremonies. That was a common practice. In other words, they were thrown into blazing furnaces, a rather gruesome and traumatizing experience for a young child I would say. Child sacrifice was done to please the gods and to extract their blessings upon the nations in abundance of crops and for victory on the battlefield."

Davy was horrified at the thought of a child enduring such brutality.

His attention was momentarily diverted by a hummingbird at a feeder outside the window.

"The high priests were magicians, witch doctors and shamans from around the world. That is why it is called the Babylonian Mystery Religion. They had exclusive mystical knowledge, the dark arts. The magicians you see on television today, their tradition traces back to Nimrod, the magicians of Egypt, the Druids, and the Incas. They are the enlightened ones, knowing the mysteries of the universe, the Illuminati. The uninitiated depend upon the keepers of secret knowledge to survive in a hostile world. They are the gatekeepers into the spiritual world. This gives them great power."

"Magicians are part of the Babylonian Mystery Religion? I always thought magicians were just entertainment. We just understood it is all about clever tricks being performed."

"Clever tricks, yes, the modern magician. But the whole implication is they have secret knowledge and magical powers, dark spiritual power. Isn't that the image of the magician, right out of the Mystery religion?"

"Well, I guess I will view magicians with a whole new perspective now."

"There is so much you don't know, don't have a clue. Ignorance is cured by knowledge. You have much to learn. Baal, Moloch, Wooden, Murdoch, Quetzalcoatl, Krishna, Osiris, Horace, Apollo, Thor, Zeus, Zoroaster, Achilles, Buddha; these were some of the many names that referred to Nimrod and his decedents. The Oracles of Delphi, the gods of mythology all refer back to them, Nimrod and Ishtar, even their descendents, one way or another."

"The things you tell me, I've had no idea."

Emerald smiled as if to say I know. "There is so much more. The Seven Wonders of the Ancient World all refer to Nimrod one way or another."

"The Seven Wonders of the Ancient World, all of them?"

"All of them, the Seven Wonders described by Antipatros, the Greek historian in the second century, the Great Pyramids of Egypt, the Hanging Gardens of Babylon, the Statue of Zeus, The Temple of Artemis, the Tomb of King Mausolus, the Colossos of Helios, and the Pharos Lighthouse built by Alexander the Great. The pyramids and ziggurats built around the world came from Nimrod and his mystery religion. The Tower of Babel was a prototype. It was a temple to the gods of astrology. It was also, a place to wage war of rebellion against Jehovah and his host in heaven. He was the first to proclaim that God is dead."

Once more, the phone buzzed. "See, I'm doing good to get twenty minutes of conversation in between phone calls; somebody always wants something."

He lifted the receiver. "Hello. Oh, hi Jerome, good to hear from you. What's going on?... No kidding? It sounds like we have a problem, a very serious problem.. You do, huh?... Okay, we need to eliminate the problem, quickly, efficiently, no mess... Good, I knew I could count on you. That's what I like about you. I can always count on you... Right. Thanks my friend."

Hanging up the phone, he continued, "All the great kings of the earth and all those who control the great wealth descend then from Nimrod with direct linkage, all of them down to our time. They were never citizens of the countries they ruled, no, they were all foreign invaders, enslaving the native populations. It's bred into their genes and is passed down to our day. You can always tell descendents of Nimrod because they have an insatiable obsession to dominate others. Some became bankers and industrial tycoons. Some became coaches. Have you ever known sports coaches with dominate personalities who felt like they had to win every time? Surely, some come to mind. Some became Union thugs. Others became military generals, some of the world's greatest generals-some of America's best generals."

Emerald laughed. "Hell, some became great religious leaders. All the great kings were related, descended from the same system, the same family, the Babylonian Mystery Religion. They always married within the system. Never dilute the sacred blood line by letting those who are unworthy infiltrate. It would have been blasphemy to marry a common person, one not descended from the gods. The kings were all descended from divinity, don't you see? That is why the kings of ancient Egyptians, Romans, and other old civilizations insisted on being worshiped as gods."

"If you have to be descended from Nimrod in order to rule, then how could I ever inherit your position? I am not descended from royalty."

"Oh, but you are. The blood of Nimrod flows through your veins on both your maternal and paternal lines. You carry the blood of kings, all the great kings of history."

Davy was stunned. "What makes you think such a thing? How could you know that?"

"I told you, I know more about you than you do yourself. I have researched this all very carefully. You carry the bloodline of Nimrod. You may not understand fully, may not appreciate the significance of Nimrod. No one understands the spirit of Nimrod today better than Hollywood. Hollywood today is a poor imitation though, nothing more than a gold plated cesspool, a poor imitation of the original indeed. But, you will understand with time."

Davy was confused. "But I thought you courted the stars of Hollywood. That's what Travis told me."

"Yes, indeed. Every tool is fit to be utilized by the master craftsman. I use every resource to the greatest advantage for our purpose. They deserve to be used. The irony is that all the great religions of the world, both branches, have borrowed so heavily from each other that it is sometimes difficult to tell them apart. Even Christianity has been heavily influenced by Nimrod. Still, the different religions continue to fight for the dominion, to force their own views on the others. Satan and God were together at one time, though even now they continue to war with each other."

"That I understand."

"There are two world perspectives; one is that Jehovah is God, that he created all things, including humanity. Therefore, he is worthy of our worship. The other view, the humanistic view which traces all the way back to Nimrod, holds that all things came into being as the result of natural selection. In other words, the survival of the fittest. It is the natural order of things. Therefore, the strong have, not only the opportunity to dominate the weaker, but an obligation to do so. It is part of the process of the survival of the fittest that moves society, moves humanity to ever higher levels of achievement. The goal is to someday achieve a utopian world."

"So, what do you believe, I mean which perspective?"

"I'm thinking, wouldn't it be great to combine the two perspectives, to experience the best of both worlds, God as God, and man as God, both being the same person. If I can bring these two world positions together, God and humanism, then I will be the greatest God ever."

"That seems a bit of a contradiction, an impossible achievement."

"For others, perhaps, but if I accomplish that, I would deserve to be God. Besides, there is a greater challenge, the ever-present specter of death. If I can overcome the obstacle of death, then I will indeed be God. It's a tremendous challenge, to be sure, but I'm thinking with the mystical power of ancient relics, perhaps, yes, indeed perhaps, but that has yet to play out. We shall see, we shall see. The point is, if I achieve immortality, then so will you. You wouldn't be able to become the leader of the world then, but you would sit at the right hand of God, and more important, you will have immortality."

"Mystic powers?" Ancient relics? Immortality? That seems rather incomprehensible."

"Yes, that's what makes life so interesting, the monumental

challenges when the stakes are so high, when failure is potentially devastating and the outcome is in doubt; that is exhilarating indeed."

Emerald was staring directly at Davy, and his words seemed to have spiritual power, the kind that comes from an unknown world. "I am, even now, the third most powerful man the world has ever known. I expect to pass Alexander the Great soon, and I now consider it to be a realistic possibility to someday surpass Nimrod, as incredible as that sounds. I have advantages Nimrod did not have, that is, modern technology which will allow me to accomplish things he could never dream of."

Emerald often smiled softly; it was beginning to annoy Davy.

"I tell you, there is not a president elected, a dictator selected, a war engaged, or a peace negotiated unless I approve, unless I participate in the early planning stage. I have absolute veto power. My power reaches into the halls of every government on earth. I can with little effort if I wish, influence the happenings of the most remote places on earth and the decisions in city halls on a local level. This is all made possible by modern technology, and it is all accomplished with total anonymity for all practical purposes."

Either he is the most brilliant man I have ever heard, or the most delusional, thought Davy. "That sounds impossible. How can one man control so many people?"

"Modern technology. There is more than the public could ever imagine. For instance, every plasma screen television carries a miniature video and audio receiver. We can spy on any home or office that has a flat screen television if we believe we have reason to be suspicious. You wouldn't believe some of the technology we have in play."

"Wow!" Davy whispered softly.

Emerald continued, "For the past three years, we have planted an electronic chip in every cell phone sold in the entire world. We have every cell phone conversation recorded in electronic storage. We can track the location where every cell phone has traveled anywhere in the world. This is all safely stored information. The same with all automobiles produced in the last two years. We can track the vehicle's location on a daily basis. We have recorded every conversation within the cars. Why do you think the government became involved in the production of cars?"

"That sounds like a lot of excess information. How could such massive amounts of information be of any use, particularly when so much of it is idle babble?"

"The value is in the ability to retrieve the information we need. Suppose we wished to destroy someone's reputation. If you can pry into every idle word and action, track their every location, you can destroy just about anyone. Think back over your own life. Are there no moments that would cause you great shame?"

Davy laughed uneasily. "That kind of information could be dangerous, especially in the wrong hands."

"The wrong hands, indeed. That is why we have such extensive security measures in place, so this kind of information never falls into the wrong hands. But, that is only a part of the technology we have available. Anyway, can you imagine the wealth and power one would have if he could bring all these warring children, all these religions together in harmony, no longer wasting vast resources and lives in war but working together to make the world a better place to live? We could eradicate poverty, murder, disease, political corruption, and all the scourges of civilization. Every person, those fit to live, would live in health and luxury, and we would have peace such as the world has never seen, nor even conceived. It will be a utopian government on earth."

"If you can do that?"

"I intend to accomplish that, Davy. Nimrod's spirit will empower me."

"I don't understand how that can happen. How would you receive power from Nimrod's spirit?"

"I have communed with Nimrod, numerous times. He comes to me occasionally in a vision when I enter a Peyote induced trance in a sweat lodge. I will be greater than Nimrod, but only in this world. He is now God of this world, in spirit. I will bring it all together. I am a man obsessed to make it happen, that is, if I live long enough. If not, then that is where you come in. I will leave the unfinished business in your hands. I have confidence in your ability. We will be like Moses and Joshua, like David and Solomon. Like God and Jesus. The work of God is often too much for one man. You may well become the wealthiest, most powerful man in history, perhaps all of this culminating after I am gone."

"That's pretty difficult for me to grasp, really difficult. With all due respect, sir, do you think this is possible? There seems to be more hatred worldwide now than ever before. You're talking about a millennium of peace and prosperity while the religions of the world seem to prophecy Armageddon. Even the scientist community is constantly predicting the end of the world. You spoke of the terrible weapons that will soon be produced and the hatred and anger between nations. How is it possible to heal such animosity?"

"First of all, you must realize they all have something in common - the human carnal nature, greed, and fear. Greed and fear can divide, but they can also bring people together. And then they also have a common history, a common heritage. They have a spiritual relationship if you go back far enough. The divisions have resulted from the vainglory and arrogance of men. But, they all trace back to a common spirit and reality in time. So, they have a spiritual connectedness. All the religions of the world have borrowed so heavily from each other through the years, they are no longer that far apart. It is mostly the selfish ambitions of ruthless and self-serving leaders that contaminate their followers. Only petty jealousies divide them. Envy and greed often cultivated rage, to be sure, but not as insurmountable as one might think."

Davy found he doubted himself, wondering if he understood the difference between reality and insanity, or if it was possible for him to do so anymore.

Emerald studied Davy before continuing, choosing his words carefully. "There is something else I must tell you, a carefully guarded secret. Perhaps this will help you to better understand. In my possession are two special items no man has seen since antiquity, religious artifacts that will enable me to achieve my goals.... the Ark... and the Throne."

"Excuse me, sir; did you just say the Ark and the Throne?"

12
ANCIENT RELICS AND MYSTIC POWERS

"Yes, Davy, the Ark of the Covenant and the Throne of Nimrod. It is impossible to govern the world without spiritual assistance, too much resistance; the people are too stiff-necked. But, I have them both. For the first time since they both vanished in ancient history, they are now together, the greatest spiritual and government symbols, now reunited, the power of the God of Abraham and the spirit of Nimrod, together. The resistance of the world will be subdued and all people of the earth brought together by the Ark and the Throne. They will be harnessed by great spiritual power such as the world has never seen. Massive wealth and power goes to the man who is able to tap into that power. I believe I will be fully able to do so. However, it might come to fruition after I am gone. You are the chosen one who will reap the great benefit, the way Solomon did from David. That man is you, Davy."

"Wow! That is so incredible! I didn't even know there was such a thing, the Throne of Nimrod."

"Of course, such is the ignorance of the world. But power comes with knowledge. I will teach you much."

"You're telling me you have the Ark and the Throne? Not replications, but the actual items? That's hard to believe."

"I'm talking about the actual Ark of the Covenant that came down from Mount Sinai. I'm talking about the same throne upon which Nimrod sat, the same throne discovered by Phillip of Macedonia and upon which Alexander the Great sat. Why do you think there has never been another Alexander the Great since then? I'll tell you why, because the Throne was lost, the seat of world government. They have both been lost to history, until recently, and now, I have them both. It is through the spirit of Nimrod I shall rule."

"You mean that right now, somewhere in this world, you have access to them both, the Ark and the Throne?"

"Not just somewhere, Davy, right here in this very house, in a concealed room below."

"A secret room in the basement? I had no idea. I have never seen anything that gave evidence of a secret room."

"It is very well concealed, such as you would never suspect. There is no possibility you, or anyone else, will ever stumble upon it, even if you searched diligently. But, even if you did, there is only one key, and I have it. There is only one way in and I am the way. There is an entire floor below the basement that is patterned after the Tabernacle. I have built an Altar for each relic, and only two people in the entire world have ever seen them, that being Marti and myself. I am, even now, developing a priest in training, a priest from Iraq to attend to the Ark and the Throne that sit on the altars. I need a priest who can extract maximum power. That's where Babylon was you know, in Iraq. That's where Nimrod had his throne room and ruled the world. That's where his heir, Nebuchadnezzar, ruled, and then Belshazzar. Daniel served in the sacred court and that's where Alexander died. Those are no mere coincidences."

"Where in the world did you find them?"

"The Ark we found at Stonehenge, perhaps where you would least expect to find it; then again, maybe not. Ancient Israelites, the Ten Lost Tribes, traveled to England. The Druids were apostate Israelites who adopted Assyrian religious practices and brought their corrupted worship of Nimrod to England. They hid it, at Stonehenge until some day in the future when it would be retrieved by a great world leader, a messiah who would be worthy to receive it. Not only did we find the Arc there, but also the treasure of Solomon. The Throne of Nimrod we found at the Money Pit in Nova Scotia."

"The Money Pit in Nova Scotia? I have heard of that. People think that pirates buried treasure there, and then booby trapped it with the ocean."

"Not pirates, the Knights Templar. They brought the Throne of Nimrod to Nova Scotia and hid it for safekeeping. They hid it and the great Templar wealth. That's why King Phillip and the Pope had them murdered you know, because they wanted the Templar wealth, that and they feared their power. It was destined for the Throne of Nimrod and the wealth of the Templar to be rediscovered in the end times, by the one prophesied."

"The Knights Templar? Sure, I know who they were. They started with the Crusades and were decimated by King Phillip of France. I read all about that in the *Divinci Code* and other books that came after."

"They existed long before the Crusades. Nothing comes out of nothing. You have to know their prehistory. They were originally the royal select guards for Nimrod. They were sometimes called Genie after certain Babylonian spirits of great power. He entrusted his life to them, kind of like the Swiss Guards for the Pope, only more effective, more ruthless."

"Genie, you mean like in the Arabian Knights?"

"Exactly, one and the same."

"Royal guards to Nimrod? Wow! That's hard to believe, so unreal."

"In a sense their legacy is preserved by the Free Masons, a weak replica. The thing is, they still continue, in stealth and in power. But the real action takes place with the Illuminati and the Rosicrucian. I will teach you all about them in time. You will even meet some, at the right time."

"That's all so hard to believe, the Knights Templar burying the The Throne of Nimrod and The Knight Templar Treasure at the Money Pit. But people have tried to find the treasure of the Money Pit before, big investors, people with lots of money."

"Big investors, indeed, including President Roosevelt and actor John Wayne, people with access to lots of money."

"So why were you able to find the treasure of the Money Pit when others of great wealth were not able to do so?"

"I had a map."

"A map?"

"Yes, a map. One that told what treasure lay at the bottom of the Money Pit, one that revealed the secret to retrieving the treasure. I knew it was the Throne of Nimrod and the Templar's Treasure that lay hidden there. Knowing that whoever possessed the Throne would be able to harness great spiritual powers to rule the world, I was willing to invest much more than anyone before. It was an excellent investment. The treasure was immense. It would have elevated Canada to a world superpower. It would have paid off the United States' debt easily. But now, I have the treasure of the Knight Templar, as well as the wealth of Solomon. I now control the world through my great wealth and political muscle. I will soon rule the world, the entire world, and I will do so openly."

"Where did you get a map of the Money Pit?"

"I found the map at the Newport Round Tower of Rhode Island."

"So, why the Newport Round Tower? Did you have a map that led you to the map?"

"I had developed an interest in both the Money Pit and the Round Tower. I had reason to believe they were related. I developed a hunch; perhaps it was the Spirit of Nimrod whispering to me. I knew that once a year on the winter solstice, a beam of sunlight shone directly on the key stone, the splendid illumination of the egg stone. I thought that was surely significant. So, one night, I had a team of master masons remove the key stone. It was a big deal, removing the stone and replacing it without damaging the building, or leaving tell tale signs the stone had been disturbed. I broke the hollow stone open and replaced it with an exact replica."

Davy scratched his head. This all sounds like some kind of mythological film out of Hollywood, but that's all fantasy. Things don't happen like this in the real world."

"Oh, it's all real. On the inside was a parchment with a map and instructions. It told what was at the bottom of the money pit. No one knows the keystone has been disturbed and changed. There are all these people with all kinds of theories, but no one knows. Someday, perhaps investors will once again attempt to claim the treasure, but they will find nothing. I already have it."

"That is an incredible story. I can't believe Canada and England would allow you to take such valuable treasures. I think that countries like Russia, China, and Iran would try to steal it, so they could rule the world."

Emerald laughed. "They had no choice. They were totally unaware they had been found and removed right under their nose, even though both countries were sponsoring their own archeological excavations. Steal them, hell yes, if they knew they existed. Powerful people in every country on the face of the earth would kill for Nimrod's Throne and the Ark of the Covenant. So, now you understand the importance of stealth."

"But how?" Davy felt like an overheated circuit breaker reaching a point of overload.

"Just like getting your prenatal records, only on a larger scale, of course. You infiltrate their forces, you pay the right people. People are like putty in my hands. The Canadian Prime Minister and the Queen Mother would have both been plenty pissed if they only knew what I took from them."

Davy could only shake his head and exclaim, "Wow!" He could feel the hair standing up on his neck.

"Let's see, where does that lead us now? Oh yes, when I make my move to publicly present myself as the legitimate ruler of the world, I will make Babylon once more the seat of world power. I will rename it the Emerald City. I will rebuild the Tower of Babel. I will rebuild the original Babylonian Hanging Gardens. I will rebuild all of the Seven Wonders of the Ancient World. The City of Emerald will surpass the grandeur and splendor of ancient Rome, Egypt, Alexandria, Constantinople, Babylon and Solomon's Jerusalem. It will surpass Paris, New York, all the modern cities. It will be the greatest sight the world has ever seen. The main street to the palace will be of pure gold. It will be a testimony to my ability as the greatest king of them all. It will be the most spectacular monument ever built to honor a man. Someday, perhaps you will rule the world from that great city."

"You would change the name of Babylon to The Emerald City?"

"Besides, being a grand monument to me, it will be necessary. There would be too much resistance to the revival of the Babylonian Empire, especially at what some will consider as the last days. The Emerald City will be much more palatable to the masses of the world."

"I thought you operated through stealth? How can you build such a monument to yourself if the world doesn't even know you exist?"

"Timing is everything and everything at the right time. When I am ready to fulfill my destiny as the greatest leader the world has ever known, I will no longer need to operate in stealth. I will have absolute control. It will no longer matter who knows. Besides, I have patiently waited for nearly one hundred years to experience my much deserved recognition as a great leader and for saving the world. A hundred years is a long time to wait for glory, don't you think?"

Words defied Davy, but Emerald continued.

"The ancient Jews were taken to Babylon, Daniel being great among them. He served first Nebuchadnezzar, then Belshazzar and later the Persian King Darius, all part of the Babylonian Mystery Religion. Daniel was a priest for both the Jews and also for a select group of Babylonian priests. They formed into a hybrid religious sect, instructed by Daniel concerning the secrets of God. It was their descendents, the Magi that brought treasure, Daniel's treasure, to the Christ Child. This small group has descended down to this very day, only a handful of them exist, and I have secured a descendant of the original priesthood who is even now being trained as priest for both the Ark and the Throne. When he arrives, he will live in the secret rooms serving those sacred relics, conducting holy services before them every day for the rest of his life. He will never again see the outside world, will never again see any people, only Marti and me, and then you. That will be his only purpose in life. His name is Amaladzar."

Davy laughed internally at the thought of a priest whose name rhymed with salad bar. "It's hard to believe someone would agree to do that. Is it of his free will?"

"You don't know these people. He considers it a great honor. These sacred relics have great power. Davy, I have found that by returning every three months before those items, I renew my energy. I draw energy mostly from Nimrod's throne and little from the Ark. Hopefully, Amaladzar can remedy that. The power from the Throne is one of the things that has kept me youthful and filled with energy, that and Antoinette's magic with her herbs and cooking and such. I believe that I will live to the age of one hundred thirty eight, at least according to our present calculations. Perhaps with new revelations and developments, I could live to be one hundred and fifty, or perhaps even two hundred. I might even attain immortality."

Davy found it all so hard to believe.

"But even so, I presently continue to age, ever so slowly, so I know the day will come when I must die if I am not able to discover immortality before that happens. No one knows when that will be, so I must see to it that you are ready. I'm sure we will have adequate time, but I feel the need to move rapidly. You are my hope. You are the hope of the world. Only two people know about the Ark and the Throne within the secret room, and now three, counting you. You must never tell anyone, not a single soul. I trust you, Davy. No one else must ever know. What you do after I am gone is your business. You will have gained great wisdom by then."

"Can I see them?"

"You may, but not until you are ready. You must be prepared."

"But, I don't understand. How did you find them? How did you come about such relics without anyone knowing, and how was a secret room built, and how were they transported, all without anyone else on the face of the earth knowing?"

"Of course others were involved. Something of this magnitude would not happen without others being involved. It was a tightly guarded secret, all of it, enforced by the threat of death. All who were involved, with the exception of Marti and me, all met an untimely death. I call it the enforcement of Providence. The story you ask is a long an interesting one. I shall tell you someday, but for now, let us just say that providence has handled all the details. Perhaps I shall write a book someday, one that will never be read by anyone but you. Only Marti and I are left. We are the chosen ones, and now you, of course. It is imperative that you tell no one lest you suffer the same fate as the others. Do you have any questions, my son?"

"I have a hard time believing the Ark and the Throne are hidden right here in your estate. I've not seen anything that would indicate a hidden room."

"The sacred room is under the altar of rocks in the Dome Room, three stories deep. You will never find the entrance, or any other evidence of the room for that matter. Three huge electrodes connect from the artifacts below to the altar of rocks above transmitting energy into the atmosphere, similar to the Tesla Coil effect, except that his coil projects high voltage electrical energy into the atmosphere and this, this special adaptation of the Tesla Coil creates spiritual energy, which is much more powerful."

"Nikola Tesla, I know who he is. He was a genius with electricity. I read all about him."

"Of course, brilliant indeed. The thing is, to be a great leader, there are times you have to be ruthless. You have to be willing and able to wield power. I know this is a bit much for you, but you will eventually understand and absorb all I am saying. Any other questions?"

Questions? Of course I have questions, thought Davy. *How could I not have questions?* He drew in a deep breath. *I will be a different kind of leader when my time comes, a good and decent one who has the good of the people of the world at heart. I may have to play the game, as Emerald says, until I am in that position, but I will be different. That is my destiny, to be a benevolent world leader. I will be magnanimous to the poor people, the masses. My time will come. I will be different.*

Davy's thoughts returned to Emerald. "I'm just so overwhelmed. I don't have any questions at this time, but I'm sure I will later on, many questions. Right now I feel like a duck wobbling around after being whacked on the head with a stick."

Emerald laughed and said, "Abraham Lincoln, talking about General William Rosecrans after he was humiliated at the Battle of Chickamauga during the Civil War. That is very good, Davy. I like Lincoln. That's what I like about you; you're a well-read and creative intellectual, though you don't exactly flaunt it. You have a way of disarming people, making them underestimate you. So then, let me close by saying this, I can tell you that even though I may not see you for months at a time, you will be in the forefront of my thoughts daily, I will be much aware and fully involved in your daily life and all decisions that affect you. I am your God as well as your new father. Now, I must get back to business, I have much work to do."

He warmly shook Davy's hand and said, "I am so glad to have you in the family, my son." He suddenly stopped talking, and as abruptly as he had interrupted his work to greet Davy, he now as abruptly returned to his chair at the desk, took pen in hand, and began making notes on his paperwork, seemingly oblivious to Davy's presence.

Davy felt a little awkward, but said, "Thank you Emerald, sir, thank you very much."

Emerald seemed not to notice, so Davy slowly backed out of Emerald's office and then headed down the spiral stairs in a state of wonderment of all that had just taken place. He had the sensation he had just returned from Alice's Wonderland or Dorothy's Oz, perhaps even from some wonderful realistic weird dream.

Davy wondered why he had been chosen as heir. Why not Travis? He had so much going for him. But for all his qualifications, Travis was a technocrat, a highly skilled geek. *I am a mover and a shaker. I am Choleric, a Sensation Type. I am dominant. I am imaginative like Napoleon. I motivate people. I make the trains run on time. I believe Emerald has chosen wisely.* The first person he met downstairs was Travis.

Davy was startled from his trance as he met Travis in the great cathedral room in close proximity to the altar of rocks where he sensed spiritual vibrations.

Travis studied Davy for a moment, a grin on his face. "So, you've had your visit with Emerald?"

"Yes, I just came from there."

"You were up there over two hours. That's impressive. Is he awesome or what?"

Davy laughed. "Oh, he's awesome, all right. He's unbelievable."

"The thing is," said Travis, "no matter what he's talking about, he always blows you away. The next time, he will be talking about something altogether different, and it will still blow you away. You get the feeling he only shares with you a little bit of what he knows, only what he wants you to know." Travis clasped him on the shoulder and grinned reassuringly.

Davy quickly excused himself and retreated to the sanctum of his apartment where he continued to ponder the unusual happenings in his life and to wrestle with the great internal struggle going on inside his mind. Before leaving the Great Dome Room, he paused at a large bookcase, perhaps drawn by spiritual powers. There he discovered an interesting book of relatively small size, black, old and worn. He took it with him, and once safe in the comfort of his room began to read *The Mythology of Nimrod and his Babylonian Mystery Religion: Fact or Fiction?* by Malcolm Bernard Hostelmiester, PhD. The introduction read:

Having now received news of my imminent demise from terminal cancer, which I had thought was benign, I must hurriedly put together this information I have researched from the Book of Jasher,* son of

Caleb, plus classic mythologies and various other scattered ancient historical sources from around the world. After considerable study, I am forced to prematurely share my knowledge and understanding with the present political and intellectual world. The name Nimrod means the rebellious one after his spiritual father. It is said that Nimrod also means the great illumination.

This book is short and powerful, and the information is vitally important as it relates to the role Nimrod's Spirit will play in the return of the Babylonian Mystery Religion as it affects future attempts by tyrants to rule the world, and what some consider as the end of the world apocalypse.

I have written factual information in story form to help the reader better grasp that incredible story. I originally anticipated a large book but by necessity will attempt to write five chapters, the last being of vital importance as it will provide the vital knowledge for salvation of the world from that great evil. I fear the demonic forces of hell shall be loosed to prevail upon the earth. I pray to God that I may finish that last chapter, the hope of civilization. I have made arrangements for whatever I write to be published regardless of how much I accomplish. I can only hope to complete the entire work so the world might be saved from ravages of the Spirit of Nimrod and his Babylonian Mystery Religion. God help us all. - Malcolm Hostelmiester.

The next page had three graphic illustrations. From top to bottom were a snake named Alpha, a spider named Consort, and a rat named Omega. Davy wondered at the significance of the pictures which caused him to shudder. He turned to Chapter One, The Golden Age of Nimrod.

* Some references taken from the Book of Jasher published by Digit Read Publishing Co.

13
THE GOLDEN AGE OF NIMROD
(Chapter 1: The Mythology of Nimrod)

Nimrod led his elite corps of one hundred warriors down from The Tower of Babel. "We have killed him; God is dead. The mighty men of Nimrod have ascended The Tower into the heavens. We have stormed his gates, and we have destroyed God with our arrows. See, are we not drenched in his blood? He is dead!. Go spread the news from every mountain. God is dead! Nevermore shall the men of earth fear the wrath of God and his judgment upon my people. I have conquered and taken his throne. I am now the supreme God."

***

In days of antiquity, there reigned a king by the name of Nimrod, the mightiest king who ever lived. He was renowned amongst the nations as a great and mighty hunter; great in strength, great in stature, great in intellect, and endowed with an abundance of audacity. It was widely believed that he took on the spirit of his quarry which empowered him to kill the largest and most vicious of all animals that roamed the forests and the plains. Others said the clothing he wore contained great magic, power from the gods.

He wore the loin cloth of Adam, made by Yehovah from the skins of animals to hide his nakedness. The loin cloth containing magic was given to Nimrod from his father Cush, and it was given to Cush by his father Ham who had stolen it from the rightful owner; Ham was a thief. Nimrod claimed that Elohim did not make the skins for clothing, but that they were made by Moloch, because Moloch was his chosen god. His name was also Baal and he had many names among nations.

Ham never wore the magic skins publicly due to the fear and shame of being a thief, though he desired to do so. Likewise, Cush never wore the skins because of fear and shame. But Nimrod had no fear nor had he any shame. Neither was he afraid of any man nor beast, no nor even of any spirit, and he wore the skins and some said that was why he was a great hunter, because he wore the skins on the hunt. He prevailed against all manner of beast on every continent.

Not only was Nimrod a great hunter, but he was a great warrior, using his hunting skills against his fellow man killing many for sport, and he ruthlessly subdued all his neighbors. Nimrod organized those he subjugated in villages and towns and built walls about them and fortifications, and he devised armaments and weapons such as the world had never seen; therefore, he was able to subdue all the people of the earth.

Nimrod raised up mighty men before him to do his bidding in business and in war and he became a great man upon the earth, even a god to many. Some hated Nimrod for his atrocities, but others admired Nimrod and worshiped him. They wished they could be like him and sought to curry his favor to secure positions of wealth and authority. They wished to avail themselves of his financial and religious system. They worshiped Nimrod, but he was a murderer and a thief. His rule was absolute.

Also, in those days the earth was sparsely populated and some nations had hundreds of thousands within. Their numbers would increase to millions in a short time as men lived several hundred years of age, each generation having children for a time span of over one hundred years, and their children doing the same so that the population of the earth increased dramatically.

If a man and his family, or his tribe, wished to do so, they could leave the locality where they lived and move to a new area and settle in lands that no man claimed, and none disputed them because there were few people on the earth. Nimrod was glad to have people who would prosper and increase the wealth of his empire.

In those days gold was found upon the face of the earth, in fields, in pastures, and in the forests, and men searched and found the gold because of its beauty, and every household had gold, and some made it into jewelry. Others fashioned goblets and all manner of utensils, and others built gods to place upon their mantels and to worship them.

In later days, all the easy gold was consumed from the face of the earth and men were forced to labor for it in remote places. But Nimrod coveted the gold and claimed it for himself. He decreed that all men should bring their gold to him, and that any man who held back so much as a featherweight of gold should be put to death, and all the people gave their gold to the tax collectors of Nimrod because they wished not to die, for every man feared Nimrod.

He took the gold and plated the walls of his throne room and all his personal armor. All the vessels and utensils were made of gold, and his throne was made entirely of gold, except for twelve fine emeralds that were embedded in the throne. Even the seventy steps that ascended the throne were plated with gold. On either side of the stairs leading to the throne stood a dragon, one on either side.

The dragons were made of gold, each standing the height of two men, with emeralds for eyes, and they were fearful to behold. Each man who approached Nimrod was made to bow down before the two dragons, the one on the left and the one on the right. The wings of the dragons were spread so that whoever approached Nimrod must first pass under the wings of the dragon before their emerald gaze. There were also two dragons crafted into the throne, one on either arm, and a dragon was inscribed onto the back of the throne. The outer rooms were also fitted in gold and gold plated candle sticks and fine ornaments glittered throughout the castle and idols also. All his men servants and all his maid servants were decked in fine gold.

In Nimrod's living quarters all the furniture was plated with gold and many fine ornaments, so they were referred to as the rooms of gold. Nimrod's crown was finely crafted gold and contained a single emerald, the largest the world had ever known.

Nimrod had golden bands upon his wrists and also upon his ankles. He wore several golden chains about his neck, the largest containing a large emerald and on his fingers he had three golden rings. Upon one ring was engraved a rat, upon another a spider, and upon the other a snake. Also, his wife Semiramis was bedecked with gold, with golden chains about her neck, golden earrings, and golden rings upon all of her fingers. Gold was even braided into the locks of her hair. No man or woman has ever been so covered with gold unto this very day as were Nimrod and his wife Semiramis, or Ishtar as she was widely known. She was Nimrod's consort, and the black widow spider was named after her.

This was the golden age of history, and no man, nor even any single nation, has ever possessed such qualities of gold since that time. He also gave gold to his friends and chief officials, and it was during this time that men began to place great value upon gold. All men sought after his gifts of gold and his approval. He was called Nimrod the Great Benefactor for enriching his friends, but he punished his enemies until they all disappeared or were intimidated into silence. He was also called Eldorado.

The throne weighed so much that none could move it, but it was constructed by skilled artisans so that it fit together like a puzzle and one arm could be removed, and another arm removed, and so forth so the chair could be dismantled and moved as the need arose. However, it was finely constructed so none could tell it could be broken down into parts. And there were twelve large emeralds imbedded in the throne of gold, because Nimrod loved emeralds. It was Nimrod who first named the Emerald Isles.

Nimrod subdued the nations of the earth and he exacted heavy taxes and regulated their going to and fro, but he also gave them protection from the wild animals and from each other, and he created a great society, and built magnificent buildings and great gods. All the people of the earth worshiped Nimrod and wished to be like him, only greater, but they could never be, because he had the power of the spirit and that spirit was the god of this world. Nimrod decreed that The System was God and The System should be worshiped by all.

Everyone who worshiped The System, therefore, prospered, but those who did not worship The System were abused and put to death. He named The System the Babylonian Mystery Religion and set magicians over them, because the magi understood all the mysteries of the universe. Therefore, all the people bowed down before him, and worshiped him. In all things he was glorious, but profane. It was Nimrod who built The Tower of Babel in defiance of Yehovah.

14
PARTING IS SUCH SWEET SORROW

The next few weeks passed quickly enough without any unusual or spectacular events to create intrusion into their daily routine. Davy was disappointed the three of them no longer had the supreme level of emotional bonding they had felt that first night. Perhaps they would never again do so. Even so, he treasured the memory of that first night. He worried the experience might fade into some fog-like memory, like the one he held of an early and precious Christmas moment that had once been so vivid. His life experiences had taught him that life has a way of working things out, at least on its own terms. Whatever will be will be. Que sera, sera, as they say.

Emerald was home three nights and two full days. Davy saw him one time only, the time of his interview. Emerald's departure was as sudden and as mysterious as his arrival. The mansion had turned into a beehive of activity for those two days. The guest houses were filled at all times, the offices on the hall adjoining Davy's apartment were all occupied with men entering and leaving. Drivers made routine round trips to the airport shuttling very important people. A few flew directly in and landed on the helicopter pad. Six stuffed leather chairs in the alcove down the hall from Emerald's office cushioned those anxious souls who waited their turn for some precious appointed face time with the great man.

A harpist and a pianist played soft music in the background and a butler kept them supplied with martinis and hors d'oerves. A therapist gave them a foot bath and rubbed their feet with fragrant oils. A crew of attractive girls ushered the guests to their destinations throughout the mansion. Some of the distinguished gentlemen skimmed through magazines while others scanned their laptops and still others talked on cell phones. Half a dozen armed bodyguards manned their stations throughout the house.

Davy remembered Marti's advice to avail himself to the experience and insights of those who filled the halls and offices, to mine their experiences to his own best advantage, as Marti had put it. Davy considered he had done a pretty good job, to the best of his ability, but afterward felt he could have done better. The next time he would do better, much better. And then, they were gone, all of them.

The large quiet mansion belonged once more to Marti, Antoinette, the household staff, and to Davy, Sarah and Travis. As much as Davy had enjoyed the excitement, he found himself relieved when they were gone. In a sense, they had intruded into personal space that belonged to Sarah, Travis, and him. He was glad they had their own space back. So much of Davy's recent life appeared to be a progressive dream state.

The classes for Sarah and Travis had ended and the classes for Davy had not started yet, so they had plenty of time to relax and hang out together. They swam daily, used the bowling alley, the squash court, the tennis court, the exercise room, the sauna, and the running track. Once or twice a week, they watched a full length feature film on the big screen in the theater room. Davy never missed a chance to watch Texas A&M or the Dallas football teams and occasionally the Spurs. At one time, he had dreamed of playing for both football teams. Almost every day he spent some time in the F-16 flight simulator, fulfilling another of his fantasies.

Usually about three times a week they would go to the stables and each saddle a mount and ride the trails through the woods. Sarah and Travis had been schooled in the equestrian arts and shared their knowledge with Davy, who was a fast learner. He loved the horses. He would receive his own equestrian training in time. Once or twice a week they would ride those same trails, but only on bicycles, or dirt bikes, or sometimes on four-wheelers. Davy loved the time they spent together, but his favorite time was when they would hold their discussions, late into the night, sharing their lives with each other. It was during those discussions they bonded and grew deeper into each other's souls.

After Davy's first powerful assessment of Sarah's sensuous beauty, he had determined, aided by his great inner strength, that his safest, his surest course of action was to develop a brother and sister relationship with her, one of respect, and then let it lead where it may. Davy had promised his mother to hold women with high respect. That is a promise easily broken if one's mother was still alive, but how do you break a promise to your deceased mother? He was strongly committed to the idea that romantic love should be based on a foundation of respect.

Perhaps he was not good enough for her. If he should be so lucky their relationship would someday develop into a romantic one, then better they should build a solid foundation of friendship first. Davy considered he was sailing on uncharted waters, at least as far as she was concerned. Davy's mastery of his own lustful inclinations was no easy matter, but he grew stronger therein as the days passed.

It was with great surprise when a couple of weeks later, he received the latest news from Sarah. "You're doing what?"

"I'm leaving. In three days I will be leaving to fulfill my destiny, going to nursing school. Marti told me about an hour ago and the arrangements have already been made."

Davy wrapped his hand around the back of his neck. "Wow! This is all happening so fast. It's like I don't have time to absorb anything."

"I know. Things happen that way around Emerald's world. Like I said, he moves at the speed of light."

Sarah held Scarlet lovingly and softly scratched behind her ears.

I sure wouldn't mind being that dog, thought Davy, *please God, just for a little bit.* Davy smirked inwardly at the thought. Sarah didn't have a clue.

"How do you feel about this, now that you are actually going to be leaving all this behind to fulfill your dream?"

"I suppose I have mixed feelings, you know, visiting new places, forming new relationships and having enough money this time to participate in their activities. I had lots of friends before, in my old school, but I always knew when money was involved, there were a lot of things I couldn't do with them. Now, the possibilities are exciting."

Davy nodded in a show of support. He was happy for her; he disguised his sorrow.

"I always wanted to be a nurse, even when I was a little girl. I would pretend to be a nurse when my little cousins came over and I would take care of my patients. I would pronounce them sick with the flu and make them stay in a little makeshift bed I had arranged. I used ice-cream sticks for thermometers. I took their temperature about a hundred times, keeping them in bed while I gave them plenty of water to drink. I suppose it was lucky for them I didn't know anything about rectal thermometers."

"Someday, if I get sick, you are the nurse I want taking care of me." Davy laughed.

Sarah smiled politely and continued. "They always tired of the game before I would. Sometimes I would be somewhat insistent before they would openly rebel and quit the game. As I think back, they probably had to go potty because of all the water. I suppose I was rather annoying at times. I have to smile when I think of those times, those good times. It's been a long time since I've seen my cousins."

Sarah laughed and Davy grinned with understanding. "I sure understand good times with cousins, especially Harold and Carlos. We were close. It's been a long time since Harold and I have gone hunting. I miss that. I'd love to see them again, both of them."

She continued, "I also have a feeling of sadness. I fully understand the privilege of living at Silverstone Estates. It's been a wonderful experience, like living in a magical kingdom. There are no financial worries and I have lived like a queen. I know I'm leaving that all behind. Most people have never experienced anything like it, so I know how lucky I have been. And then, there's you and Travis. You have become dear friends to me, precious family such as I have never had. You don't know how much that means to me. I'm going to miss you, really miss you."

Davy had a warm feeling that flowed throughout his being. He considered reaching over and giving her a simple kiss, but was afraid of his own powerful feelings. He was committed to being a gentleman. He thought of how his mother and little sister would have been proud of him. He had no intention of ruining such a precious relationship on an emotional whim of the moment. Sarah saw him as a brother, as family, and he respected that. His desire for her would forever be subordinate to her needs. Unknown to Davy, manhood had stood up on its hind legs within him. Some of our most momentous internal moments pass unnoticed, unappreciated, by us and by others.

Sarah continued, "My world is about to change. Four years in nursing school will be tough. Hopefully I will see you and Travis during the holidays, or perhaps summer vacation, but who knows where you will be by then. And when I graduate from nursing school, my world will change again. I want to be a nurse for poor people, where I am needed most, for those in most desperate need."

For the first time, it dawned on Davy that he and Sarah were going in opposite directions. His world in a life of high finances would certainly not be in close proximity to sick and poor people. He was swept with a chilling dose of reality. "In school, you will probably meet your life partner. You will date and marry someone who has the same life goals that match your own. I will be happy for you. I only hope you get someone who deserves you." The thought of what he had just said weighed heavily upon him.

Sarah smiled in appreciation for his obvious concern. "Who knows what the future holds? I just believe that everything works out in the end."

The next three days went by altogether too fast to suit Davy. *That's the problem with good times; they pass too quickly.* He felt the time had been fast forwarded as one might do a DVD, and he found himself driving Sarah to the airport in one of the long black stretch limos that were always available at Silverstone Estates for such purposes. It suddenly dawned on Davy that this was the first time either of them had left the estate since he had arrived. Davy realized how secluded their lives had been.

Now, she waited for a private Learjet to fly her to her destination. At school, she would shed her aura of wealth and would become just one of the girls. Her financial attachment to Silverstone Empire would end six months after she graduated. Davy knew the next few minutes would pass as quickly as the rest of the days had flown, unrealistically fast.

The porter carried her luggage and her dog in its cage, and Scarlet shivered, normal for the nervous animal. Sarah called after him, "Be careful with Scarlet. She scares easily."

Davy and Sarah exchanged their final farewells as the pilot looked at his watch for the third time.

"I'm going to miss you," said Davy. "Really, really miss you."

"That is so sweet of you," she said as she gave him a hug, a warm hug that lasted several seconds. "I'm going to miss you too. You have become such an important part of my life."

Davy smiled and said, "Rapunzel, Rapunzel..."

She smiled back and replied, "Throw down your rabbit." They both laughed.

She had taken no more than ten steps away from him when he called out, "Sarah."

She turned to look at him one last time.

He could no longer restrain himself, "I just want you to know that I love you. I will always love you, more than you could ever know." He swallowed sharply and wondered if it sounded too brotherly.

She ran quickly back to give him another parting hug and kissed him on the cheek. Then she was gone. He watched the pilot and Sarah board the small jet. He watched it taxi out, wait its turn, and then take off down the runway. He watched as it climbed into the sky, taking the love of his life with him, watched until it disappeared into the distant blue of the sky. He wondered if his parents had ever felt such intense feelings for each other. Finally, feeling empty, he turned and headed for the car. Already, he longed for the next time he would see Sarah. Tears came to his eyes. He didn't know how he could hide his love from her the next time.

Perhaps the next time would be the right time for him to tell her how much he loved her. With the fickleness of life, who knew when that would be, or even if he would ever see her again. He said a small prayer to Yahweh that he would see her before long. He thought about how hard it would be for him to hear someday she was getting married. He wondered how he could go on without her. Perhaps he should have been more honest in expressing his feelings for her. Perhaps she had wanted him to do so. What if this was a missed window of opportunity that would never come his way again? Sometimes in life an opportunity only comes once, and if missed, is gone forever. Davy wondered if his self imposed restraint was born of love or fear.

He threw the thought from his mind. He gently touched his fingers to the side of his face where she had kissed him, and then he thought of Shirley Marie. It had been a long time since he had thought of Shirley Marie. He had a deep crush on her when he was in the second grade, but he was too bashful to tell her so, or to show it in any way. She didn't seem to even know he existed, and then one day, without any apparent reason, she came running up to him and kissed him on the cheek. Perhaps the other girls had dared her; he didn't care. Maybe she really liked him and he should have told her he liked her.

She moved to another school the following week and he never saw her again. Davy was adamant that his mother was never to wash the spot of Shirley's kiss. She humored him for a full week, and then one day before he realized what was happening, she washed his cheek. He had been so upset he had pouted for a couple of weeks. It took him several months to get over his grudge entirely, but he finally did, and eventually forgot all about her. He wondered where Shirley Marie was now. But Davy knew that no one could ever wash Sarah's kiss from his face, for it had penetrated to the depth of his heart and was thus safely protected from the abrasions of the world.

As Davy approached the limo, he saw paper stuck under the windshield wiper. He was surprised as he was unaware of any parking violation he might have made. He was chagrined about paying a fine with money he couldn't afford, but then he realized he didn't have those kinds of worries any more. He had access to money now. He wondered if Marti or Emerald could fix it for him, but discarded the idea as he thought it lacked class. Upon closer examination, he found a note inside of an envelope. Strange, he thought as he removed it. Hand printed, the note read:

Beware!
Beware!!
Beware!!!
Things are not as they seem and you are in great danger.
Please destroy this note as it places me at risk.
God speed and protect you.
A Friend

Davy examined the back of the note and the envelope in a futile search for more information. Perplexed, he read the note two more times in his car before folding it and placing it in his shirt pocket. He would have to think about this some more. The note was quickly forgotten as his thoughts returned to Sarah.

In the days that followed, Davy continued to live the good life, but it was no longer the same without her. The very next day after she left, he e-mailed her a short message. Later, he received a reply. He was disappointed. It did not have the feeling of intimacy he thought they shared, nor did her next reply fare any better. He reasoned she was too busy, too distracted to sit down and give him a thoughtful reply. Perhaps the close relationship he thought they shared was less than he had supposed. She was so attractive and friendly; she was probably forming new friendships, perhaps even closer and more intense.

The third day after her departure, feeling particularly lonely, he went to her apartment and laid on her bed trying to recapture the feeling of her presence. He was intrigued by the cute and dainty decorating touches of a woman's hands, the hand crafted pictures and doilies pasted on the walls. After laying there for a while, he sat up to leave and noticed her Bible sitting on the table by the head of the bed, her grandmother's Bible. Opening the Bible, he found a folded sheet of paper upon which she had written his initial several times. Underneath the initials she had penned; *Davy, Davy, Davy, whatever shall I do with you? You are dashingly handsome and there is no denying the chemistry I feel when you are near. I sense the animal magnetism each time you touch me. I would love to pursue that romance and see where it led, but for a vow I made to God. I can not leave his calling. That is a tough decision, but one I know I must make. God give me strength.*

His first thought was the next time he saw her, he could press the issue and she would melt under his charms. But then thought he would be destroying her dream, perhaps even her faith.

He knew how important her Bible was to her and how disappointed she would be when she realized it was missing. Perhaps she would believe it lost. Davy had good reason to e-mail her again.

Sarah returned his e-mail later that day saying she was aware she had left it, for him as a keepsake from her. *It is a gift I want you to have.* He was surprised she would give it up, but it was certainly something he would treasure. From that time on he kept it on the table at the head of his own bed. He read a few pages every evening before bedding down for the night. Never did he feel closer to Sarah then when he was reading her Bible. He usually slept with it under his pillow, though sometimes he went to sleep holding it, a great source of comfort to him. Even with this most precious gift, Davy's life was no longer the same without her. He used the note of warning from the windshield as his bookmark.

Davy started his class with Shahiek, three days a week, three hours before noon and three hours after noon in the same room he had first met Sarah and Travis. There was home work to do and projects to compete, much of which involved the internet. He found several of the subjects fascinating, for instance, how to appear to have disappeared from the face of the earth without leaving any evidence behind, and how to secure a new identity, including a past, family history, and documents such as a social security card and driver's license. Others were titled How Political Miscalculations Created an Unanticipated World and Financial Controls are More Powerful than Armaments. Davy had access to a number of websites he would never have guessed existed, indeed, few people ever have known about. All this was done under the watchful eyes of Shahiek.

If Davy felt the loss of Sarah's companionship, and it was a sharp loss indeed, he had ample time to draw ever closer to Travis. Davy had never thought about how it would have been different if his older brother had not died a few days after being born. If you've never had an older brother in your life, looking out for you, giving you guidance and protection besides companionship, then you never know what it's like to miss having an older brother. But Travis played the role with such love and concern in wisdom that Davy wondered how he had ever managed without one. Not that he actually needed one; after all, he was quite independent and self-sufficient without any family at all. It was just so nice to know that someone cared and was looking out for him.

During one of their long conversations, Davy showed the Bible to Travis and shared the message from the e-mail she had given it to him for a keepsake.

"Sparkle gave you that?"

"Sparkle?"

Travis laughed. "I call her Sparkle sometimes, just habit."

"Cool," said Davy. "It certainly fits."

Travis asked, "You miss her, don't you?'

"Of course," Davy responded, "don't you?"

"Sure," said Travis, "but not nearly as much as I think you do."

"Oh," said Davy, somewhat surprised. "You don't think you like her as much as I do?"

"It's not that I like her less; it's just that you like her more, lots more."

Davy thought a minute and then asked, "Really now, was it so obvious you could tell?"

Travis laughed. "You did a pretty good job of concealing it, but I could tell."

"Do you think she knew?"

Travis chuckled. "She's pretty intuitive. I'd be surprised if she didn't know."

Davy thought for a moment. What about you? You ever fall for a girl, you know, head over heels type of thing?"

"Not really."

"What, you don't like girls?"

"Oh, it's not that. Believe me, I like girls. It's just that my mother and father married when they were freshmen in college. When I was born, mom had to drop out of school and take a job to support dad and me while he continued his studies, particularly while he was pursuing his master's and doctorate. Mom couldn't get a good job because she didn't have her education yet, and part of what she made had to go to day care for me. They had to do without meals at times. Sometimes she would mix water in my milk bottle so I wouldn't be hungry."

"Wow, that's like crap city."

"Oh yes, you bet. That didn't work so well and apparently I cried a lot. It was pretty difficult on my family to live that way. My mother suffered a lot. She often cried herself to sleep. She made me promise that I would never get married until I could provide for a wife and children the way they deserved to be taken care of."

"I'm sorry. That had to be tough for a baby not to have enough to eat. It must have been tough for your mother to see you hungry; must have been difficult for your dad too."

"In some ways it was worth it. Eventually, my father made good money, but it affected their marriage. In some ways they never really got over it."

"I'm sorry, man."

"I don't want that to happen to me. I don't want it to happen to my wife, my children. I am determined I will never get married until I am financially responsible. So the safest thing is not to show any interest in girls until that time. Otherwise, I will fall in love, get all crazy, and next thing I'll know is we're married. You shouldn't have a family until you can do it right. It's not been easy. I really like girls, but I've been pretty darned determined."

"That is precious."

"I've noticed that when young couples are in love, they look into each other's eyes and believe their love will last forever. But they get caught up with having kids and struggling with enough money to get along, and next thing you know, a heaviness sets in, and then resentment. Love is replaced by bitterness. I don't think I could handle that. When I get married, I want it to be forever. I want to be a good family man. Having a family is important to me. Someday I will have a family."

"That's good."

"I determined never to date a girl until I could provide for a woman and child the way they deserve. A man has a responsibility. Soon, I will be making good money. I will begin to date, and then marry. Someday, I shall tell my wife every day how much I love her. She will see it in my eyes. I don't want my children to see their parents argue. Every child should live in love."

"That is beautiful. I have learned so much from you in the short time we have known each other."

"I appreciate hearing you say that. I have also learned much from you."

When Travis later told Davy that he, too, would be leaving for his first year of college, Davy was afraid the next two weeks would go by altogether too fast. He was right. The next thing he knew, he was driving Travis to the airport in a black stretch limo. Travis would be taken to his destination in a private Learjet. As the jet disappeared into the blue of the sky, Davy felt incredibly alone, not unlike when his family had died.

When he returned to his apartment, he sought relief by returning to the book of Nimrod.

15

INNOCENCE AND EVIL
(Chapter 2: The Mythology of Nimrod)

The moon was full and the wind blew softly in the Fertile Crescent. The time of deliverance had come and had successfully been fulfilled. Having finished her pressing midwife duties, Dorinda turned her attention to pampering the mother. The new babe had nursed and now slept contentedly in his adoring mother's embrace and under her loving gaze.

She counted his dainty little fingers and toes and said, "Abram, I know you will make your father proud. Someday, perhaps you will become a great general serving Nimrod, even as your father now is. Today you are an innocent babe, but your destiny is greatness. I know it shall be so, and your father Terah will be proud to call you his son."

Terah, meanwhile, had returned to the festivities in the great hall, the hall of the gods in his palace where the nobility had gathered to celebrate the birth of his firstborn son. No father was ever more proud of an offspring than was Terah that night.

"Yamar, Bemini and Latinius, my dear friends," he exclaimed, slapping one on the back. "What a great honor to have Magi here tonight for the birth of my son. Do you come representing the court of Nimrod, or is the privilege of your visit for personal pleasure and honor, as from friend to friend?"

"Ah, our dear friend, Terah," said Yamar, "can it not be both? We three travel these many miles to celebrate the birth of your firstborn. Because you are our dear friend, we would not miss it for the world. But, you will be pleased to know we deliver the official blessing of Nimrod on this sacred occasion. You may consider it indicative of the great esteem you hold in the eyes of the great Nimrod, as one would expect for his favorite general."

"Then upon your return, let the great Nimrod know I am truly honored to receive his blessing upon the birth of my son. As I live and serve the great Nimrod, king of all the earth, so shall my son serve him, and the gods willing, my son will become a great general in service for the great and mighty king."

With that, Terah turned to the great god that stood in the banquet hall, the god that was chief deity over the other eleven that stood around the room, and lifted a golden goblet in a toast.

"May Moloch bless my son to become a great and mighty warrior, one willing to fight for the glory of Nimrod, even to die for him if necessary, and that willingly, for the glory of the great king and his glorious kingdom. Long live Nimrod, the great and powerful Nimrod."

Upon hearing the toast to Moloch and the requested blessing, Yamar, Bemini and Latinius bowed before the great god with their foreheads touching the marble floor and they all said in unison, "Great is Moloch and great is Nimrod and may the kingdom last forever."

As the three Magi returned to their feet, Terah said, "Thank you my friends. Many great men are here to honor the birth of my son, my heir, but none of them are as dear to me as you are this night. My heart is thrilled to have you bear witness and share this momentous occasion with me."

But, while Terah valued their friendship, he said this because the three Magi were close to the heart of Nimrod, and Terah was an accomplished politician as well as a great general, and they were also wise in their own way. The four shared fellowship and conversation, even intimate conversation, but the midnight hour came and passed. Most of the visitors had vacated after the arrival and announcement of the birth and with adequate celebration, so these four, exhausted from a long and demanding day, also retired to their suites. The next day the Magi would have a long and grueling trip as they returned to the court of Nimrod.

As the Magi walked the balcony on the outside wall to their suite of rooms, they were astonished at a phenomenon in the sky. Behold, they saw a bright star traveling slowly east to west. No sooner had that star appeared than a second bright star appeared traveling behind the first. And, no sooner had the second star appeared than a third star appeared traveling behind the second. No sooner had that happened than a fourth star appeared, brighter than the other three together, and the fourth star traveled faster so it caught the third star and devoured it, and then caught the second star and consumed it, and then likewise the first star, so only the great star remained of the four, and it grew even brighter.

The Magi wondered at the phenomenon and were astonished and when they came to their rooms, they were astonished still.

"What do these things mean, this great sign in the heavens," asked Bemini?

"It must be a message from the gods," said Latinius.

"And surely, it concerns Abram, the son of Terah as this unusual sign happens on the very night he is born."

The three Magicians then entered into their wizardry, consulting the spirits of the gods and they communed concerning the matter, after the custom of the select college of magicians that served Nimrod, and they were in agreement.

This is the message they ascertained that the newborn son of Terah should someday become a mighty warrior and a great king, and he would devour the great kingdom of Nimrod, and he should destroy Nimrod himself and his seed after him, for Terah was from the tribe of Shem and not from the tribe of Nimrod.

Then said Latinius, "We must tell Nimrod."

Bemini said, "But if we tell Nimrod, he will kill the child and perhaps Terah, our good friend."

Yamar then said, "If we fail to tell Nimrod and he finds out the thing and knows we did not tell him, then will he have us thrown into the fire and we shall die, we and our entire household. Let us therefore tell Nimrod and let him do what he will do."

Upon their return to the Palace of Nimrod, they told him all concerning the birth of the child and of the signs in the heavens. When he asked them of their interpretation, they told him all their heart, that someday Abram would devour Nimrod and his kingdom. Now, the king was such he feared no man, no, not even any spirit, no, not even any evil spirit, because he himself had a fearsome countenance and because he tolerated no opposition to live. He therefore called Terah before his magnificent court.

Terah appeared before Nimrod and knew nothing that had transpired before concerning his son and the heavenly signs the Magi had seen. As he approached Nimrod, he prostrated himself three times and said,

"Oh great Nimrod, may you live forever, and of your kingdom may there be no end. Great is the name of Nimrod. Holy is the great Nimrod. All power upon the earth to Nimrod, and all things belong to Nimrod. Great is the name of the almighty Nimrod."

Terah remained in his third bow until Nimrod bade him rise for to do so before receiving permission from Nimrod was to risk immediate decapitation.

"Come now, Terah the great warrior and my favorite general, and stand before Nimrod, even the great Nimrod. Come before me and answer what I ask." Terah arose and approached Nimrod.

"Of course, almighty Nimrod, ask and I shall answer with all my heart, for never have I held anything back from you, my king. I will tell you all you inquire."

Nimrod then revealed all the Magi had told him. He gave Terah a hard stare before continuing. "Therefore, bring your son to me and I will give you great riches, and I will make you the greatest king under Nimrod, great in all the earth. Then will my kingdom be saved, your life be spared, and you will not die."

Terah in response said, "Oh great and mighty king, I have a dilemma that troubles me greatly and I am at a loss to know what to do. Answer me out of your kingly wisdom that I might resolve my situation and I will then answer you of your inquiry."

Nimrod answered, "Say on."

"Oh mighty king, you in your magnificence have in past times given to me, your servant, a white horse, a prize worthy as a gift would be from such a great king. It is a white horse of such beauty as I have never seen in all my days except in the stables of Nimrod, only there have I seen such a beautiful stallion. It is as I would expect from such a magnificent benefactor. I have therefore cherished this white horse which you have given me, not only because he is a superior horse, but even more so because it is a gift from the mighty Nimrod. Therefore have I greatly cherished this animal above all my possessions, even above my wives."

"What you say is true. Therefore, whatever could be your dilemma?"

"Then comes a man to Terah, one of your kings of great wealth, one who controls a great fleet of merchant ships, comes to visit the court of Terah in the city of Ur. I showed him all I had and proudly showed him my precious white horse, the one given me by Nimrod, thus my dilemma."

Nimrod waited with a stone face.

"He wanted the white horse, and offered me great riches, such as I have never seen. I said within my heart if I sell the magnificent horse, I will have greater riches than I could ever need, more than I could ever hope to have. But then I thought this is a gift from the great Nimrod, and I should not sell it for any amount of riches. Therefore, oh great Nimrod, tell me what I should do and solve my great dilemma. What sayeth thou, oh mighty Nimrod and wise king?"

Nimrod was indignant and his anger waxed hot. "You would dare sell a gift you have received from the great Nimrod. Others would rather die than give up a gift from Nimrod. How dare you be such an ingrate? You shall never sell the white horse, no not even for all the wealth in the world, no, not even unto death. It is settled, the great Nimrod has spoken."

"Indeed master, I am grateful, for your wisdom is above all the kings of the earth and above all the wise men, so who could ever doubt the wisdom of Nimrod. So, now you have answered my question, so shall I answer yours, even in your own words. The great gods in their generosity have given me a son, one without equal of countenance among all the babes upon the earth. You offer me riches and power in exchange for my gift from the gods. By your own words, I would be an ingrate if I did so. Therefore, I will not bring you my son."

"You would mock the mighty Nimrod?" His eyes glared.

"I ask of your great mercy. I would never mock the Great Nimrod. I knew no other way to approach you. I again appeal to the magnificent benefactor. Let me keep the child, heart of my heart and flesh of my flesh."

Nimrod rose to his feet in anger and his face was red, for no one dared dispute the great Nimrod and deny him in this manner. He considered sending him into the heat of the fire, except this was his greatest general and he preferred not have him killed. Therefore, he said, "I will give you three days to reconsider and then I will require your resolution to the issue. Perhaps you will have regained your sanity by then. So, three days then. Go now, and leave my sight before my anger consumes me and both of us should regret my actions!"

In three days Terah sent a message to Nimrod that said, "I will not deliver my son, my beloved son. Gazing into his eyes, I cannot bring myself to do so. Being a father yourself, surely you understand. I am your most fervent servant. I appeal to your magnificent generosity."

Nimrod sent a message to Terah by his fastest steed that said, "By an oath before all the gods, all that presently live and all that have ever lived, if you do not deliver me your son before the sun sets three days hence, if you do not deliver your son, then this I will do. I will send my mightiest warriors against your house and they will destroy all the men, and all the women, both aged and babe, and all between. They will be hacked into pieces and left for the jackals, the wild dogs and the lions. I will salt the earth so no foliage can grow forever, and I swear by the host of gods that so much as a dog in the city of Ur shall not survive. Therefore, the seed of Terah shall disappear from the earth, and his name will be removed from all records and will be an abomination forever and ever.

The next day Terah laden his camels with provisions, and with a heavy heart took men worthy of his escort, traveled to the palace of Nimrod, and carried with him his son.

Nimrod received him gladly, kissed his cheek, and placed upon his shoulders a lavender robe. He took the child and thrust its head upon a stone in the palace so its brains and blood ran out upon the marble floor. The royal dogs were fetched and they licked up the brains and the blood. The dogs fought over and devoured the child. Thus did Terah take his son to Nimrod so Nimrod's kingdom should be saved to perpetuity and protected from the evil of the child as foretold by the Magi.

Nimrod sent Terah away with great riches more than any man had ever received at the hand of Nimrod and commanded he should be given ruler-ship over new territory, such as he had done for no general before. Nimrod was pleased and Terah was satisfied. What Nimrod did not know was that Terah had not delivered Abram, but delivered his newly born son by a servant maid. For Terah did not consider any other child to be his first born son, but only Abram who was born of his favorite wife. So Abram lived and Nimrod soon forgot the incident entirely.

From that day the three Magi, friends of Terah, no longer came into his presence because they could not look him in the eyes.

16
A GRUESOME DISCOVERY

"Emerald will be returning tomorrow," Marti told Davy.

Davy was rather surprised. "Is that unusual, for him to return so soon? I mean, he was here less than a month ago. I thought he didn't come back that often."

"With Emerald, anything is possible, but yes, it is unusual for him to return this soon. However, there is a reason; there is always a reason for everything that Emerald does. In this particular situation, it just happens that he is not well."

"Not well?" responded Davy with concern. "What does that mean, exactly?"

"Emerald has a heart condition. He'll be having heart surgery. They are flying a heart specialist into town. Emerald hasn't lived to the grand old age he has without having the best medical attention. The heart surgeon is world renown Dr. Cotillion. This is all being kept low key. The press will not be informed, only a select few. You can tell no one, not one single person."

"Of course. Will Emerald be all right as he travels on his way back home? What if he has a crisis on the plane?"

"Emerald will have a heart specialist accompanying him on the plane, along with two nurses. His private jet has built-in medical equipment, everything he might need in an emergency. But, there shouldn't be a crisis. Emerald usually operates one step ahead. When he thought he might be having trouble, he had an early diagnosis, so they were able to schedule surgery without inordinate risk. Certainly, time is a factor, but it should be okay."

"Heart surgery sounds pretty serious. Is there a possibility Emerald might – well-you know, not make it?"

"Heart surgery is always a serious deal. Emerald has had several heart surgeries, and he has always responded well. I expect him to do so this time also, but you never know. Life at best is a crap-shoot."

Davy bit his lower lip in quiet contemplation. "If something were to happen to Emerald, if he died or something, I was just wondering, what would happen to me? Would my situation, and that of Sarah and Travis, would this all come to an end? I don't want to be so self-focused at a time Emerald's life is at risk, but I can't help wonder how it would affect me."

"Not to worry, Davy. Every contingency has been anticipated. Your finances have been set up for the next eight years in a trust fund. Besides that, he has highly capable people, loyal people placed in strategic locations. I am not in one of his power front-line positions, God knows, I don't want that. But, I do have considerable influence with them all. I am the coordinator, the facilitator. They look to me for direction from Emerald. I will insure that you move forward to assume your position as Emerald would have it, as his heir."

"You know about that?"

"Of course. Emerald shares everything with me. I am his eyes and ears. I will keep things on track until he is back on his feet, or until you are ready to assume full leadership if that becomes necessary. You will progress as fast as you are capable and as fast as you wish. I will, at the right time, turn my loyalty from Emerald to you. Let's just hope that everything goes well with Emerald, and it probably will. It always has. But, if not, you could wake up in a couple of days as the unofficial ruler of the world, the richest, most powerful man alive."

Marti grinned at Davy's sudden realization of the possibilities that fate could thrust upon him, all of the wealthy and powerful men of the world at his beck and call to determine the fate of nations. Davy found it hard to fathom. He was not prepared. He was not properly trained. He didn't have this kind of experience. What did he know about world governments, about political intrigue? He didn't want the responsibility of having the destiny of billions of people resting on his shoulders.

The rest of the day Davy spent in quiet, thoughtful solitude. His was an uneasy and troubled soul. Was he up to the task? Would his training be adequate, especially with such a short time for him to be trained? What if a major crisis developed on the international scene? Would he have a clue how to prevent that from happening or how he was supposed to respond? He worried he would be responsible for the collapse of world governments, or even of starting a war. What if a nuclear missile was launched? What would he be expected to do? Would it be possible that he could be responsible for the destruction of the world, the annihilation of mankind?

He wondered how Sarah and Travis would react to his selection as Emerald's heir. After all, they were there before he was. Would they be glad for him, or would they be jealous? If he were to take over Emerald's empire, he would see to it they were taken care of very well. Surely, they would know that.

Another thought crossed his mind as he contemplated the axiom, "Heavy hangs the head that wears the crown." Davy knew there were numerous evil people in the world, those who would kill without so much as a stir of conscious in order to take over the great empire. How many, a thousand, ten thousand, a hundred thousand? Who knew? *That's a lot of people who might want me dead. It would only take one to get the job done. Would I know how to survive such evil?*

Suddenly, Davy longed for the good old days when he ran carefree and lived on the streets. The monumental problems he thought he had then now suddenly paled by comparison.

When a person is programmed a certain way through genetics and environment, how does one suddenly change his entire lifestyle in such a radical fashion? What if he was not comfortable in his new position, what if he detested it, would it make any difference? For the time being none of that mattered. Destiny had a mind of her own, and it seemed to him he was on a small boat shooting some violent rapids and had no way to control present events in his life.

At the same time, he had a nagging worry that the whole thing might fall through and he would find himself cast back onto the streets, unworthy of the role, unworthy of companionship with Sarah and Travis. He was sorely troubled and again had fitful sleep that night with more dreams that included lightning and rolling thunder. He awoke the next morning surprised to find the mansion apparently empty.

Davy showered and entered his walk-in closet. He had to laugh as the closet was larger than his childhood bedroom. He pulled out and considered several pair of dress slacks and a cocoa colored knit sports shirt. He selected a pair of brown wingtip shoes he had not worn yet. He was getting used to wearing expensive clothing and enjoyed the experience. He didn't even need a good reason for wearing nice clothing, just because he wanted to. He caressed a couple of silk ties and wished he had a good occasion to wear one of several three-piece suites available. Daily, sometimes twice daily, he would shower and change clothes, depositing them in the clothes hamper, and daily, almost magically, they reappeared, folded or on hangers, starched as needed, conveniently available for his selection and use.

He wandered about the huge, silent mansion looking for someone who could provide him with some information on Emerald. He roamed the house, calling out for Marti, for Antoinette, the staff, anybody at all. He searched inside and out. No one answered. He remembered as a boy returning from school and calling for his mother, and how abandoned he had felt if she did not answer. Children just assume their mother will always be home when they return from school. He was surprised the feeling was returning so strongly to him now. He felt uncommonly lonely. The vastness of the mansion seemed to magnify the feeling, a feeling that seemed so inappropriate for an adult.

As Davy passed the spiral stairs on the west wing, the one that led to Emerald's living quarters and office, he wondered about Emerald. Had he returned to the house? Was he upstairs, even now, perhaps in bed? Was Davy alone in the house with the most powerful man in the world? Or, did he go directly to the hospital? Was the cardiac operation already over, or were they just now preparing for it?

He had so many questions going through his mind. He stared up the spiral stairway and again thought about Emerald, about their visit, how surreal it had seemed. Even though it had taken place less than a month ago, it almost seemed like it never happened. Davy felt like he was in a dream, the kind where you are standing in the presence of God, talking to him, face-to-face, and then you wake up and it seems so real that you believe you were actually in God's presence, yet you're not sure.

What is reality, anyway, and how do we even know we are real, or sane? Sane people know they are sane, but people with deep psychotic problems believe they are sane also. Some people really do believe they are Napoleon. Others believe they really are God. So, how do we know we are not just a figment of someone else's dream or imagination? How do we know we are not some character on some great galactic video game, perhaps one designed by God, one he would delete at the end of the day? Davy wondered how he could be sure he had truly met with Emerald. How could he be sure that Emerald was even real? Of course he was real. How else could Davy explain the mansion and his own presence there?

As Davy stared up the spiral stairway, he almost seemed to be in a trance, and he gradually realized that he was feeling a pull, an urge tugging at him to go up the stairs. He had only been up the stairs one time, the time he had been invited for an appointment with Emerald. It seemed to Davy that to go up the stairs without a proper Invitation was a breach of trust and so had never considered doing so before. He would never betray the man to whom he owed so much.

He wondered if it was a spiritual pull, perhaps from the gods of wealth and power. If so, then Emerald would want him to be obedient. Perhaps it was nothing more than his insecurities playing tricks on him, or maybe it was simply greed, and that somehow, he was succumbing to the force of a lower nature, or even an evil one. He was uncomfortable feeling powerless to resist the pull, and so he slowly climbed the stairs, and as he rose ever higher, felt himself entering a different spiritual level. He walked down the hall and hesitated right in front of Emerald's office. Entering the office, he wondered if he should remove his shoes, for surely this was hallowed ground, particularly if he was under the influence of whatever financial gods might be involved.

Davy walked behind the large desk and sat down in Emerald's chair. His eyes lit on a new gilded plaque which said The Most Glorious Human Achievement is Victory over Adversity. Davy smiled, picked it up and examined it closely. He was disappointed to see that neither he nor his mother was referenced. Even so, he had to smile at the thought he had contributed a quote that sat on the desk of the richest, most powerful man in the world. That seemed a worthy accomplishment. *I shall add Mother's name someday, when I have inherited the position*, he thought.

He spread his fingers and swept them slowly across the surface of the rich wood. He allowed time for the sensation of wealth to soak into his finger tips, to rise up through his arms and fill his soul. On a whim, he then reached his hand under the desk and ran his fingers along the inside corners. Reaching even further back, he felt a hook with a key hanging thereon. Retrieving it, holding it in his hand, he observed it closely, and then he fitted it into the keyhole of the top center drawer. It unlocked and he slid it slightly open.

He then slid his hand down the right side of the desk, opening each of the three drawers in succession and then closing them. He started to do so with the drawers on the left side when it dawned on him how incredibly stupid this was. Emerald would be offended, and rightfully so. It would not matter that Davy meant no harm. It was just curiosity, the foolish indiscretions of youth, but one that could be more than enough to derail his future. He quickly closed and locked the drawers and returned the key to its hiding place.

Davy was sitting in the chair of the most powerful person in the world. Of this he had no doubt, for the spirits witnessed to him. He could feel the spirit of Emerald rise up into his very being. He wondered if it were possible that Emerald had died. Was this some sort of transfer of power and wealth by the gods, of leadership from one to another, like the transfer of Elijah's mantle to Elisha? He sat mesmerized, transfixed by the moment. He thought how unfair it was that his life had moved so fast, farther in the last month than most people experienced in a lifetime. Even so, he was glad, exceedingly glad.

It was at this moment of intense introspection that Davy heard a bump, or at least he thought he heard a bump. Perhaps he had felt it more than heard it, he wasn't sure. Suddenly, he felt vulnerable. He should not even be in Emerald's office. What might be the ramifications of being discovered here? He didn't think it would be such a big deal actually, but then he had been wrong before. He certainly had been terribly wrong when he had misjudged the reactions of Satan's Little Brothers to some friendly ribbing. His self-insistence he was doing nothing wrong prevented a blatant act of hiding, but discretion indicated the wisdom of blending into his surroundings so he should not draw attention to himself.

He sat motionless, trying to figure out what he had heard. It was fairly dark inside the office, mostly light from the hall filtering in between the flowers and vines so he had a perfect camouflage of shadows. He waited in the stillness of silence, and then he heard it again, a dull, low, faint thud. It was real this time; there could be no denying that. And then, equally suddenly, he saw the wall begin to move on the far side of the hall. He watched in wide-eyed amazement as he saw a section of paneling telescope into the adjacent piece of paneling revealing light from an inner room.

Leaping lizards, he thought, *this is the sort of thing you see in Little Orphan Annie or perhaps in Harry Potter, but never in real life.* Two figures emerged into the hallway. One was Marti and the other was a stranger Davy had never seen before. Marti carried a stainless steel container by a handle on top, the lid securely fastened by over-center latches. The other gentleman carried a larger stainless steel container with handles on the sides. They were talking as they entered the hall, but Davy only heard muffled mumbles.

Marti reached up and twisted the nearest crystal wall lantern. The inside light switched off and the door slowly closed. Davy did not move a muscle. He could still hear them talking as they walked down the hall and descended the stairs. He heard the massive front door open and close. Waiting for several minutes, in case they came back in, Davy arose from Emerald's chair and scurried to the front window overlooking the cars parked below. The men each placed their container in separate vehicles, talked a little more, shook hands, then each climbed into their car. They slowly drove down the lane, and disappeared beyond the massive iron gates.

Davy, already stunned beyond belief by the recent overwhelming changes in his life was now stunned into a state of intense disbelief, not knowing exactly what he should do. He returned to the partition that had moved. He placed both hands on the panel as though he might discern by feel the mystery hidden by the false wall. He looked at the wall lamp, the one Marti had turned. Davy twisted the lamp even as Marti had done. "Open sesame," he whispered.

The partition began to move and a light clicked on inside. He walked into the concealed room and was amazed to the point of disbelief. The room was fourteen feet by fourteen and was painted white like a doctors office. Two walls were lined with cabinet drawers with Formica cabinet tops and above were closeted cabinet doors. A phone hung on one wall and on the plain wall there seemed to be a large appliance recessed into the wall that looked like an industrial washer or perhaps a dryer with a slide in front to feed whatever into the appliance. The room was well lit with indirect lighting. It reminded Davy of a medical clinic. In the center of the room were two stainless steel gurneys. One of the gurneys stood empty, but it was the other that caught his attention, for it was draped with a sheet which was covering what appeared to be a body.

Davy wasn't sure he wanted to know what was beneath the sheet, but he was compelled to gently take hold of one corner of the sheet and slowly pull it back. He was shocked by what he saw, a young male with blond wavy hair. As he pulled the sheet further down there appeared a face that seemed remarkably like the face of Travis; only it could not have been him. Travis was many miles from here, enrolled in school, so the thing that looked remarkably like a body could not have been him, too white, too statuesque and perfectly sculptured to capture Travis's likeness with such amazing detail. And, that body like thing was remarkably still with absolutely no signs of life, a mannequin perhaps, but certainly not Travis. That would be impossible. Travis was flesh colored and full of life. No, Travis could never hold this still. No way could this be Travis.

Davy noticed drops of water hanging on the stainless steel top and a few small beads of what looked like blood. There was a small trough that circumvented the gurney and emptied on one end into a tube that reached to a drain in the floor. He now felt alien to himself, as though he was outside his body, disconnected.

The other gurney was an exact copy of the first, except it contained no linen and no human form. Davy found himself in a trance, his actions coming from forces other than his own will or intellect. He pulled the sheet down further revealing an incision running the length of the ribcage and abdomen. The cavity was empty; therefore, it could not be a real person, too white, too still. He found it difficult to believe his own lie.

His fear for the moment overwhelmed reality. Yet, he knew. It had to be Travis. Anything else was insanity.

Davy didn't know what to make of it all. Reason abandoned him. He felt a knot beginning to form in the pit of his abdomen telling him there was something horribly wrong. He felt the knot trying to rise and he suddenly had the fear of vomiting. He was not supposed to be there. He was not supposed to see, to know all this, and the smell of vomit would betray his presence no matter how well he might clean it up. He raced from the room, twisting the light fixture behind him. He ran down the stairs and passing close to the couch, was no longer able to stifle the growing urge. He vomited on the floor.

Out the window he saw Marti pull up in the stretch limo. He didn't know what to do. He didn't think he could hide his emotions from Marti, so he quickly grabbed the decorative blanket off the back of the couch, wrapped it around him and lay on the couch. Perhaps the cover would be enough to block out the world. He heard the massive door open and close. He wondered if the door to the secret room had closed behind him. He should have checked.

Marti sniffed the air as soon as he entered and asked, "What's going on?"

"I'm sick. I think I have the flu," Davy spoke weakly behind the blanket, not much more than a mumble.

"Just my luck," replied Marti. "Vomit on the rug and the whole staff is gone for the day. But, not to worry. Actually, I was an orderly at one time, in my previous life. I've cleaned lots of vomit, wiped a lot of asses too. I can do that."

Marti disappeared and returned shortly with disinfecting cleaning supplies and quickly cleaned the mess and sprayed aerosol fresher into the air. Davy was glad the ruse of sickness gave him cover for any strange behavior he might exhibit or emotions that would betray him.

"If you are sick, you'd better go upstairs to bed. You'll feel better there. Besides, we don't need any more vomit down here. How long have you been sick?"

"Not long," Davy muttered truly feeling weak and lightheaded.

"You want me to call the doctor?"

"I don't think that will be necessary. I usually get over the flu rather rapidly. In a few days I should be okay."

"Suit yourself, but if you need the doctor, just say the word, no problem."

"Okay," responded Davy. He got up, the blanket still wrapped around him, and walked in a state of numbness toward the stairs.

"Can you make it okay?" asked Marti after him.

"Yeah, I'll be okay. I'm just nauseous and weak, but I don't think I'll vomit anymore."

"Okay. Antoinette has returned also. I'll send her up with a hot cup of her famous herb tea. She'll fix you up."

"Thanks," said Davy.

Davy undressed and was snuggled in bed securely hidden from life by his covers. It seemed forever before he heard steps approaching his room and Marti entered carrying a cup of tea which he set on the table beside Davy's bed.

"Antoinette sends her regrets you are not feeling well. She says drink this and you should feel a lot better. It will help the nausea go away. Antoinette and I are getting ready to leave. We will be gone overnight. If you need me for any reason, I left my cell phone number on the table. Call me if you need me, but not unless."

Davy grunted weakly.

"Emerald will be undergoing surgery any time now. That will last several hours, and then he will be transferred to the critical care unit. He'll be there several days and won't be in condition to receive any visitors. We'll be back before then. So, just take it easy and start feeling better. The staff will return tomorrow if you need anything."

Davy heard the door close softly after he left the room. When he heard the massive door downstairs close, he ran to the window where he saw them place luggage in the trunk, then Marti opened the driver's door and Antoinette slid in first, Marti guiding her with his hand on the small of her back. The backup lights came on; the car backed up and then drove slowly down the drive and out the iron gates.

Davy slipped his clothes on and went to his computer where he typed out a letter to Sarah, asking her if she was okay. He desperately needed reassurance from a friend he could trust. As an afterthought, he wrote P.S. Rapunzel, Rapunzel... After sending it, he thought for a moment, and on a whim e-mailed Travis asking how he was and hit the Send button.

He went downstairs and straight to the other stairs, the ones that led to Emerald's office and to the secret room. Davy twisted the lamp, watched the door open, and went inside. He had to reassure himself what he thought he had seen was real. Back inside he found it all too real, but felt like he was revisiting a dream.

The gurneys stood in the center of the room, but now they were both empty. He reached out and felt the stainless steel of them both. They were cold to the touch. He then walked around the room, sliding his hand over the counter-top, stopping long enough to open some of the drawers. He needed to continually reassure himself it was all real.

In one drawer were white linens, sheets like those that had covered that body like thing. In another drawer were surgical instruments; in another were some restraints, handcuffs, and some key-rings with multiple keys on them. In another drawer were needles, syringes, all kinds of medical bottles and other paraphernalia.

He continued around the room, stopping at the appliance recessed into the wall. Across the front was a tag that had written in small letters, crematorium model # 37K. He suddenly realized he heard the faint sound of gas flames. The machine clicked, he heard a buzzer, and the gas shut off automatically. The horror of the reality that Travis had been inside and now no longer existed closed about him like a heavy fog. But why was this all happening? He struggled to make sense out of the situation.

What if Emerald's heart operation was a heart transplant? What if he had type AB negative blood, the rarest, and needed an AB negative donor, someone like Travis. Could that have really been Travis after all?

Suddenly, Davy began to cry, deep heaving sobs with the entire body convulsing as the reality of Travis' death penetrated his resistance. He could not bear to lose family again. He sobbed for some time before he regained his composure and tried to process some kind of rational understanding.

He stared blankly. Does that mean the next time Emerald needs a heart transplant, it will come from me? How could that be possible if I am to be Emerald's heir? Was the primary purpose of the young people brought into Emerald's family to provide a heart reserve for Emerald whenever he needed one? Then I could be next, at any time, five years, next year, six months, who knows how soon. But that is not possible; I am Emerald's heir.

Another thought came to Davy. So this explains the mansion being so quiet and empty. They couldn't take a chance on the staff accidentally observing what took place here.

Davy shivered. Is Emerald's life a huge deception, about being adopted into Emerald's family, being chosen as the anointed one? Was Emerald as wealthy and powerful as he claimed? How much of all this was a lie? Why would Emerald go to such elaborate and complicated intrigue when simpler more efficient lies would serve the same purpose? What about the other young men who had been chosen by Emerald, those who had gone before, had their purpose been to provide a heart replacement for Emerald? Were they all dead now? All of the organs were gone from that body like thing that looked for the world like Travis. Had their organs been harvested and sold on the black market to the wealthy who needed organ transplants?

And then a new thought occurred to Davy. *Why was it Travis and not me? They must have gone to a lot of trouble, to make arrangements to bring him back, and I was already here. Wouldn't it have been simpler to have just used me? If so, then I should have been the one on the gurney. It could have been me inside of the... But no; I'm the anointed one, Emerald's heir. I am uniquely qualified, Emerald said so. That has to be why they didn't take me. Well, to hell with his Empire. No way I would ever want to be involved with something like that."*

Davy's head was spinning. He was in such a state of despair that he was in danger of collapsing emotionally, of entering into a physical state known as failure to thrive where one's physical body begins to shut down, a preclude to death. Then his thoughts returned again to Sarah. *What about Sarah? She doesn't have AB negative blood. Is she safe? Is she even alive?*

Davy's mind was truly in a daze, unable to process thoughts in a meaningful way, unsure what to do next. What could he possibly do? The Silverstone Empire was obviously so vast with a presence possible even into the smallest villages around the world. How could he possibly escape his precarious predicament? Then his thought returned again to Sarah, where was she? He had the sick feeling once more in the pit of his stomach. He had to know. He must rescue her if she was still alive. Slowly, manhood began to once more awaken within him and his vigor began to return, a strength he had never felt before. He knew somehow he must find Sarah and deliver her to safety, if she was still alive. He kept reassuring himself she was still alive, that it was not too late.

Davy placed his right hand on the wall beside the crematorium and bowed his head. The outer enamel jacket of the machine was warm, but not uncomfortably so.

"Goodbye, my friend. I have loved you as a brother. Indeed, you have been closer than a brother. I grieve for you; a deep, deep grieving, more than my soul can bear. I will miss you, my friend. Part of my heart has been torn asunder, ripped from my breast. You now belong to the ages. I know you were not a believer, but you were a better man than many who call themselves Christian. May Yahweh, the great giver of life, deal with you from his great compassion and grace."

Davy wasn't sure how long he had stared in a trance, but he immediately transitioned his purpose from Travis to Sarah. His face was steel as he hurried back to his apartment, to his own personal computer to check his e-mail. There was a reply from Travis. "I am doing well. Thanks for asking. Travis."

Now, Davy's mind was spinning. *If Travis was doing well, who was that on the steel gurney? Why was the reply so brief and curt? That doesn't seem like Travis.* He pulled up Sarah's reply. "All is going well. Having a great time. Sarah. P.S. Throw down your hair."

It was every bit as brief and curt as Travis's. But the thing that really troubled him was her response to Rapunzel, Rapunzel; *throw down your hair? That wasn't right. What happened to throw down your rabbit? What if someone else is writing the replies*, he wondered. Praying he was not too late, Davy ran from the room, down the stairs, across the large expanse of the cathedral hall and up the other stairs, into Emeralds office. He slid into Emerald's chair, reached his hand under the desk and fished for the key. Finding it, he quickly unlocked the desk and began to search the drawers, looking for something, anything that might give him a clue to Sarah's location.

In the third drawer he found a black ledger book wrapped with a large red rubber band. He removed the band and began searching from the front backwards. The book was a bounty of information, personal business such as would never show up on other corporate ledgers. He searched until he came to an entry marked Sarah, $10,000/Fuerzo de los Ponderosas/The Red Garter/ Guantario, Mexico.

Davy knew about the Fuerzo de los Ponderosas from his many hours playing with Cousin Carlos in the town of Escondero just ten miles beyond Guantario. He had heard many stories about this evil arm of the Columbia drug cartel, men who were noted for their brutality, men who were cut-throat in their dealings, their vicious deeds legendary. As children Davy and Carlos had played games of constable and Fuerzo los Poderosos, which had upset his aunt considerably.

She insisted they identify themselves as constables and banditos. "Those people are too evil," she scolded. But, when they were in their favorite hiding place, safely away from the oversight of his mother, Carlos told him tales he had heard of some of the terrible things they were reported to have done. Stories that made chills run up and down Davy's spine.

Finishing his search of the ledger and the rest of the desk, he found no other references to Sarah. This was the only lead he had to work on; therefore, he would go to Guantario. He was acquainted with Guantario. Take Highway 35 from San Antonio to Laredo and then follow the less traveled two-lane highway about fifteen miles into Mexico. It was a town with a population of sixty thousand.

He had been there in his youth many a summer, passing through to visit Carlos. Davy's mind thought back to the many precious moments he and Harold had spent with Carlos in a small crowded house filled with children. It was there that Davy had learned the Spanish language, so much so he spoke fluently with the local inhabitants. Davy went to the wooden chest that contained one million dollars. He pulled out ten thousand dollars worth of bills. Stuffing some money in his pockets and some in a sack, he reasoned that should be more than enough for any emergency.

Davy returned to his apartment once more to retrieve his wallet he kept hidden on a shelf in his walk-in closet. He was startled when he opened the door to see a large black sinister looking snake coiled on the floor with his head raised several feet in an aggressive stance. Davy was gripped with fear and slammed the door shut.

He was no expert on snakes, but it looked remarkably like a black mamba he had seen on an animal show on television. Black mambas, he knew, were deadly poisonous, aggressive, mean tempered, and exceedingly quick. He felt reasonably sure the snake could not get through the slim crack under the door, but that gave him scant comfort. How did the thing get in the closet? That just didn't make sense. And what was it doing in the mansion in the first place?

Davy rushed to the lounge where he retrieved from the wall one of the two swords that crossed the family ancient crest. Davy then went to the broom closet. He knew he would need a broom to confuse and distract the snake while he killed it with the sword. The snake might be too fast without a distraction. Sweat was beading on his brow as he turned the closet doorknob with his left hand, the hand that held the broom, and he held the sword ready for action in his right hand. He quickly jerked the door open, his adrenals pumping full speed.

To Davy's amazement, there was no snake visible. He slowly and cautiously edged into the closet, looking down and all around, even overhead, expecting a sudden attack at any moment. Using the sword, he slid the clothes draped on hangers apart while holding the broom in a defensive position. A snake that large would not be able to hide.

Carefully, he slid the hangers of clothes on the bar, first on one side and then the other. He found it hard to believe the snake wasn't there. He saw no cracks or holes that would allow the serpent to enter or leave. He preferred to face the reptile, kill it and know it was dead, rather than worry about a surprise attack later. He wondered if he was imagining things. He grabbed his wallet and backed out of the closet while on full alert. He was relieved after he slammed the door shut, but his heart was racing and he was greatly unnerved.

Davy went immediately down to the kitchen and pulled a limo ignition key from the key cabinet that hung on the door in the kitchen pantry. He hurried outside through the front doors and out to the cars in waiting, grateful to be out of the house, eager to be away from the snake. Suddenly he wondered at the possibility of a snake within the car. Could it be, even now, under his seat? Davy knew that didn't make any sense, but then again, it didn't make sense seeing a snake in his closet.

As he drove down the lane, he wondered if anyone would try to stop him at the gate. He reassured himself with the thought no one was aware of what he knew, so there was no reason for anyone to be suspicious. In any event, he would soon find out if he was free to leave.

17

FLEEING THE WRATH OF NIMROD
(Chapter 3: The Mythology of Nimrod)

Terah was a wise and prudent man, so he sent his wife and son to live with the grandfather of his grandfather, Eber, who was a holy man of old. Abram lived with Eber until he was fifty years of age, and Eber taught him all the ways of the ancients that were right and true.

At that time, Abram said, "I wish to visit my father whom I have never seen for I hear he is a great man and have heard much of him from my grandfather."

"Ah," said Eber. "That would be good adventure and the desire to see your father is only natural, but such adventure could be dangerous."

"And have you not taught me Godly wisdom and courage?"

So he left Eber and traveled to Ur, to the court of his father who gladly received him. Terah embraced Abram and said, "My son, my son, now is my heart glad and I have at long last seen my son who is flesh of my flesh and shall be my heir."

His mother, who had returned to her husband long ago, cried.

The men kissed each other upon the cheek and were exceedingly glad. They spent the day together sharing many stories that had happened since they parted. Terah introduced him to his chief men, but he kept the name of Abram secret and called him Shavuot lest Nimrod should discover his son. Abram's countenance was such that all the court admired him. They talked all the day long and shared heart to heart. But when Abram saw his father bow down before Moloch and the other eleven gods of stone about the great hall, he was indignant and asked, "Father why do you worship gods of stone that are made by man's hands?"

"Do you not know? These are our gods who created the earth and all things therein, including you and me, and all this from nothing. These are the gods that give Nimrod great power and also Terah his power. All that I own and all that I am I owe to these gods."

The next day, Abram had his mother make a pot of venison stew for which she was famous, and he took the stew and set it before Moloch, but at the end of the day Moloch had eaten none of the stew. Some chortled at Abram's deed, but Terah was not amused. He considered it an embarrassment.

The following day, Abram had his mother make him three pots of venison stew and set them before Moloch. Again, people chortled, and again Terah was not amused, but he left to look after his daily business. While he was gone, Abram took a large hammer and smashed the statues, all the statues except for Moloch, and he placed the large hammer in Moloch's hands. In all this, no one saw what Abram did because he drove everyone out and shut the great doors to the hall before he destroyed the stone gods.

When Terah returned and heard what Abram did and saw the smashed gods, he was angry and said, "My son, what is this treachery you have done to me and why have you destroyed my gods? Why do you bring dishonor upon my head and offend the gods, my precious gods? These are those which have created me and all the earth, even from nothing he has created us, and he gives me great power. You would offend the gods that give me even my very breath?"

Then Abram said, "I did not smash the gods of stone."

Terah's face was red and the veins stood out on his neck and he said, "But I know you did, for though no one saw you, they heard you smash the gods, and you alone were in there, so again I ask, why have you dealt treacherously with me, your father?"

"I tell you I did not. I took the venison stew and set it before Moloch as I did the day before, only I took three tubs instead of one, and set all three before him. I thought perhaps I had offended him the day prior by not bringing enough for the great god Moloch. And then I thought perhaps he was timid, so I closed the great doors so he could eat in privacy. I had no sooner done so then the other eleven gods, the lesser gods, reached out to help themselves to the stew I had provided for Moloch, and he became angry. He created a large hammer out of nothing and began to smash the other gods in his wrath."

At these words, Terah was even angrier. "Why do you lie to your father, the great warrior and general? Moloch cannot create something from nothing because he is a statue made of stone. Neither can he break the other gods because he is made of stone and cannot move. Therefore, I know that you and you alone must have broken the gods and placed the hammer in Moloch's hands because you and you alone were in the great hall."

Then said Abram, "You have spoken great wisdom; by your own words I answer you. If the gods are made of stone and if they are made with the hands of men, then they are not able to move or do anything, let alone create all of life from nothing, nor can he give you any power at all, let alone great power. How can he give you breath when he can't even breathe himself?"

But Terah did not appreciate Abram's wisdom and was angry. Terah would have killed Abram except for intervention by Abram's mother. He was also fearful, because he thought now is Abram making his move to oppose Nimrod. Nimrod's anger will be kindled against me, and he will throw me into the fires, for these are the fires he keeps burning day and night to consume his enemies, even before a great assembly of the people who must witness the destiny of those who betray the great Nimrod. I must confess to my benefactor before he hears the matter from others.

Abram fled and left the land of his father because he knew of his father's anger and of his fear. Terah straightway went to Nimrod and confessed all. "My god and king, I have sinned against heaven and against you," and Terah told him all that had transpired. He said, "I throw myself upon your mercy. I am not worthy to live, and if it is your will to take my life, then so be it, for I have failed the great Nimrod."

But Nimrod did not wish to lose his most brilliant general and said, "The great Nimrod will have mercy upon you. I know you did not do this thing of your own volition, but rather someone influenced you to do such a thing. Tell me then, who caused you to do this great evil and you shall live."

"It is true, my Lord. There was one who did influence me and that was my oldest son Haran, begotten to me by a servant maiden, and he whispered in my ear and enticed me that I brought one of my sons of my harem to you that was not Abram."

Nimrod took hold of Terah's son Haran, by his servant maid, and his loins turned to water and he soiled himself. Nimrod had him thrown into the fires, flames lapped about the man and reduced him quickly to a cinder and the people smelt the stench of burnt human flesh, but Terah was saved and served his master faithfully after that time. All the people were afraid and none dared cross Nimrod in any manner because the stench stayed in their nostrils for months and in their memories for years. Nimrod sought after Abram to destroy him, but the earth swallowed him and hid him in Canaan, so Abram lived in peace and prosperity.

18
A QUEST OF LOVE

Davy's breath was caught up short when he punched the gate code into the dashboard keyboard as he expected armed guards to come running up at any moment. However, he experienced no interference when he drove through the gates. Leaving Emerald Estate, his only life focus was traveling to Guantario and finding Sarah.

On the Loop, he passed a Vacation Bible School in a subdivision. Children ran carefree on the playground, playing their silly games, making crafts and learning Bible stories. He remembered attending Vacation Bible School as a youngster, singing new songs, cutting and pasting in crafts, being guided through the daily routine by adult instructors, absorbed in a child's innocent world.

Housewives busied themselves in yard-work and thought ahead to their afternoon bridge club meeting or televised soap opera. No one was aware of, let alone concerned about, the trauma Davy faced. He thought, *They don't have a clue; they are unaware of the great danger that lurks in their very midst. They are unaware of great evil right under their nose, the slow but sure corrosion of their way of life. They are in the process of losing their freedom and becoming enslaved.* He also thought of what Emerald had said, "They are fools, they are all fools", but Davy told himself, *They are not fools, they are just ignorant. They have no way of knowing. They are victims, just like I am; only they don't know it yet.*

As he drove down Highway 35, his mind was in turmoil and he had stomach spasms. He wondered what the chances were she was even there. He had heard Marti on the phone to London ordering a shipment of this or that sent from Glasgow to Buenos Ares, and the commodity ordered would never go through London, or even near. So what guarantee was there that even though he had a location in Mexico, she would even be there, or had ever been there? But that was his only hope, all he had to go on. He refused to consider she might not be there. He refused to believe she might even be like... he shuddered... well, like Travis. His location in Mexico was the only thing in the entire world he had to hold on to. Therefore, he would go.

Telling himself not to worry was of no help whatsoever. *If she is not alive,* he vowed, *there will be revenge. God have mercy on Emerald if she is dead.* Davy felt rage; he felt defiled. The thought of vengeance was new to him, something he never learned from his mother or father. *Nevertheless,* he repeated, *there will be revenge. And if she is alive-Yahweh let her be alive-what are my chances of finding and rescuing her?* It was possible that neither one would get out alive. It didn't matter, he had to try. If he couldn't rescue her, then what reason did he have to go on? He would gladly trade his life for hers. She had so much more to offer the world than he did. He kept appealing to Yahweh for assistance, for reassurance, for compassion, for mercy.

At last, he saw a sign proclaiming Laredo five miles ahead. He then saw a road ahead that left the highway on the right, the old highway, long untraveled except for a few local vehicles, ending at the edge of the Rio Grande River. The old bridge was torn down years ago, but the concrete pillars rose like silent witnesses to the past. Close to the river was a large machine shed, still used some by the county highway department to store various pieces of road equipment.

Davy remembered the old road and the shed fondly. He and some school buddies had driven the road, sat on the concrete abutment that had once been a part of the bridge, drank beer, tossed rocks into the river, and talked about the things high school boys talk about: their problems in school, their difficulties with parents, their post graduation plans and their problems with girls. Randy, as usual, had boasted of his dating prowess. Coming as it did close to graduation, it seemed like a rite of passage.

The old shed was just as he last remembered it, only now it was mostly empty. He snaked the black limo around several pieces of equipment toward the back of the shed so it was well-hidden. A black limo visibly parked in a county highway shed was sure to arouse unneeded attention. Davy wondered if the limo had a tracking device. He reassured himself with the thought no one had any reason to be suspicious or looking for him until the next day. He wasn't sure that would be enough time, but he couldn't worry about that now.

Davy walked up river until he came to the concrete spillway and began to walk carefully across. Downstream he saw a Hispanic wading in the river on the Mexican side casting his net for fish, trying to feed his family. The water looked cool and he knew it was deep on the States side. He was grateful to have a concrete path across the river to Sarah.

On the other side he climbed the bank and started walking the dirt road that followed the river, a road he was sure would lead him back to the highway on the Mexican side. Less than a hundred feet from where he crossed the river, he came to an isolated humble adobe with a green pickup truck sitting in the yard. As Davy crossed the yard toward the house, a friendly Mexican came out the front door, grinning broadly.

"Buenos Dios, Amigo," said the man.

Davy's Spanish was not perfect, but more than adequate for his purposes.

"Buenos Dios back at you, Amigo." Davy grinned at the man with his remarkably charming smile. "The pickup, does she run good?"

"Si, she runs very good."

"I'd like to use it, how much money, American dollars?"

"Sweet Maria, she's not for sale." He grinned widely, a gold tooth glistening in the sun. "She's banged up a little, but we had some good times together."

"Look, I don't want to buy it, just rent it. How does three thousand sound?"

"Three thousand, American dollars? That's more than she's worth. I'd gladly sell her for three thousand dollars. That's more than enough." He grinned again. "Three thousand dollars and I'd be one happy hombre."

"I don't want to buy it, just rent it. I should be able to bring it back when I'm done, but if not, you're still happy. Okay?"

"Si amigo, I'm happy already." He grinned extra broadly, handed the key to Davy and wrote a receipt Davy requested in case he was stopped by local authorities.

Davy was pleased as he drove the dirt road at having acquired a vehicle so quickly. *So far, so good,* he thought as he drove. The sky was sunny and blue with a high ceiling and a soft breeze flowed through the window. *It's a beautiful day he thought to himself, damned shame I can't enjoy it. What else can go wrong? Beautiful days are for when good things happen, when all is right with the world.* He wondered if he would ever again enjoy a beautiful day, any day, ever.

The truck ran well, and for that he was grateful. He thought of the many summer days as a child he had spent with his cousin just seven miles beyond Guantario in the village of Escondero. He longed for the days when he and Harold had roamed the hills in Arkansas. Those were the good times, when all was right with the world, when he and his cousins roamed free. He realized that the best times of his life were behind him now. He hadn't known it at the time, wishing as a youth he could be wealthy like those he saw on television or in the movies. He had been happy then. It's just that he wished his family had more money, so they could enjoy life more. He had been determined to someday make so much money his family could enjoy the good things of life. That was when he had a family.

Davy tried to clear his mind as he knew his quest ahead would require his highest functional potential. *No wonder the mansion was silent and emptied of staff,* he thought. *The silence and absence of staff had been such an obvious contrast with the normal daily activities that took place there. They could afford no unnecessary witnesses. Of course the house was empty.* His mind flashed back as he considered all the activities that had taken place since he arrived there, hoping somehow to make sense of things.

When you hurt so damned much, when your parents and your sister get killed, when your best friend is murdered, when the woman you love... he again shuddered. He wondered if the pain would ever end. Would he ever be able to enjoy life again? How do you ever return to the magic and the joys of youth? How do you put the massive genie of emotional pain back into the bottle? He could not rid himself of the pain in his gut.

The miles passed quickly, but not quickly enough. At last, he saw a sign that indicated Guantario three miles ahead. He would have given up by now, gone off and died somewhere were it not for the thought of Sarah, but, to give up on Sarah, never. He would press on until his last breath. There would be no pain too great. Failing was not an option. Davy remembered Emerald using that very phrase.

Suddenly, a greasy glob splattered on the passenger side of his windshield. *What was that?* Davy turned the windshield wipers on, but that only served to smear the greasy glob, so he quickly turned them off. Looking up through the windshield, he could see high above him buzzards circling in the blue sky, their wings spread like sails, catching a free ride on the strength of the wind currents. They were small in the sky but they formed a sharp silhouette. Fortunately, the smear did not obstruct his driving view. It was only a distraction.

That bastard buzzard, he thought *A bastard benefactor, that's what they all are.*

And then he felt a pull on his steering wheel to the right. Next came a wobbling from the front right tire. Davy was frustrated as he got out surveying the flat tire. Impulsively, he kicked the tire. *Damned, that hurt; that was just stupid.*

He limped for a few minutes trying to work out the pain. *I hope it's not broken. That was just plain stupid.*

No wonder, he thought, as he observed how shiny the tire was. The other three weren't much better, but he was grateful to find a spare in the back of the truck and a jack behind the seat. Twenty minutes later and he was on the road again. He grimaced with pain as he held his right foot to the accelerator.

As he entered town, Davy saw a filling station and pulled in. *Better to have a full tank of gas,* he thought; *never know what kind of crisis might lie ahead.* He added a quart of oil and some air to the tires, and then cleaned all the windows. For a moment he considered having all four tires replaced, but he refused to take the time. Every second was an eternity. Inside, he eyed a modest straw sombrero, and remembering he had not yet eaten today, picked up a drink and a Twinkie. The pain seemed to be subsiding a bit, but he still limped.

Paying the clerk he inquired about The Red Garter. The clerk stared at him over his glasses for a moment and said, "The Fuerzo de los Poderosos, huh?" The clerk hesitated in a moment of thoughtful silence before continuing, "Keep going on the highway just like you're going, and when you come to Main Street, take a right, go about six blocks and take a left on Las Veras. You will see it about one block, on the corner, on the right. You can't miss it."

"Gracias."

"And Amigo, be careful."

"Muchas gracias," said Davy, picking up the sombrero and snacks he had just purchased, sticking the change in his pocket.

He had a feeling of foreboding that was intensified by the clerk's behavior. Davy continued on his way, the drink and Twinkie sitting untouched on the seat beside him. He turned right onto Main Street and then left on Las Veras Street. And there it was, just like the clerk had said it would be, The Red Garter.

The building sat on the intersection of two streets, yellow stucco with a large neon sign showing a sexy woman's leg wearing a red garter. The red garter repeatedly flashed off and on. Three stone steps, well worn by traffic, had an iron railing leading to the porch. The parking lot was sparsely filled. Davy stared at the building, said a quick prayer, and stepped out of his truck. He placed the modest sombrero on his head, steeled himself, and walked to the front door.

Entering as unobtrusive as possible and looking around, he found himself in a large room with a bar on one end and cafeteria tables on the other. Beyond the tables he saw a stage with two scantily clad girls who were grinding on brass poles. On the bar side of the room he saw several round tables, some of which had card games in progress while others were empty. Some of the tables had a modest pile of money sitting in the center, but one table had accumulated a rather sizable sum as the players raised their aggressive bets. Their coarse conversation and loud laughter cut the room like a knife. Sitting at the bar were several customers, each with an attractive girl worming drinks from their marks. He thought the men looked sleazy; Davy felt dirty.

Moseying up to the bar, he waited to be served by the bar maid who was wearing considerable makeup, but too old and heavy to be attractive.

"What will it be stranger?" she inquired in a gravelly voice.

"Just a beer for now."

She popped the cap from the bottle with authority of experience.

"Your girls are attractive, but they look so young. I am surprised at how young they are."

"They have to be," she said. "We receive some very powerful people here, important people. We have to keep them happy. That is our job."

Davy's gaze fell and he stared at the bar top. His normal proclivity for conversation eluded him.

"We get two kinds of customers here," she said; "those who the organization wants to entertain and others who are running away from something, usually from themselves. So, which are you?"

It was as much a statement as a question, so Davy felt no inclination to respond. He felt disgusted and wondered about the sordid stories the girls might have to tell, the sad stories that brought them into such despicable circumstances.

"First time here?" she asked.

"First time I ever had reason to be here."

"Well, enjoy your drink," she placed the beer in front of him. "Let me know if you want some action."

"Not right now." He threw down his money.

"Suit yourself; it doesn't cost anything to look."

He took the bottle in hand, turned around, leaned against the bar and took a couple sips of beer. He watched as a couple of girls entered the bar and began to work customers for drinks. He noticed the girls all wore a plastic smile, lots of lipstick, sensuous perhaps, but flaccid, the smile giving an exterior message without revealing the wearer's inner emotional sentiment. But, none of that mattered to the patrons. Davy was filled with disgust.

Another customer with a girl in hand left through the same door the other two had come through. Davy turned back to the bar deeply troubled. He took a large sip and wondered why he was even here. Even if she had been here, what were the chances she would still be here, or even anywhere close by? She could be anywhere in the world. Was somebody just going to blurt out they knew where Sarah was? He reminded himself this was the only clue he had. He silently vowed he would not leave until he had found her, or had gained pertinent information of some kind. He would not let the trail end here, not now. How could he live with himself if he did?

An hour later, Davy still stood at the bar drinking his third beer. He was overwhelmed with helpless feelings and was gripped with despair and unbearable pain. His brooding demeanor kept the bar maid from attempting conversation with him except to bring him a fresh bottle as her job required.

Davy took another large drink and again turned around, hoping against hope that he might see something, anything. He was astounded to see Sarah. She was leaving through the back door, followed closely behind by a customer. Davy stared in disbelief. Why had he waited so long without checking for her? He was consumed with rage. He would have ran after her, but he knew it would only result in death for the both of them. Even so, it took all the strength he had to restrain himself. Davy felt dirty. He hated himself. He hated Emerald. He hated the world. He was there as her protector, as her rescuer. He had failed her.

Davy felt so helpless and traumatized he wanted to die. He dropped his head into his hands and bit his lip, to the point of drawing blood. Again, he had to resist the impulse to rush to her aid. As much as he agonized, he would have to wait. He didn't know how he could stand the pain of knowing what was going on. But that was such a selfish thought. How much more she must be going through at this very moment. He could not indulge himself in his own misery. *I must be strong for her sake.* He recovered himself and raised his head back up, fighting back the tears. *I must be strong for her sake*, he repeated.

Davy was more vigilant now. He was watching when twenty minutes later her customer left, by himself. Davy stared at the man with anger, intense hatred such as he had never before experienced. He watched as he left the Red Garter. He considered following him and killing him, but he could not abandon Sarah. It was perhaps ten minutes more when he saw her again enter, this time with another girl. They were talking, having no awareness beyond their own conversation. Both wore a somber expression beneath the plastic smiles.

His heart broke at the sight of Sarah. She now had a bruise on the side of her face. The girl beside her was attractive with a nice figure, but clearly quite young which caused him even more sadness.

"How about her, the girl in the yellow dress with red flowers?" he asked.

"Anita?" She stopped wiping the counter."

"No, the other one, in the yellow dress, with flowers."

"That would be Anita," she replied with some annoyance.

Again, Davy was filled with rage, an emotion he fought to control. *They have kidnapped her and sold her as a sex slave. They have stripped her of her dignity. How dare they change her name to Anita and destroy her identity.*

"She is a classy girl, fresh too; that will cost you. Not often we get fresh meat."

Squelching his hostile emotions, he asked calmly, "How much?"

"You have expensive taste. She is too much for you."

"How much?" He was more forceful now.

"Five hundred dollars. You got five hundred dollars?"

Davy peeled out the money in one hundred dollar bills.

"Follow me," she said, rolling her eyes and scooping up the money.

Davy pulled the sombrero low over his forehead and lowered his head. The last thing he wanted was for Sarah to recognize him in surprise and give away he knew her. He knew it would not be good, but, if she did, she did, and he would deal with it the best he could. He wondered why he had not purchased a gun. How foolish.

As they approached the girls, Sarah's countenance immediately darkened and she looked at the floor. The younger girl had the look of a scared fawn, one that suddenly realized it had been cornered by a predator. Sarah instinctively and protectively stepped in front of the girl and said, "Here I am, take me."

"Actually, you are the one he wants," said the woman. "Anita, you have a friend. Show him a good time."

Sara said in a low voice, "Follow me," She turned, leading Davy through the door in the back of the room, still gazing at the floor.

"Have fun, kids," the lady called after them.

The young girl had shrunk back into the woodwork.

Davy followed her down a long hall and through one of many doors that lined the hall, his eyes fastened on her, longing to reach out and touch her. She seemed so vulnerable. The room was small, had a freshly made bed on one side, and the walls held several large sensuous pictures of women in various stages of undress and in seductive positions.

Sarah stopped at the center of the room with her back still turned toward Davy, and said softly, "You may take off my blouse, if you wish." She spoke in almost a whisper.

Davy stood there, unsure of what he should say, so they both stood for ten seconds or more, waiting in tortuous silence. He saw her shiver. At last, he said, "Sarah, it's me, Davy."

She temporarily froze, then turning around and seeing it wasn't a hallucination, immediately hugged him about the neck with a desperate hug that was so tight it was on the verge of being painful.

Davy hugged her back, warmly and with all the tender love he could show her. "It's going to be okay. I came for you, to get you out of here." Over and over he kept repeating, "I love you, dearly love you, more than you can imagine. Elohim loves you. God loves you. I love you. You must understand that I love you dearly. I'm going to get you out of here. Everything's going to be okay."

For ten minutes she held him in her tight grip, not saying a word, frozen in his embrace of genuine love, he ministering to her immediate emotional needs. He began to carefully change the purpose of his words, never losing the feeling of tender affection.

"We need to get out of here. Somehow we have to get out. I need for you to loosen your grip. It's important for us to leave as soon as possible."

He took her arms in his hands and began to slowly peel them back. She loosened her grip with the greatest of reluctance. At last, she said, "You are in great danger. They will never let me go. They will kill you if you try to rescue me. You must leave quickly, so go, now. There is no way to get me out of here alive. Go now."

Davy saw the fear in her eyes, the sadness, the hopelessness, and his heart was broken. "Sarah, I'm not leaving here without you. I will die first. And if they do happen to kill me, then know this: you were loved."

Again, her arms gripped Davy and once more he began to assure her. In all of this she showed no emotion. There may come a moment in one's life when the ability to express emotion dies. Davy made an oath to himself that not only would he rescue her, but he would see to it that she was emotionally and spiritually healed, even to her former self. He could not fight back the doubt it might be impossible. He was able, with some effort, to again coax the release of her grip.

"We have to get out of here. It's imperative we leave as quickly as possible. We have to go now. I need you to be strong for me. If you can be strong for a little while, we have a good chance to get out of here. I need you to be strong."

"There is only one way we can get out. Do you have a car?"

"I have a truck, a pickup truck."

"Then you leave first. On the alley behind the building is a dumpster. Wait for me there. It is part of our job to empty the waste baskets, keep the trash hauled out. Nobody is motivated to do it, so there is always trash to take out. I will bring some out then jump into the pickup. But that is the easy part. They will come, they always come. They will hurt me if they find us, hurt me badly, in front of the other girls. They always make an example. We are chained by our fears. They will kill you. I am afraid."

"Fears be damned. I'm getting us both out of here. I will not leave without you."

"Please be careful. And may God have mercy."

"Now is not the time to be careful. Now is the time for boldness and for wisdom, great wisdom." He grabbed her chin in his hands and said, "I need you to be brave. Can you do that for me?"

She nodded without saying a word.

"Good. And now would be a good time to say a prayer."

"I will. I have prayed every day. I have been determined to have faith and hope, but there comes a point when even hope can die. I will pray. Go quickly now, Davy, and God speed."

"Good girl. If ever God hears prayer, this would be a perfect time for him to do it now." He smiled into her face and then he was gone.

Davy pulled the green pickup truck beside the dumpster and waited for what seemed an eternity. His watch showed at least twenty minutes and he was starting to worry. His heart started to pound, perhaps he would never see her again, but suddenly, Sarah came around the corner carrying two large black trash bags filled to capacity. She tossed them into the dumpster, walked quickly but discreetly to the passenger's side and climbed in, Davy having already opened the door to receive her.

She slammed it shut, and he instructed her to duck down so she couldn't be seen. He knew time was of the essence, so he left as quickly as he could move the old truck without drawing attention. He retraced the route he had taken toward the Red Garter, and had turned left onto the highway before either of them spoke. Sarah sat upright in the seat.

It was Sarah who broke the silence. "Hardly anyone ever tries to escape; they are afraid to try. The men always return rather quickly with the runaway girl. The first time they bring a girl back, they hurt her badly, in front of the other girls of course, being careful not to do visible damage. They slap her around; sometimes they break some bones. They place a plastic bag over her face so they can't breathe until she passes out. They do this repeatedly. Each time she believes this will be the time she dies. They put her tied and gagged in a dark hole in the ground for three days without food or water."

Davy was at a loss for words. What could he say?

"The second time a girl tries to escape they torture her slowly, burn with cigarettes, scalding water, until she dies. They know how to destroy a person's will, her desire to live. I have not seen it myself, but it's horrible to hear the girls tell about it. They all live in fear. It's the fear that keeps them chained. The girls have lost all hope of ever escaping. There is nothing worse than having no hope. May God have mercy they don't bring us back. It is better for us to die." Fear radiated from her face and her voice was desperate.

Davy reached over and squeezed her hand reassuringly. "We're going to be okay, I know we are. I can feel it. We're going to make it. I promise you that. There's something else I want you to know. You are loved, really and truly loved for the beautiful person you are."

She squeezed his hand in response, but her face was still a mask. "Scarlet is gone," she said soberly.

"I'm so sorry. What happened to her?"

"I don't know for sure. They took her from me as soon as I got there. The girls said they probably used her to bait their fighting dogs. That is such a terrible thing to happen to a dog, a sweet dog like Scarlet. Poor Scarlet."

"I am sorry, so terribly sorry." His words, he knew, were not adequate.

That was the last word spoken for several miles. Davy was torn between two practical emotions; one was the desire to get the hell out of there as fast as possible, to cross the Rio Grande before anyone knew they were gone and hoped the threat would end there. The other emotion was the fear of being stopped by a highway constable. Hopefully, he wouldn't even see a patrol car on this lightly used two-way highway, but who knew when one might appear? Davy split the difference, driving over the speed limit, but hopefully not so fast he would get stopped, which was a pretty good plan, except he kept unconsciously increasing his speed at times. He tried to keep his eyes open for patrol cars.

They were about five miles from their turnoff point, the dirt road that led to their river crossing, when he suddenly slowed down, realizing too late that the car cresting the hill had a set of lights on top. Perhaps, he thought, his speed was low enough it would not be a problem. Perhaps he had slowed down quickly enough. Perhaps the radar was not turned on, even if the car had radar. Perhaps the officer had more important business than stopping a car that wasn't going all that fast over the limit.

His heart fell as he saw in his review mirror the car hit its brake lights, slow down, make a small turn, back up, swing back into the lane behind Davy, and his lights began to flash. Sarah gave Davy a look of desperation. He considered for a moment hitting the gas pedal and making a run for it, but he knew it would be futile, attempting to outrun a patrol car in that old pickup. No, it was better to take his chances and risk the hand of fate rather than be hauled into jail where they would certainly be discovered. He pulled over and stopped. His big concern was the law would think he had stolen the truck, and there was the potential they could still wind up in a Mexican jail. He knew how corrupt authorities could be.

He pulled his wallet as the patrol car stopped behind him. Davy removed his license, wrapped five one-hundred dollar bills around it and the rental receipt for the truck folded around the outside. As the officer approached his window, slow and intimidating, he said, "You were speeding, Gringo, very fast." Davy handed him the license pack. The officer silently unfolded them, looked at the bills, the license, and then read the receipt. The officer broke with a wide grin, returned two of the three items and said in broken English, "You were going a little fast. No problem. Slow down, but don't let it happen again. Have a nice day, Amigo."

Davy responded with, "Muchas gracias, muchas gracias, muchas gracias," with an emphatic display of appreciation.

After the officer entered his car, turned around, and headed the other way, Davy and Sarah could breathe again. He held his truck to the speed limit from thereon. He could not risk being stopped again. Their journey to the turnoff road seemed like an eternity. They were less than one mile from that destination when Davy saw in the distance of his rear-view mirror a patrol car appear over the hill at a high rate of speed, red lights flashing. He pushed the accelerator to the floor. He was going for broke this time. The siren began to wail.

"They know you are gone. We have to make it all the way to the river. He won't dare cross the border into Texas."

Sarah cupped her hands to her mouth. Any words she might have spoken stuck in her throat. When Davy turned off onto the dirt road, his tires leaving black skid marks on the highway and throwing a cloud of dust as the tires hit the dirt road, he almost lost control of the pickup. He knew it was about a quarter mile to the crossing and the patrol car was quickly gaining. It was now a race to the border, a race for their lives. Davy hoped the huge dust cloud his truck was leaving behind would slow the patrol car down a bit. The owner of the truck curiously emerged from his house to investigate the commotion.

The truck skidded to a stop not far from the river bank. Davy and Sarah made a dash for the concrete spillway, their path of escape across the river. They crossed as rapidly as possible, Sarah in front and Davy close behind. She almost lost her balance once, but Davy quickly grabbed her blouse and stabilized her, keeping her from falling into the waters below. They reached the far bank as the patrol car skidded to a stop. The officer pulled his gun and fired four shots in their direction and then followed in pursuit across the river, across the spillway.

Davy and Sarah ran to the highway shed, raced to the car, and quickly got in. Davy's hand was shaking as he, with some difficulty, inserted the key. He backed his car around equipment, out of the shed, and had just shifted into drive when the officer rounded the back corner of the shed, not twenty feet away. The limo threw dirt and gravel as Davy hit the accelerator. The officer shielded his face with his free arm and then emptied his gun into the rear window, confident that would end the chase. He was totally perplexed when the rear window stayed intact.

Soon, they were back on the highway, headed north. Davy and Sarah were appreciative of their escape, for they had overcome tremendous obstacles. Perhaps they were receiving some kind of spiritual assistance, who knew. But they were still in great danger. They had nowhere to go, no resources or support system, and then there was Emerald and his vast network that could find them no matter where in the world they might go. They were hopeful, but their future looked bleak. Perhaps two runaway kids were not important enough to spend time and resources in pursuit. They were emotionally and physically drained, but for the moment, they were safe. They still had hope. He continued to give Sarah reassurance she was worthy of love.

Somehow, they needed to disappear off the face of the earth. Davy was grateful this had been a part of his studies under Shahiek.

19

THE BABYLONIAN MYSTERY RELIGION
(Chapter 4: The Mythology of Nimrod)

Many years passed and Abram had a grandson, and the grandson became a man, a mighty hunter in his own right. Nimrod was still king and was powerful for those were the times when men lived for many years, even hundreds of years, and the grandson was called The Mighty Red Hunter who is descended from Seth. He was as great a hunter as Nimrod once had been.

Then said the grandson of Abram, "This Nimrod is an exceedingly wicked man and brings a curse upon all of the earth, and Elohim has instructed me to chase after Nimrod and to slay him, and he would give me strength and wisdom." Therefore, he set off after Nimrod.

But Nimrod dreamed a terrible dream of fearful lightening the result of spiritual warfare. He dreamed that a Mighty Red Hunter would come upon him to slay him and he awoke from his dream and he experienced fear for the first time. His heart was pounding such his chest hurt and great drops of sweat ran down from his head and his body so that his bed was drenched. Then all the people wondered at the radical change they saw in Nimrod, for none saw him express fear before. Some said he feared because a spirit had left him, but others said he was so because a spirit had entered him.

Nimrod then fled from the descendant of Seth. Across Asia he chased after him, and across Europe. He continually drew closer. Nimrod had an insane fear which astounded the nations.

Nimrod drew near unto the Shrine of Vati-canikulus, which was another name for Temple of Moloch, and sat on a hill and there were six others. In desperation and in fear he cried out as a calf whose throat is being cut and held onto the image of Vati-canikulus so his pursuer should not kill him, but The Mighty Red Hunter fell violently upon him with his sword and slay him. He cut the body into ten pieces and sent one each to the ten kings who ruled under Nimrod so they should know the same fate awaited them if they continued their evil ways. But Nimrod's phallus he threw into the sea.

When Nimrod's wife, Semiramis, heard what was done, she lamented and was sorely grieved because she loved Nimrod for he was a great and powerful man and a god to the entire world, and she was his goddess. She went to the sea and begged of the sea to return to her the phallus of Nimrod, so Neptune sent a messenger from the deep and the messenger returned the phallus to her from the ocean depth.

She took the phallus to the Shrine of Vati-canikulus and she built there a large obelisk that was an image of Nimrod's phallus. Semiramis caressed the obelisk and kissed it and the phallus she held in her hand came to life through the power of the gods and she conceived and bore a child. She then buried the phallus before the obelisk along with the ten pieces of his body she had retrieved. That great shrine had been built in the honor of the god Moloch, which was also a name of the god of this world. The body of Nimrod was buried at the shrine of the god he worshiped.

Semiramis said, "The child I carry is the child of Nimrod, and it is his returned spirit so Nimrod himself shall be reborn and he is a great god, the greatest god above all others. It is his son, but also the reincarnation of Nimrod returned in the flesh." She called her newborn son Osiris, Horace, Hercules, Thor, Zeus and many other names that are passed down among many nations even to this day. Some of her names were Lilith, Isis, Dianna, Aphrodite, Venus, Astarte, and Ishtar. Easter Island was named after her, and they raised many stone idols there for the glory of Semiramis and Nimrod because it was a vortex of spiritual activity. Also, the great cities of Samaria and Nineveh were named after Semiramis.

Now, Semiramis was cunning and conniving and she thirsted for power and glory, so she declared herself the queen of heaven, the consort of the great god Nimrod, even the great god of the heavens. She made Nimrod god over all gods and she made herself equal unto him, and she commanded all the people to worship them in their great temples. Nimrod became the great sun god and she the great moon god, and they were gods above all the other gods, even down to the end of days, so men searched the heavens to answer the great mysteries of life. Even to this day, the names of many mythological gods refer to Nimrod and

Semiramis, and many religions worship them still. The sun god and the moon god still rule the nations.

Semiramis was a beautiful woman, even into her old age. Some claimed she was the most beautiful woman who ever lived. She was Nimrod's mother, but she poisoned her husband, and she seduced Nimrod, and married him. As Nimrod's mother and as his wife she corrupted him even more than his natural inclination. She exploited his evil for her own glory. When her child was delivered, the one she claimed conceived by Nimrod, she called him Osiris. When he came to age, she seduced him and married him also. Osiris was therefore her husband, her son, and her grandson; he was all of these to her. Then Semiramis seduced the kings of the earth so she might exert power over them and manipulate them shamefully, and she called her son god, but said he was really Nimrod reborn.

She set up idols and temples. The priestesses serviced the men who worshipped there. Eggs and rabbits were incorporated in their fertility rites. Many children were born to the temple prostitutes, and they had no place for them. They sacrificed the abundance of babies in temple worship to their gods. The idols of Moloch were heated to cherry red and the babies were placed on his hands. They were then devoured into his fiery stomach. Their bones were retrieved and placed into pottery and plastered within the walls of the temples, for they believed the sacrifice of innocents hallowed their temples and pleased their gods.

Some of the prettiest girl babies were kept to become future priestesses for the temple worship. The people drank and made merry. Semiramis had all the power of Nimrod and more. Her spirit would return many years later in such women as Jezebel, Cleopatra, Evita Peron, and many others including Antoinette, wife of Emerald. They set up idols in groves and covered the woods with holly and gold. The groves they called Holly Woods.

Then Semiramis said, "It is the great commandment, from this time forth all of the kings of the earth shall be descended from Nimrod and there shall be no king who does not carry his blood. Some who carry Nimrod's blood will fall out of the ruling class and will marry with the common people, and someday such a one may lead a revolt and shall secure a ruler-ship. If he is worthy and if he carries Nimrod's blood, then it will be well and the ruling class of kings and gods will accept him, but if he is not worthy or if one carries not the blood of Nimrod, then all the kings of the earth shall rise up together to destroy the usurper who carries not Nimrods' blood."

So it has been done to this very day, even as happened to Napoleon and many others who would be kings, but were cast down by the descendents of Nimrod. The kings of the earth, therefore, were never from the nations ruled, but were always strangers who ruled over them, descended from Nimrod, and they ruled all the earth and enslaved all the people who did not carry Nimrod's blood. Some who carried Nimrod's blood became great kings and others who fell from the ruling class became lords of thievery and piracy and organized crime, while others became Communists. Others became great religious leaders, it was their nature to dominate others and to create much dissension.

Semiramis called a vernerable council of the kings and queens: their top advisers, great generals, prominent priest and priestess, the College of Magicians and The Masters of the Great White Lodge, all from around the world. After a grand banquet she stood and addressed her subjects. "My children, my children, listen to me. I am Lilith, even the great Lilith. The System is God. The System is always God. As God's holy instrument on earth, I am The System. Whoever defies The System, I tell you, whoever defies The System shall be thrown into the eternal fires of Nimrod and their souls shall suffer there forever. Those who are most loyal to The System shall become the anointed of The System. The System is always God and Nimrod and I are always The System."

The people responded as one, having been properly cued, "Holy are Nimrod and Semiramis. Holy is The System."

She began her incantation.

> Queen of heaven, Queen of hell,
> Horned Hunter of the night.
> Lend your power unto the spell
> Work my will by magic rite.*

The people responded in unison, "Holy are Nimrod and Semiramis."

"I pray the spirits; come now Baal, Zeus, and Thor. Come now Marduk, Apollo, Neptune and Beelzebub, Quetzalcoatl, even Gilgamesh. Let the spirit of Nimrod be impregnated upon the earth, government without end. Let the Spirit of Nimrod rule forever without end.

The people said, "Come Avatar, come Great Spirit of Avatar."

A dozen large drums of animal skins and hollowed stumps kept a rhythmic beat that reverberated to the inward parts of their being. The audience lifted their arms and hands and swayed and danced to the music as those who are spirit possessed.

In a room beside the banquet hall, six girls five years of age were ushered onto a stage. They were dressed as little angels and were all giggles and happy they had been chosen of the temple children to meet Nimrod in person. Their joy was quickly turned to horror as the priests fell on them with knives and slit their throats. They were hung upside down with hooks in their heels so their blood could be collected in golden vessels. The blood was then mixed one part to nine parts wine and stirred with incantations by the priests.

The potion was delivered in golden goblets to the participants and Semiramis lifted her golden chalice and proclaimed, "We worship thee almighty Nimrod. Come Avatar."

"The people responded, "Holy is Nimrod. Come Avatar."

The incantations continued until the potion of wine and blood was gone, the group engaged in a great sexual religious orgy. More young angels, in their early teens, were brought into the grand hall to satisfy the lust of the men and they were violently abused. Some died later. Late into the night most of the guest passed out in a drunken stupor from wine and power.

The next day, Semiramis had Terah killed because he did not carry Nimrod's blood; his head was bashed in and he was cast into the fires, so he died after the manner of his sons before him, for he had delivered his sons deceitfully to Nimrod. All the kings of the earth who carried not the blood of Nimrod were also eliminated.

The kings and queens of the earth then intermarried to insure the blood of Nimrod would pass from generation to generation in purity, without becoming contaminated with common blood and so a seed of Nimrod would always sit on the seats of world power. They called themselves children of the gods and they called themselves Aryans. But eventually, the Throne of Nimrod became lost because of the deceit and contrivance of evil men, but Nimrod's sons continued to rule all the nations.

The Throne of Nimrod was recovered by the Genie, who were an elite core of the Magi who had the spirits of demons called Genie, and they had been the personal body guards of Nimrod. They continued to serve Semiramis and they in time became worshiped as great spirits by the Persians, the Arabians, and even the Knight Templar. They served the Church during the Crusades, but only because they wished to control and to take over the church in the full power of the government of Nimrod, but they hid the Throne of Nimrod from the Church.

When the Church found out what the Knight Templar intended, then King Phillip had them all executed, as many as he was able, so the remaining Knight Templar went into hiding and eventually became the Illuminati. It is their purpose to ensure, even to this day, that the seed of Nimrod rules the world. It was the Knight Templar who hid the Throne of Nimrod in the Money Pit against the day of the reincarnation of Nimrod when the Spirit of Nimrod should rise up to reclaim his world throne.

The government of Nimrod never left. It has always operated in stealth in every country and every religion awaiting the day when it should again rule in absolute power and regain its rightful position, and the kingdom of Nimrod in the latter days would be more glorious than the original, a time when the streets approaching the palace of world power would be all paved in gold.

All the kings of the earth, then, were related and they all descended from Nimrod. The kings considered themselves to be gods and demanded to be appropriately worshiped, and they were also priests unto the people, so that the kings imposed the Babylonian Mystery Religion upon all the nations, even unto this time, but always in stealth. This was all prophesied by sages of old.

It was the Spirit of Nimrod, then, who would raise up a man of Emerald when the time was fulfilled, and the Spirit of Nimrod should once again rule the world in majesty and in glory with an iron fist.

---

* Incantation from Man, Myth and Magic published by Marshall Cavendish Corporation.

20
A BITTER DISAPPOINTMENT

As they headed north, Davy was careful to set the cruise control on the speed limit, not one mile over. The last thing he wanted was to be stopped by a Texas Ranger. They were feeling a little more positive about their situation, but they both understood the magnitude of obstacles that still confronted them like some ominous dark storm shadow that threatened to obliterate their future. Davy's mind was working furiously to come up with a plan. He wondered how intrusive exactly was Emerald's network of control and information. Did it really reach down into local levels as he had indicated? Maybe he was dishonest about that too.

Since crossing the river and gaining access to the highway, they had begun to converse a little more than they had while feeling the grip of fear in Mexico. The Fuerzo los Poderosos were vicious and evil people who delighted in their decadence. They would as soon kill a man as look at him, just for sport; this Davy knew. For whatever faults Emerald might have, he did seem to have some redeeming qualities, and he did appear to be a decent person on some levels, even if wildly misguided in other areas.

Surely he would not be as vicious, as vindictive as the Fuerzo los Poderosos were. Perhaps he would not even pursue them. What were two young people to a man of such wealth? He would not miss them; he had more important business to attend. Wouldn't that make more sense? Besides, Emerald could always find other young men as victims to supply his needs for heart replacements. Davy felt guilty with such a thought, so he quickly dismissed it from his mind. He was feeling much better about their chances of getting away now. If he used his head, perhaps things could turn out all right after all.

As they traveled, he remembered how he had considered the day to be such a nice day as he had traveled toward Escondero, but how he was unable to enjoy it. But, now he considered the possibility he could salvage some of the beauty of the day, in spite of the great evil that had gone before. Now, they could see the prospect of hope. Perhaps he and Sarah might yet have a good life together. Perhaps they might yet... but Davy was too exhausted to continue. He would need all his energy to deal with the reality of the moment.

Ahead on the four lane highway, in the left lane coming toward them, Davy saw a car on the shoulder of the road, a black one, and beyond the car he could see the flashing lights of a patrol car. He was grateful it was someone else being stopped, not him. Not that he wished ill on anyone, it's only that the worst they had to deal with was a ticket; whereas if he and Sarah were stopped it could mean... he could not finish the thought. His mouth felt dry.

The officer was returning to his car and turned the flashing lights off as they passed. Davy had a foreboding feeling when he saw the car that had been pulled over was a black stretch limousine. He watched the progression of events through his rear view mirror. The State Ranger pulled out onto the highway, turned on his flashing lights, and then crossed over the dividing meridian and headed north toward Davy. The flashing car quickly reduced the distance between the two.

Davy turned on his right turn signal and pulled over to the side of the road, once more with a sick feeling in his stomach. Sarah found it difficult to breathe. The sun was just setting, bathing the sky in soft orange and dark purple. Davy was unnerved by the stern face of the officer, though it was partially concealed by the Ranger's wide-brimmed hat and sunglasses, and the fact that his hand rested on his gun holster. The officer walked up to Davy's window and asked for his driver's license, which he quickly produced.

"Was I doing something wrong, officer?"

"Would you step out of the car?"

Davy sensed it would be a huge mistake to even appear to be resisting. When Davy was out, the officer instructed him, "Turn around, spread your legs, and place your hands on the car." His speech was metal hard and he patted Davy down for weapons.

"I don't understand, officer, was I doing something wrong?"

The officer roughly pulled one arm behind his back and slipped on handcuffs. He did the same for the other arm. He led Davy to the police car and placed him in the back seat. He then returned for Sarah, who was beside herself, ordered her out of the car, and similarly placed her in cuffs and led her to the back seat. She said not a word.

"I'd like to know why we're being treated like this. Did we do something wrong?"

The officer started his car, eased onto the highway and turned the flashing lights off.

"How about our rights? Aren't you going to read those to us?"

The officer lifted his radio mike and reported to headquarters, "This is Ranger 212. I've found the Silverstone fugitives on northbound 35."

"This is Ranger Station. Copy that. Congratulations. Be careful; they may be dangerous."

"Will do. Send someone out to pick up the car; it's by the ten mile marker between Bad Luck Ditch and Hope Road. In the process of bringing them in."

"Roger that. Good job. Captain will be pleased. Ten-four."

"Thanks. Ten-four."

On the way back, Davy and Sarah spoke little and what they did came in whispers. They looked at each other often, but words seemed to fail them. As they approached San Antonio, Davy noticed they did not exit on the road that led to the Texas Ranger Station, but he was not about to inquire of their destination. They took the bypass around the city, turned north on 10, off on Beaumont, and then again on Crystal Lane. Stopping before the massive iron gate of Silverstone Estate, the officer reached out the window, pushed a button beside a speaker, and patiently waited until someone triggered the gates to open. Davy surmised this was not the first time the officer had followed this routine.

They drove up the lane and parked at the top of the driveway circle. Davy remembered the first time he had made the trip up the lane and considered how different the trip was this time. Then, he was full of hope. He remembered his early skepticism, brief though that may have been, and how confident he had been about getting out of any difficult situation. He had so much self-confidence at that time. He only had himself to worry about, but now there was Sarah. She was his first obligation. What a difference time can make.

He wondered what thoughts were going through Sarah's mind. He didn't mind whatever evil might happen to him, but he could not bear the thought of anything happening to Sarah. She had suffered enough already. The only information they had shared the last half of the trip was with their eyes, the fear of what might lie ahead and the compassionate love they shared for each other. Davy thought about making a run for it, and he would have done so if it hadn't been for leaving Sarah behind.

Escaping was not an option.

"Okay, everybody out," the Ranger ordered as he opened the door. They walked to the front door, which opened as soon as they approached. All three entered where they were met by Marti who exchanged greetings with the officer, but ignored Davy and Sarah. Two other officers stood behind Marti. The small group was led by Marti through the cathedral room, *the cathedral room that was supposed to have been my spiritual womb,* so Davy reflected on Marti's earlier comment. The cathedral room now felt more like Davy's spiritual tomb. The altar of large rocks now reminded him of a pagan gravestone. He could feel spiritual power emanating from the altar.

They approached Emerald's spiral stairway. Marti started up first followed by Sarah, but Davy suddenly suspected where they were going. He remembered Travis, and instantly firmly planted his feet, refusing to go any further. There was no way he was going into the secret room.

One of the officers pulled his gun and pointed it toward Sarah's temple. "You have about five seconds and I'm going to blow her damned brains out!"

Davy wilted, "No, no, please don't do that. I'll cooperate."

There was much that Sarah did not know-about Travis, the secret room, or the reason Emerald had brought them into his organization. She walked in a stupor. He saw no reason to cause her more distress if it was not necessary, no, not until she had to know.

Davy followed them weakly up the stairs, being shoved by two officers behind. The door to the secret room stood open and they all entered. Davy stared at the two stainless steel gurneys and felt chills go up his back. He didn't say a word, nor could he. He and Sarah were directed to two wooden straight back chairs, solid chairs, sitting back to back, and were instructed to sit down. They were handcuffed to the chairs, one cuff from Davy's right hand, through the chair, and then to Sarah's left hand. Their other hands were similarly cuffed. They had a cuff on each ankle which was shackled to the chair. The three officers were dismissed.

"You sure you don't need our assistance?"

"The chloroform and I can handle it from here. Thanks for the offer." They disappeared down the stairs.

Marti nodded at the two young people. "Welcome home Davy and Sarah, so good to see you. Your arrival is fortuitous as it seems Emerald has rejected his heart transplant. So, you're in the on-deck circle, Davy. You're the next batter up. It turns out you are the one who is going to be the magnificent benefactor. You will be providing a magnificent, strong, young heart for Emerald."

"So, you killed Travis, and for what? For nothing! You wasted the life a good and decent person, one who had so much to offer, so much to give."

"Not wasted. His harvested organs will help others to live. The sacrifice of his life will give life to many. And, that is beside the financial benefits, of course."

"What's he talking about?" asked Sarah, although she suspected the truth.

"Why did you do this to Sarah?" shouted Davy. "What is ten thousand dollars to a man with Emerald's wealth? Why would you do such a vile thing?"

"Actually, it had nothing to do with ten thousand dollars, certainly that is small change to Emerald, although when you are as obsessed with achievement as Emerald is, everything counts on the score board. But, the main reason is building alliances on the world scene. The Fuerzo de los Poderosos is an important power-base, even though most people here in the States have never heard of them. Important people around the world know and fear them though. That translates into power."

"What could such evil people mean to Emerald?"

They have needs which allow Emerald to endear himself to them. They need distribution routes for their drug traffic, routes that are safe and effective. They need arms supplies. They need women, beautiful women. The Fuerzo los Poderosos supply many of Emerald's needs. They have great power. They are the most feared terrorist in the world, and influential people in high places have a dreadful fear of them. That works to Emerald's advantage. And, of course, this business arrangement is lucrative for Emerald, far greater than Sarah's price of sale. Basically, she is a pawn in a much greater game. In games played at this level, people are expendable. You always have to be concerned with the greater good of humanity."

"If you send Sarah back they will kill her! Please don't send her back!" His plea was a piteous wail, and his soul was in anguish.

"Not to worry. I have no intention of sending her back. She has already served our purpose with the Poderosos. I know what they would do to her. They would torture and then kill her. No, that would be inhumane, an absolute waste. It's not like I have no feelings at all. Certainly, we can't let her go free, she knows too much. She will serve humanity better as a donor of organs, as Travis did. We all have to die sometime. There is a very lucrative black market for organs from healthy young people. More importantly, the recipients are powerful men who will be greatly indebted to Emerald."

"I don't believe what I'm hearing."

"We will harvest and sell your organs also, besides the heart which will go to Emerald. He, of course, gets first dibs on that. You are making quite a contribution. It is a magnificent thing you are doing. Your life will be lost, but many will be saved."

"How can you do something like this?" shouted Davy. "How can you think like this? How can anyone be so evil?"

"It comes down to a matter of priorities. Emerald is too vital in the world situation. If he were to die, civilization could fly apart. What you are doing is for the good of the world. It is no different than a soldier who sacrifices his life protecting the ones that he loves, no different than Jesus giving his life for the sins of the world. What you are doing is magnificent. You must accept that. It is your destiny."

"You're sick. You are nothing more than hateful people all wrapped up in yourselves. You are no different than the people you are trying to protect the world from."

"Nothing personal, Davy. The world is divided into lions and lambs. The job of lions is to feed on lambs. That's what they do, that's how they live, and that's who they are. The purpose of lambs is to provide food for the lions. Emerald and I are lions. You are a lamb. You were born to be a lamb. You're whole purpose in life is to provide food for lions. You are either one or the other. That's the way your God made it. That's just the way it is."

"You don't care; you don't even care. You honest to God don't care!"

"He who gives a damn places himself at a great disadvantage. To survive in this world, it is imperative you don't give a damn, that is, if you are going to be a lion, a highly successful lion."

"There is no way I could ever be like you."

"Then that proves my point. You are what you are."

Davy felt anger rising within him, not so much for himself, but for Sarah. She sat with her head slumped in a state of resignation.

Davy voiced his strong objection again. "You can't do this to Sarah! You can't do this to me!"

"Why not? Do you think someone is going to save you? There is no one else on the estate, only us. I am sorry, but no one can help you."

"Emerald has chosen me as his heir, to take over the operation and carry on his work. As Emerald's future replacement, I have every right to give Sarah clemency."

"Oh please."

"You just want me out of the way so you can take it over."

Marti laughed a muffled, thoughtful laugh.

Davy continued, "That's it, you're making sure I don't stand between you and taking over the operation when Emerald dies."

"Okay, number one, all I have to do is ask him for it and it's mine. Number two, I don't want the damned thing. I have all the advantages in my present position without the headaches and risks that go with the job. You couldn't force me to take it, it would be a life of hell. Number three, when you are in that position there is always someone who wants you dead so they can take over. Death walks in the shadow of power. Tyrants are unbelievably paranoid. Emerald has had at least six of his top generals assassinated because he became afraid of them, because they accumulated too much power and became too strong."

Davy struggled against his restraints, which resulted in intense pain. He quit when Sarah cried out, the cuffs cutting into her wrists.

"I figured out a long time ago that the only way to be safe around Emerald was to have absolutely no interest in the position, don't learn the details of how to make things work. That's why I'm the coordinator. I line others up to do the actual work. That's why I'm the only one that Emerald trusts. It has worked pretty well for me, which is why I'm still here. And number four, if I wanted to take over, all I had to do would be to deliver the wrong heart for his heart operation. He would've been dead long ago and I would already be head of the operation, at least if someone hadn't killed me by now."

"How can you live with yourself, being so vile and hateful?"

"I'm not hateful. Actually, the lion loves the lamb. You don't hate what gives you sustenance. You love what gives you life. It's the lamb that hates. The lamb hates the lion, the one that takes its life. It is the lamb that is filled with rage."

"I thought we were friends."

"The truth is, I think you are a good and decent person. I really liked you. You have tremendous talent and ability. You probably could have done quite well in the organization. Unfortunately, Emerald needs you now. This is the way you can best contribute to the overall good. You are going to be Emerald's magnificent benefactor."

"Why me?"

"You are the only available option. Besides, you have a strong, young healthy heart, even more than Travis's heart, I am sure. We did want to have time to better prepare you through proper nutrition and herbs to cleanse and strengthen your heart even more, but you are an excellent specimen even so. You are going to be a magnificent benefactor, not only to Emerald, but to the entire world. It's quite an honor when you think about it."

"I don't believe you. I want to talk to Emerald. I can't believe he made this whole thing up, an elaborate hoax, the story he told me about being chosen his heir, the anointed one. No one would make up a lie that involved and complicated. I don't believe it. I want to talk to Emerald. I won't believe it until I hear it from him."

Marti laughed again, the passive laugh that follows a thought. "I'm afraid that is quite impossible. He can't talk to anyone right now, and when he will be able to, you won't be able to talk to him, or anyone else. As for telling a lie that big and complicated, Emerald has always said, if you're going to tell a lie, tell a big one. People are suspicious of little lies, but they never question the big ones. The bigger the lie, the more involved it is, the more people want to believe it. No, if we had told you small lies, you would never have believed. You were even skeptical of the big lie, which is unusual."

Several times Davy started to struggle against the restraints, but quickly stopped when Sarah winced in pain.

"Emerald has become very accomplished at telling great protracted lies. It's funny how people seem to get caught up in their talent for lies, kind of sucks them in. He was always expanding his scope for prevarications, that's the word he likes to use, prevarications, directing people. He has become almost compulsive in his efforts at creative prevarications, very strange."

"You'll never get away with this." Davy's caustic comment was as much a plea to providence as a statement. He glanced briefly at the crematorium.

"Davy, there is something you should probably know."

Davy did not inquire; he only stared.

"Emerald is your father."

"He could never be my father; I would never accept that. We signed no papers."

"No, I mean, he really is your father; your biological father."

Davy found the comment so offensive he felt he had been punched in the gut. "No, I don't believe that. Why would you say such a thing? Why would you even suggest that?"

"Emerald is indeed your biological father. His blood flows through your veins. Your father and mother never knew. He was also the biological father of Travis. You and Travis were half brothers."

"That is crazy talk. That is impossible. Stop doing this to me."

"Your mother was hospitalized for a gallbladder operation before you were conceived, in there for about a week. She was artificially inseminated then with Emerald being the donor. Neither she nor your father ever knew. They always assumed he was the natural father."

"Stop saying things like that. Don't take my father away from me. You've already taken everything else. Please stop. Why would he even do such a thing?"

"I'm sorry Davy, I really am. The thing is Emerald really liked you; he was fond of you. He thought you might really have what it took to become his heir. Of course you had a long way to go and there was to be fierce competition for the position, but you were clearly in the running."

Davy groaned such as only one in deep agony can do.

"It was necessary for him to artificially inseminate many women so he could have his own offspring available to provide for his heart transplants. Not all of them had the right blood type, so he had to work the odds, had to have enough on hand so he always had someone available. The unfortunate thing is he needed you now, and you are the only available compatible heart for Emerald. You have the blood of Nimrod in your veins. I just thought it might help to know you were saving your father, that's all. Maybe I shouldn't have mentioned it."

Marti looked somber; he almost seemed to care.

Davy dropped his head in anguish and wondered if in such emotional pain he would even live until the surgeon arrived. He heard Sarah moaning, "I don't want to die. I want to live. Please don't let me die."

Marti picked up the phone and dialed. "We're ready to go. How soon can Hawthorne be here?' There was a moment of silence and Marti became highly agitated. "What in the hell do you mean he can't come. What's going on?"

There was another moment of silence and Marti' agitation abated. "How long has he been in the States? When does he go back? Okay then, so how good is he, that's the question?" Another pause and then, "Are you sure? You know we want the best for Emerald." Another pause, "Okay, send him over, but if things don't go well, it's your ass. Understood?"

Marti hung up the phone, the anger still lingering on his face. After a moment of thought, he picked the phone up again and dialed.

"Antoinette, where's the title of authorization papers?" Again there was a brief pause and then his anger flared again. "What in the hell do you mean, you can't find them? We need them! They should be right there where I told you." He regained his composure a bit, "Okay, I'll be right down. They have to be there somewhere. I'll find them." He left through the open door.

Davy saw this as an opportunity. If he was going to do something, it would have to be now. Surely this would be their last opportunity to escape, as remote as the possibility seemed. But, even if they did get loose, they still weren't likely to get far. It didn't matter, a poor opportunity was better than none at all.

"Sarah, we have to scoot our chairs; we must, quickly now."

Sarah lifted her head from her swoon. "Why? What are you talking about?"

"No time to explain now, just do what I say. Let's scoot that way, together now, toward the cabinets, the one in the center."

Together, they scooted, a little at a time. Sometimes working together they made progress, and other times they were out of sync and wasted both energy and time. But, slowly they made progress, inch by miserable inch. It seemed forever, but at last Davy was close enough. He had enough slack in the cuffs so he was able to pull the drawer open and reach inside. Fishing around with the cuffs cutting into his wrists and Sarah wincing, he felt the ring of keys he had seen on a previous visit. He carefully removed the keys with great difficulty, being ever so careful not to drop them. If he dropped them, hope would be dead.

And then, he began searching for the right key, he hoped to God there was a right key, working his way around the ring, trying each key in turn, inserting it into Sarah's cuff, using his right hand to her left. He was always fearful of dropping the keys. Sometimes, he lost track of where he was on the key rings so he was never quite sure how many of the keys he had tried, or if he had missed one. One key after another he tried with grueling effort, until he heard the cuff click open. His heart jumped. He transferred the key to her now free hand and in a moment she had her other hand free and then her ankles. And then she freed Davy.

"Thank God we are free," exclaimed Sarah. "Now we can get out of here."

"Not yet," said Davy, remembering Davenport and the perimeter of armed guards, electronic security and the attack dogs.

"Quickly now." he instructed her. "Sit down in the chair like you're still cuffed." He moved the chairs so she was facing the still open door with the empty chair behind her. Searching quickly, desperately through the drawers, he found a bottle of chloroform, doused his handkerchief, and concealed himself the best he could beside the open door and waited.

He had no sooner done so than he heard Marti approaching, his footsteps echoing in the hall. He was whistling an old melancholy Hank Williams song. His quick walk carried him several feet into the room before he looked up, saw Sarah, and in an instant realized something was wrong. An instant was all it took for Davy to lock him in a strong grip from behind with the chloroform hanky over his nose and mouth. Marti knew immediately he was in trouble and gave a hard yank on Davy's arm to dislodge the chloroformed hanky, but Davy's strong arms held firm. In a rapidly accelerating panic, Marti took several quick steps with

Davy on his back, turned while lunging at the cabinet, sending sharp pain up Davy's back, but he held fast.

Marti spotted the sharp corner of the cabinet on the other side of the room. A sharp corner gouged into Davy's back should do the trick. With all the strength and quickness he could muster, he started for the sharp corner, took three steps, stumbled, regained himself, took another step, again stumbled and fell limp to the floor. Davy held the chloroform in place long enough to insure that Marti was unconscious, but he wanted to make sure he didn't kill him either. Sarah jumped from the chair and ran to help subdue Marti, if needed. It was not.

"We've done it. We're free," said Sarah.

"No, not yet. There is still more to do. Antoinette will alert the guards when she discovers we are gone, as she surely will. We will be quickly recaptured. We still have a lot to do before we can consider ourselves to be free. I have to think."

They dragged Marti to the far side of the gurneys and found a sheet and covered him.

"Okay," said Davy, "now sit back down again." Sarah complied.

Davy grabbed the phone and dialed the kitchen. When Antoinette answered, he shouted into the phone, in his best Marti imitation with just a tinge of panic, "I've got a crisis; get up here now! Hurry!" and slammed the phone down before she could ask questions.

He once more took his place beside the open door with chloroformed hanky in hand and waited. Shortly Antoinette burst into the room, stopped and surveyed the scene. That was all Davy needed, that one moment, and he held the hanky firmly in place on her face as he had done to Marti before. She was more of a scrapper than Marti, digging her nails into his arms, trying to bite his hands, kicking at his shins, pulling at his hair. Even so, she quickly slumped to the floor.

Davy and Sarah stripped them naked and placed them each on a gurney. They fastened restraining straps across their shoulders, necks, and legs, and for extra security placed cuffs on their wrists and ankles. They had no sooner covered them with sheets than they heard the brass knocker banging on the great door echoing through the dome.

"Quickly now, leave by the back stairs and stay out of sight." Sarah did as she was told. He went to answer the door.

The man at the door introduced himself as Alonzo and said, "Herb sent me. I am replacing Hawthorne and I'm here for the extractions." He carried a small black bag and had two stainless steel tanks that contained liquid nitrogen.

"Glad to meet you," said Davy. "My name is Marti. I hope to hell you're as good as Hawthorne."

"Hell yes, probably better," said Alonzo, amused at his own comment.

"Well, you're certainly as cocky as he is. Come on in. Here, let me carry one of those for you."

Alonzo followed Davy up the spiral stairs and into the secret room. Marti was starting to stir a little bit and was mumbling and turning his head side to side. Davy was glad to see he was alive, but unnerved he might awaken enough to tell Alonzo who he was. He quickly grabbed for the chloroform bottle.

"No need to do that," said Alonzo. He opened his black bag and pulled out a syringe and a small bottle.

Marti was still groggy, but able to mumble, "No, no, there's been a mistake, a terrible mistake."

Alonzo filled the syringe and gave Marti a shot and then Antoinette. It seemed to Davy to take forever before he accomplished this, but the shots quickly took effect.

"Sweet dreams," Alonzo said as he removed the syringe from Antoinette.

"How long do you think it will take to do this?" Davy had no desire to stay around and watch the procedure. He still remembered the sight of Travis.

Alonzo said, "Should be close to two hours, real close. It's easy taking them out, it's transplanting them back in that takes the time and gets a little tricky."

"I'll be back in two hours then."

"Works for me."

"Call star twenty six on the phone if you need anything. I'll be right up."

Alonzo nodded and Davy left. He returned in exactly two hours. The bodies had been recovered with sheets and Alonzo was cleaning up and putting things in his black bag. The stainless steel gurneys were wet with beaded droplets of water.

"Everything go alright?"

"As slick as snot."

"Good, good, glad everything went okay. Is the heart in good shape? That's the important thing."

"Absolutely, should work quite well for Mr. Silverstone."

Davy carried one of the stainless steel boxes, the small one, downstairs and Alonzo carried the other one, down and out to Alonzo's car.

"I need for you to drop Emerald's heart off at St. Luke's Baptist Hospital on your way," said Davy.

"I'd really rather not. I wasn't figuring on doing that."

"I've had something come up that needs attending. You have to deliver it."

Alonzo reluctantly accepted both containers. Davy rehearsed the directions to the hospital, no room for mistakes in this situation. Alonzo's car drove down the lane and disappeared out the gates. Davy breathed a sigh of relief and whispered under his breath, "Good luck Emerald; you're going to need it."

Davy and Sarah were a buzz of activity as they packed a few bare necessities, nothing more than would be noticed as missing, as they prepared to leave quickly as possible. Their first order of business was the cremation of the bodies, which had to be done in succession, one at a time. Operating the crematorium was no more complicated than running an automatic washing machine and the simple instructions were mounted on the front. Davy explained the death of Travis and what he knew about Emerald. Sarah mostly listened in silence.

"How horrible." She placed her fingers to her mouth. "Poor Travis. Our dear, sweet Travis. He was so good to me, such a sweetheart. He really cared about people." Davy saw tears well up in her eyes.

"Yes, I know. He was such a genuine person. I felt so close to him, closer than a brother. I miss him terribly."

Davy bit his lip in contemplation. "Emerald has a worldwide network. His control of authority runs deep. We've just seen that with the Texas Rangers."

Sarah responded, "Then how shall we ever escape?" She wiped the tears with the back of her hand. "Even if Emerald dies, no matter where we go, they will track us down. There is apparently no place in the world they could not find us if they wanted badly enough."

"Maybe not. They will think we are both dead, our organs harvested and our bodies cremated. They will have no reason to look for us. It will be Marti and Antoinette they will be searching for, and no matter how hard they look, they will never find them for they are the ones gone, cremated. I'm sure we are not the only ones who noticed how friendly Marti and Antoinette were with each other. They will be under suspicion for Emerald's death. There will probably be an intense search for them. People who operate in the Silverstone Empire won't want a lot of loose ends floating around."

The last thing Davy did was to retrieve the wooden box that contained the million dollars, less the ten thousand he had taken earlier, of course.

"But, it's not right to take the money," Sarah objected. "Tempting as it is, it is still stealing. We shouldn't do that."

"I don't look at it that way," responded Davy. "It's just that much more money to support an evil system if we leave it. The more we take out of the system, the less money there is to be used for evil. It's like a war between good and evil. We have to use all our resources to overcome evil with good."

Sarah seemed unconvinced.

"Besides, Emerald placed us in a position where we need it to survive, so it's only fitting he should finance our escape. He should bare that financial liability as he is responsible for our desperate situation. He gave it to me. He said I could take it any time I wanted it, if I ever wanted to bail out. I sure as hell want out now. So I'm taking it because it's mine. Not that he ever expected me to take it, but that's his problem. In any event, he will be dead soon after the transplant, so I don't think it's going to help him where he's going."

The logic finally satisfied Sarah. Davy donned Marti's golfing cap and shirt and Sarah wore one of Antoinette's floppy hats and dress with large polka dots. It was their hope they would look enough like Marti and Antoinette they would not be identifiable on the security cameras outside the house.

They loaded the car and climbed in. They both looked back one last time at Emerald's mansion and gave a heavy sigh. Their look-back was brief as they had no desire to be turned into a pillar of salt. In spite of the evil they had experienced, they still had many memorable pleasant memories. They drove down the lane hoping they would not be recognized by security; no reason for them to be suspicious at this point, especially with the tinted car windows. For better or for worse, their lives were about to change once more.

21
VITAL INFORMATION LOST
(Chapter 5: The Mythology of Nimrod)

Note from the Editor:

The end came quickly for Doctor Hostelmiester. Unfortunately, he expired before he wrote this chapter. He had named this chapter The Key to Saving this World from Nimrod and the Babylonian Mystery Religion. His notes mysteriously disappeared. He left only these two illustrations.

On the bottom half of the page was an illustration of a lifeless lamb with its throat cut draining blood and another of a majestic lion wearing a crown. Below the illustration were two words: Our Hope.

22
REGENERATION

They drove several miles in silence, feeling emotionally drained. On the distant horizon they saw a single brilliant flash of lightning in the night sky.

"What now?" asked Sarah.

"I'm driving to northern Montana to find Cousin Harold. He has forty acres secluded in the mountains, lots of woods. He's always loved hunting and trapping, and said when he got old enough, he was going to move to Montana and buy a small remote patch of ground. He plants a garden and raises his own beef and deer for meat. He doesn't trust the government, doesn't even have a social security number. He conducts all his financial transactions through friends and acquaintances."

"That sounds kind of weird. Is he a militant, you know, belonging to a radical militia or something like that?"

"I suppose he is a little weird. He's a loner, and I guess loners tend to be weird, at least in the eyes of some. But he does have his own circle of friends and he certainly has it together. He knows what he's doing. And he's as genuine a person as I know. It's like we have a spiritual connection. The thing is, he believes it's dangerous to be a militant, to draw attention to yourself, so he just quietly goes about his business. The last thing he wants to do is to get into a butt kicking contest with the government. He'd rather be transparent so they don't even know he exists. He says that fighting the government is like fighting the mafia. Come to think of it, that sounds like what Emerald said."

"Do you think he'll help us? Can we trust him?"

"Oh yes, you can bet we can trust Harold. He and I are buds from way back. We spent six weeks one summer with Carlos in Mexico on his family farm, and the next summer we would spend six weeks with Harold on his family's farm in southern Arkansas. The third summer we spent at our house. We were more like brothers than cousins, pretty close, had many precious memories. That's where he learned to hunt and trap from the time he was a child. He loves being outside with nature in the backwoods. He used to take me hunting and trapping when we were young, and I learned quite a bit about all that. We had some great times together. I'd trust my life with him in a heartbeat. The further removed you get from the memories of your childhood, the more precious they become."

"Do you think the organization will find us there?"

"Not likely; they don't even know we are alive. We're supposed to be dead, cremated, both of us. Marti and Antoinette are the ones they will be looking for, but they are the ones cremated, so the search will be fruitless. The organization doesn't even know we exist now. So it will be wasted effort. Even if they were looking for us, they would have to be seriously lost to find us there, and even then they would almost need a miracle. We'll be incredibly secluded, and any necessary trips to town can be done by Harold or his friends. We can hide out there for as long as we want. The danger will be getting from here to there."

"I hope you're right. I never want to see them again, ever. What about the limo? Will they be looking for the black stretch? It's a long way to Montana, and I'm sure we would be spotted long before then."

"We're going to ditch the limo. I have access to a car."

"You have access to a car? I don't understand; how would you have access to a car?"

"It belongs to Harold. He took a pickup truck to Montana loaded with all of his worldly possessions and the money he inherited from his grandfather. He used some of his inheritance to buy the ground. He's been after me to come out and visit him, wants me to bring his car. It's old enough it shouldn't have a tracking device."

"A tracking device; what do you mean?"

Davy told her what Emerald had told him about electronic tracking devices on all new cars.

"This whole thing is just so crazy," she said.

Harold said he'd pay for the gas if I came. I reckon we don't exactly need gas money now that we have Emerald's money."

"Where's the car?"

"It's in an old shed on some property his great aunt owns, out past the edge of town on a small run down ranch. She lives in a nursing home now and never goes to the shed, so she won't miss it, or get all excited it's gone. Harold can give her a call and let her know he has it."

"How long has it been sitting there?"

"About two years."

"Do you think it will still run?"

"It should. I'd go out and start it up every month or two and take it for a short drive to keep it running smooth. He told me I could drive it any time I wanted, but I didn't want to take advantage of him, so I hardly ever did, unless I really needed it."

"How many miles does it have?"

Davy laughed. "It's has close to two hundred thousand."

"That is a lot of miles. Do you think it will get us to Montana?"

"Probably. It's about twenty years old, but he's mechanically inclined and took good care of it. He loved that car, kept it running like a top. I don't think getting there will be a problem."

They drove a while in silence before she asked, "Do you think Emerald is still alive?"

"Who knows? It's possible he's not dead yet, but he could be. I have no idea. You can bet we'll hear about it on the news whenever it happens."

"It will be on the radio," she stated as a matter of fact.

"You can be sure of that, at least if the organization wants the public to know."

"As I think back," said Sarah, "Emerald seemed to be larger than life. He had a personality of epic proportions. I get the feeling there is more to this than I understand."

"Perhaps it has to do with the prophecy, the prophecy of Nimrod's heir."

"The prophecy?"

Davy told her all he knew about Emerald being the returned Spirit of Nimrod.

"But how can that be? It can't be the fulfillment of prophecy concerning the return of Nimrod, because Emerald is probably dead, or shall be shortly, and if he is dead, then prophecy has not been fulfilled."

"I don't know. There are just so many things I don't know. We don't know Emerald is dead, at least not yet. And if he is dead, perhaps the Spirit of Nimrod could raise up another like him. Perhaps the Spirit of Nimrod could even raise Emerald back to life again."

"That is scary." said Sarah, "He could still be alive. Perhaps a new Emerald would be worse than the one we knew. Do you think all this has anything to do with the end of the world? Is this the coming of Armageddon?"

"The way I understand it, the Babylonian Mystery Religion is supposed to be resurrected at the end of this age. I don't know what all that means, but the thought certainly has a greater impact on me now."

"If Emerald is dead, then maybe the Spirit of Nimrod is dead. Do you think it can return?"

"I don't know how to answer that. We can only hope not. But if you believe in Armageddon, then the Spirit of Nimrod has to return, probably to raise up another Emerald, perhaps even the same one. The next one could be ever worse than our Emerald. That has to happen if Armageddon is to be fulfilled. The Spirit of Nimrod is the ultimate stealth operator and the origin of deception by massive propaganda campaigns, the perversion of religion for evil purposes."

"I believe in Armageddon, but this is all so overwhelming. He was such a horrible person. He was a real snake."

"It's funny you should say that." Davy then told her about the snake he had seen in his walk-in closet.

"What does it all mean?" she asked. "We all three saw something like that. I saw the spider, Travis saw the rat, and then you saw the snake."

"Not only that, but in the front of a book about Nimrod, I saw illustrations of a snake, a spider, and a rat."

"You can't be serious?"

"I am, quite serious."

"This is just so crazy. There is so much I don't understand."

"Life is kind of that way; there is always much we don't understand. There are several possibilities though. You mentioned that somehow it might have been a sign from God. Travis mentioned it might have been evil spirits. There have been myths of people, particularly evil people, who could transform themselves into creatures of some kind. I don't think that could have been it, because then he would have known I knew what he had done to Travis and was on my way to rescue you. If that had been Emerald, he would never have allowed me to leave."

"Unless he was too sick to stop you. A heart operation is a pretty serious operation. If Emerald was really sick, maybe that took away energy, away from the snake."

"That's true. There is at least one other possibility. I can't help but wonder if the herbs that Antoinette used in our meals could have caused us hallucinations. I have read some novels where evil people used hallucinogens for mind control so their victims couldn't realize what was going on."

"That is an interesting thought. What do you think it was?"

"I just don't know. There are some mysteries in life you never figure out. We may never know. I can tell you that as a writer, that scene about the snake sure made an indelible impression on me. It was incredible vivid imagery. I'm inclined to believe that somehow this is all connected to the end of days. If so, then we will have to deal with the returned Spirit of Nimrod again. At least, that's the way I understand the Apocalypse."

"That would be so terrible, I hate to even think about it," said Sarah. "What made him like that?"

"What do you mean?"

"He had so much going for him. He seemed like a good and decent person who wanted to make the world a better place for everyone. How could someone like that do the things he did? In reality, he was a horrible creature."

"That is strange. It seems the more a person wants to fix the entire world, the more they screw it up for everyone."

"Why can't people just leave things alone, and let everyone be who they are? I think we would all get along just fine if people like Emerald would just stay out of the way and let everyone do their own thing."

"To tell you the truth, I found myself getting sucked into that way of thinking, like somehow I could help to save the world, and in the process become wealthy and powerful. It all seemed like a good thing. The process corrupts you, I think. Maybe it was the blood of Nimrod that flowed through his veins that made him who he was. Maybe he just gave himself over to the spirit of evil so he could experience wealth and power. Who knows?"

"What a horrible thing, to have the blood of Nimrod flowing through your..." She caught herself and glanced toward Davy.

"You're right. It is a terrible thing, to know I have Emerald's blood in my veins, the same DNA as Nimrod."

"You don't know you carry Emerald's genetics. Marti could have been lying to you."

"I just don't know. I would like to believe he was wrong. But even if I do, I still carry the blood of Seth, from my Mother. That I know. And, my Dad is my real father because he cared for me and loved me. Emerald tried to take my heart by force, but I give my heart willingly to my father because I love him. He is my real father because my heart belongs to him in a way it could never belong to Emerald."

She squeezed his arm.

He continued, "But the thing is, I don't think whose blood you carry is as important as the decisions you make, or the character you develop. All I want to do now is to be an insignificant person, just to sit by the side of the road and be a friend to my neighbor, the person at the end of my arm. I'd like to reach out a helping hand to the person I see in most need. If I can just ease one heart from aching, I will have done much."

"That is such a wonderful thing for you to say, Davy."

"The thing is I learned it from you. I learned it from you and my mother, from my father too. I learned it from my grandparents, some teachers, and others who have been kind to me on my journey through life. And they all learned it from others. There is much goodness in the world in spite of overwhelming evil."

"Then," said Sarah, "We must pass it on. We will be an example for those who follow, and they can in turn pass it on to others."

"That's good, I like that."

Davy thought for a moment and said, "It's kind of strange, when you think about it, people who want to be rich, powerful and famous; they want to build a legacy to leave behind, and to build glorious monuments so the world will adore them after they are gone, but the monuments they build for themselves are a testament to their stupidity and are likely to be for their eternal shame. It's sad, when you give it some consideration, how badly they miss the mark. And the sad part is the world has no idea what is going on. Everyone is a victim of their own ignorance."

"Perhaps you could warn them."

"How could I do that?"

"You like to write, don't you? Maybe you could do it by writing and exposing them. You would become sort of a benefactor to the world, the whole world. You could become a magnificent benefactor for humanity, for the decent people of the world."

"Me, a magnificent benefactor?" Davy laughed nervously. "I don't know how I feel about that right now."

"You could do that, Davy, I know you could."

"I'd like that. I don't know about the magnificent benefactor part, but I would do what I could. It would be a monumental challenge. It's not easy getting published. And it would be terribly risky. We'll have to wait and see if that is my destiny. For today, our only challenge is to survive, to make it to Montana."

"Just remember, Davy, I believe in you."

Davy shook his head and said, "People want to be successful, they want to be successful in the worst way, but it's better to be productive. When you are successful, you prosper, but you may fail on a greater level. When you are productive, everyone benefits. That is true success."

They parked the limo on a remote section of a street on the edge of town with no streetlights. Davy walked the three quarters of a mile to the shed in the country, leaving Sarah behind to see after the black limo and their possessions. It was ten o'clock in the evening with a full moon and Davy was able to see adequately, so he traveled rapidly and with surety of foot. He could not help worrying about Sarah being there by herself out of his sight. He would never forgive himself if something happened to her.

At the shed he unlocked the latch that held the door and pushed the sliding doors open, a harsh grating sound of tin against tin crying in agony to the moon. A sense of loneliness and sadness settled into his emotions. Inside, feeling carefully in the shadowy darkness, he retrieved the key hanging on a nail hidden behind a board, slid into the car, inserted the key and engaged the ignition.

The motor turned over twice before starting to run, as smoothly as ever. Davy was glad. He removed the car and shut and locked the doors behind him. He soon returned to the site where he had left Sarah and the black shiny car. He breathed a sigh of relief to see she was okay. They quickly transferred their belongings and Davy used a rag to wipe away any fingerprints they might have left behind. In a short time they were back on the highway headed north.

"If," asked Sarah, "they find the limo, won't they know where to look for us? What if you left some of our fingerprints behind?"

"I'm telling you, they're not going to be looking for us. Even if they find some fingerprints inside the car that would not be unexpected, so it wouldn't be a big deal. After all, we did ride in it from time to time. The thing is we are supposed to be dead, remember?"

Sarah was intellectually satisfied with the answer, but her emotions weren't fully convinced.

"Now," said Davy, "for the first time I'm beginning to believe we can make it all the way. For the first time since we've left Mexico, I am starting to have real hope."

"Oh, I do hope so," said Sarah. I'll feel a lot better once we're out of Texas, but I won't really feel comfortable until we've reached the remote woods of Montana. That's still a long way to go. Anything can happen. I can't help but think of Chief Joseph as he led the Nez Pierce. He was a Native American, you know. They evaded the Cavalry for so long, and then when they were almost to the Canadian border, their lives ended in tragedy. They were so close, but it might as well have been a million miles. They were captured and imprisoned in a reservation, at least the ones who lived. King Louis the IV and Queen Antoinette almost escaped to Austria before they were recaptured, returned to Paris, and beheaded."

Davy was worried about Sarah. She was no longer the cheerful beautiful personality she was when he first met her. There sometimes comes a moment when emotional pain may be too great to bear and live.

This he knew from experience. He wondered if she could ever be the same again. He wondered if he could ever be the same again.

He thought it ironic how young people wished their lives away, never appreciating the magic of the moment, longing for an enchanting future made from the stuff of fairy dreams, one that seldom worked out that way, and even sometimes ended up as a hellish nightmare instead. If young people could only know what the future held, they wouldn't be in such a hurry to get there. He reflected on the joy and many happy hours of his own youth, now only a memory from the distant past.

"I think," said Davy, "when Elohim calls a person to some great commission, to a great purpose in life, he always tries them first in fire, sometimes more than a person thinks they can ever bear. Perhaps he is calling us to a greater purpose. If so, his spirit will raise us up. He will give us strength to overcome. What purpose could be greater than healing people who are broken physically, emotionally and spiritually, those who are down trodden, destitute, and scraping the bottom of life's barrel?"

"That's all I ever wanted to do. I'd like to hold all the children in the world who are hurting and let them know they are loved. In Mexico I saw so many children who were sick, malnourished, and unloved. I saw so many women who were abused, abandoned, betrayed, and without hope. Perhaps I have found my calling, or my destiny as you might say."

"That's good, overcome evil with good. I like that."

He vocalized his next thoughts. "We need to spend the money wisely. We can use it to put us both through school as nurses."

She watched him with interest and affection, staring at his face, in the dimly lit interior of the car.

He continued, "We'll have to change our names and obtain papers of identification of course, but I learned how to do all that. After we graduate and receive our nursing license, then we can go some place to work together. We can help people who are desperate and need medical attention. It would be nice to fulfill our dreams as a team. You were the one with the worthy and noble goal. It can become our dream. We can spend our lives making the world a better place to be, as nurses, both of us."

"I'd like that. That could be my destiny in life, my purpose."

"Yes, and my destiny as well."

"I'm not so sure about that. Maybe it's not your destiny."

"What? Why would you say that? It could be our destiny together. You don't see me as a nurse?"

"It's not that. I love the idea of working with you as nurses for indigent people. It's just that I..." She groped for the right words. "It's just that I believe you have another destiny, a higher calling."

"That's interesting. Why would you say that?"

"I don't know. It's just a feeling I have. I believe you have a higher purpose in life. It's just something I feel."

Davy considered her words in silence as they drove. "You know, it's funny, but I wanted so much to be wealthy. I wanted to be rich and respected, not in a bad way, but in a good way. I wanted to contribute to the betterment of the world. Now that I think about it, I guess I was not much different than any other person who wants to be rich. The process corrupts you. The thought of being, you know, one of them... It makes me sick to even think about it. There's no way I ever want to be one of them."

She placed her hand on his arm. "There's something that worries me, worries me terribly. A girl, Lolita, she was one of the girls back there, you know, The Red Garter. She is only fourteen. She is beautiful, but frail. I don't think she can make it. I'm afraid she will kill herself. She is such a wonderful girl, a precious person. I can't get her out of my mind. I'm just worried sick about her. I wish there was some way we could get her out."

"Is she the girl who was with you back there when I saw you?"

"Yes."

Davy thought in silence as they rode for several miles. "We can probably do it, but it will be quite risky."

"I know, but we have to try. Please?"

"As soon as we get situated, I'll figure something out. We would never dare to return ourselves. That would be suicide and getting ourselves killed won't help her. I'll make arrangements for someone to get her out. It can be done, but it'll have to be done right. We'll have to be careful, make sure nothing traces back to us, but it can be done. We'll make it happen. I promise you."

She squeezed his arm again and snuggled her cheek into his shoulder. "Thank you, Davy. Thank you so much. I knew you would want to do that. Every day will be an eternity for her. There is no way of knowing when it will be too late."

"I promise you that will be accomplished as quickly as we can do it."

"Thank you. That means so much to me. When the girls are no longer attractive enough to attract customers, they are discarded. They become a pariah to the local population, because they are prostitutes. They have no way to make a decent living except to continue as a low-class prostitute, until they are so despised they can no longer do even that. They can't marry anyone respectable. They waste away into poverty, starvation, and sickness. Their life is over. Rape is worse than murder. It kills your soul and destroys your spirit. They have no hope, no reason to live."

Davy said nothing. How he wished for the right thing to say, something to make everything better, to make her pain go away. He hated himself for not being able to say something comforting.

She continued. "When I was there, I grieved for myself. Now I grieve for those I left behind, every single one. I know the evil I saw there is only a small amount compared to the evil that happens every day around whole world. Right now at this very moment, someone is getting murdered, someone is starving, someone is diseased, some child is being abused, and whole communities are being destroyed."

Davy's heart was touched.

She continued, "When I was back at the Estate, I didn't have a clue of the suffering that was going on at the Red Garter. When I was there, it didn't matter that elsewhere in the world, young people were enjoying themselves at a dance or eating with friends at the soda shop. How can I ever enjoy life now that I'm aware of the suffering going on around the world? I just saw one small insignificant part of it all, but that one little bit-it was just so painful."

"There is just so much evil in the world, more than I could ever have imagined. It seems like all the powerful people, all the rich people are evil. Such great evil just overwhelms the goodness, just crushes it."

"But there are good people too, people like your parents, like my grandmother. There are lots of good people who don't give in to the evil around them. It is just that you never hear much about them."

"I don't know. I just don't know. It seems like the good people are the ones who suffer the most. I think I understand now. They refuse to compromise their values to The System. The System is evil. It all makes sense now. The only way to rid the world of evil is to eliminate The System. Maybe that's why we need Armageddon, to cleanse the world of such great evil."

"I would like that. It would be wonderful to live in a world without evil."

"Maybe it's necessary to experience man's inability to govern ourselves before we experience ruler-ship by someone who is capable and who cares, an alternative government."

"An alternative government, that is interesting."

They rode for a while in silence before Sarah said, "There is nothing sadder than a world without hope, nothing more emotionally devastating than a person without hope."

Davy pointed through the front windshield and said, "Look at the stars, how they shine. They are never brighter than in the darkness of the Texas night sky. And see, over there, the North Star. See that? It's beautiful. As long as the North Star shines brightly, there is hope."

She was again staring at Davy, a stare born of respect, of deep appreciation, and yes, even love. Davy returned the stare, looking into her eyes, and as love recognizes love, asked, "Sarah, will you marry me?"

She dropped her head and said, "I can't."

He was stunned. "What do you mean, you can't?"

"I just can't." Tears began to form. "I went through a lot down there, more horrible than you could imagine. It was physically and emotionally devastating. I'm not the same person I was before, in several ways. You deserve someone better, much better. You deserve the best."

Davy couldn't believe what he was hearing. His heart was breaking for her emotional pain. Surely, she had no idea how much he loved her. He put his arm around her, firmly pulled her toward him, and said, "Sarah, I love you so much. I have always loved you, from the moment I first saw you, and my love for you has only grown each time I've been in your presence. I loved you so much that I felt unworthy of you. I felt that you deserved someone much better than me. And so, I contented myself with the thought you would someday marry someone good enough for you. I was more than willing to sacrifice my love for you in the hope that you would find happiness in a more perfect marriage, someone who was worthy of you. It is I who am unworthy of you."

"You are so sweet. You are a wonderful person. You will make some lucky girl a good husband." Tears were now streaming down her face. She wiped her nose with a Kleenex.

Davy searched desperately for something to say, something that would make all things right.

"You remember what I said my mother told me? The most glorious human achievement is victory over adversity. That is speaking to us. She said life is precious, so precious. She is speaking to us."

"I like that. It gives me strength. Your mother must have been a special person."

"She was. She was special." He pointed with his index finger. "Sarah, I want you to do something for me. Open the glove compartment."

Sarah did as he asked. She retrieved a paper sack and took her Bible out.

"Oh good, I was afraid I had lost it. I am so glad to have grandmother's Bible again. I thought I had forever lost it." She clutched it to her breast.

Davy continued, "When you left it behind, I e-mailed you and offered to send it to you. I figured you had forgotten it. Apparently, someone replied on your behalf, I thought it was you, and told me you wanted me to have it, that you had purchased a new one. I couldn't quite believe it. But, I was so glad to have it, so I didn't question it very deeply. It reminded me of you. I read it every night, and every time I read it I thought of you. I have it marked, turn to the book-marker."

She did.

"I read so many verses that spoke of healing. I wrote down a few I thought were particularly profound. I read them over and over. They helped me to survive the pain I was feeling after you left, the angst of depression and despair."

A tear formed in his eye. "They are written on the back of a piece of paper that I used for a book-marker."

She took it out and began to read silently.

"That's a note somebody left on my windshield when I took you to the airport. Turn it over and read the other side."

"That's interesting," she replied as she finished reading the note. "I wonder who wrote it."

"I don't know. Whoever it was asked me to destroy it. I was surely derelict in not doing so, and for that I am ashamed. I could have caused someone great harm, someone who was our friend. I should have disposed of it as they requested. We must surely do so. I have no idea who wrote it. Apparently, it was someone who knew what was going on, someone who cared, a friend for sure. Perhaps we will never know. Anyway, turn it over and read the other side."

She turned it over and read aloud.

You shall find rest unto your souls. They who sow in tears shall reap in joy. Though you are as scarlet, you will be made as pure as snow. I have satiated the weary soul, and I have refreshed every sorrowful soul. For I will turn your mourning into joy, and will comfort you, and make you rejoice from your sorrow. Come unto me ye who are heavy laden and I will give you rest.

He healed them. The blind receive their sight and the lame walk, the lepers are cleansed, and the deaf hear, the dead are raised up. He cured their infirmities. He cleanses us, every bit. And God shall wipe away all tears from their eyes; and there shall be no more death, neither sorrow, nor crying, neither shall there be any more pain: for the former things are passed away. You shall return to the days of your youth. Healing comes in his wings. Though we are tried in fire, we shall come forth as pure as gold. You have turned my mourning into dancing. He heals all our diseases so that our youth is restored like the eagles. They that sow in tears will reap in joy. He heals the brokenhearted and binds up our wounds. There is a balm in Gilead. They who wait upon the Lord shall renew their strength; they shall mount up with wings of eagles; they shall run, and not be weary; and they shall walk and not be faint. A new heart will I give you.

"Those verses spoke deeply to me when I wrote them. I read them over and over and over. Now they speak to us both. We will be regenerated, made like new, better than new, better than before. We will see our families again. All things will be made right."

She squeezed his arm, a love squeeze born of affection and of pain.

Davy continued, "He will give us a new heart. Can you imagine that, a new heart? Not the way Emerald went about getting a new heart, by murdering young people, but one without any surgeons or victims. My mother spoke true; the most glorious human achievement is victory over adversity."

She shook her head yes, unable to speak.

"I think we can also say He is the ultimate Magnificent Benefactor."

She laid her head on his shoulder and started sobbing, silently at first and then convulsively so her whole body shook. Davy held her with tenderness, and after a while she went once more to sobbing in silence.

He kissed her on top of the head. "So, will you marry me?"

She nodded in agreement, still crying, her head buried in his shoulder.

He repeated, "The most glorious human accomplishment is victory over adversity. It is a spiritual gift, the essence of divinity. We have accomplished something of substance. We have been tried in the fire of adversity and refined like pure gold. We are precious in his sight. Surely, that means much."

Davy and Sarah, on a highway somewhere in Texas, disappeared into the darkness of night. The next morning they would rise with the sun, Phoenix-like, to claim their future, the first day of the rest of their lives.

Hope Lives!

AUTHOR RUMINATIONS

I was raised on a farm in oppressive poverty, but I was happy because I didn't know any better. My profession is now in the healthcare field where caring for the infirm is a purpose I cherish. I believe the most glorious human achievement is victory over adversity, the essence of divinity. I believe that life is precious, our past is mysterious, and our future is glorious.

My writings include *Mystic Waters, Legend of the Wabash, The Legend Prayer,* and *The Benefactor*, a 90,000 word novel which I anticipate will stimulate some interesting conversation. I plan to publish a second novel in the near future. I write with passion, profundity, and polypompjocosity.

Mystic Waters will have a new edition soon.
Legend of the Wabash available at floydroot.com
The Legend Prayer available at floydroot.com
Return to the Seven Houses should be available in near future

Contact floyd.root@gmail.com to request suggested questions for book clubs for *The Benefactor*.

Made in the USA
Charleston, SC
05 February 2015